Revenge of Alpha Centauri

A Fixed Star Mystery

L.N. GRUER

Published by
Hybrid Global Publishing
301 E 57th Street
4th Floor
New York, NY 10022

Manufactured in the United States of America.

Gruer, L.N.
Revenge of Alpha Centauri: A Fixed Star Mystery
    ISBN: 978-1-951943-91-2
    eBook: 978-1-951943-92-9
    LCCN: 2021920087

Cover design by: Natasha Clawson
Copyediting by: Wendie Pecharsky
Interior design by: Suba Murugan
Author photo by: Monique Feil

Disclaimer: This is a work of fiction. All names, characters, organizations, and events are fictional. Any resemblance to actual persons, living or dead, or actual events is purely coincidental.

lngruer.com

"For Susan
My own Fairy God Mother... Justice will be served."

"Astrology is assured of recognition from psychology, without further restrictions, because astrology represents the summation of all the psychological knowledge of antiquity."

Carl G. Jung

****

"Are you serious? How many carbs in one lousy cup of your salted caramel frozen yogurt?" shrieked a disheveled-looking, middle-aged woman at the top of her lungs as she faced off with a tall, creepy-skinny, pimple-faced young man behind the scale. After stupidly glancing up at the nutritional info chalked into the blackboard hanging high over the checkout, he suspected she was probably as furious with herself as she was with him. The youth, dressed in a vintage Black Sabbath silk-screen tee shirt and inky-black skinny jeans, did an impressive job pulling his tightly braided, sun-bleached hair back off his sunburned forehead. The Black Sabbath "originals" tee featured Ozzy, Geezer, Bill, and Tony surrounded by scarlet flames, including the band's baroque-goth logo with the B and S letters tangled together for better effect.

"Sorry, dude," he drawled, performing a customary eye roll, responding to the disgruntled woman without a grain of genuine remorse. "Did you change your mind? I still have to charge you," he went on smugly, adding insult to injury. The woman mirrored back the eye roll and scowled incredulously, clearly not expecting anything better from a male counterpart of the doomed species she named post-Atlantis earthlings.

"If I wanted to use up my entire week's carb allowance, I'd eat a box of Sidecar Doughnuts. At least, I'd get some pleasure out of my calories. You expect me to pay for this? Well, I'm not paying." the woman persisted, ignoring the whispers of "What a loser; she's a nutcase, what is she wearing?" coming from behind her.

"Doughnuts sound good to me," the clerk said, grinning back good-naturedly and showing a mouthful of gold teeth. "I love Costa Mesa Sidecar; on 17th street, right? Those are some expensive doughnuts. Five bucks for the one with bacon, but well worth it. My mom says five bucks is a rip off. Doesn't seem to stop the crazy ass lines..." he rattled on, ignoring the woman's scowling at his chatter. Then he said, "I have an idea. Let's take the toppings off your bill. That should lower the carbs," he joked, attempting to defuse the conflict with what his parents habitually called "an asinine sense of humor." He liked his day job, but not enough to put up with customer abuse, especially from a funky, old drama queen who wanted a freebie.

"Hasn't anyone taught you, the customer is always right?" the woman said, refusing to back down and raising her voice several decibals higher. "Clearly not. You entitled snowflakes with your white privilege are all the same. No work ethic. No customer service." With those words, the disgruntled customer, threw down a five dollar bill, flipped her frizzy cloud of maroon and gray hair over her shoulder and stormed out of the store.

"Sorry, guys," the kid apologized to the remaining patrons. "She's probably one of the addicts from the sober living place down the street, or a homeless woman from Main Beach. Welcome to Laguna."

Contents

Chapter 1

So far it's been, as I have predicted, a planetary shit storm of a birthday. I don't understand why I let myself get lured out of the comfort of my perfectly sound, one-bedroom back house in Eastside Costa Mesa to spend a half an hour in line for a jolt of inflammation-inducing, sugar-filled, frozen yogurt at an avocado-toast, acai bowl Orange County mommy hangout in Laguna Beach. I despise the $200 yoga pants mommy flock as much as their LVT backpacks. Does your baby care about a diaper bag that costs more than a drivable used car anywhere else in the world, that is, outside of coastal California?

On top of all the aggravation with the snot-nosed clerk, my two lady friends are late. I'm well aware the traffic from Inland Riverside County takes longer than Sandi is expecting, meaning I'm resigned to wait while having a snack; but I'm running out of patience with my South Laguna friend Katherine. Katherine is the one who lives locally, a few blocks south of celebrity-rich, mega-bucks Victoria Beach.

"That is what I get for having friends older than the Goddess herself," I mumble out loud while licking the bottom of the paper cup clean, hating to admit the yogurt tasted even better than Sidecar Doughnuts, and the free toasted-coconut toppings weren't bad either.

When the mommy flock, uniformly dressed in embarrassingly tight spandex, finally leaves, I plunk my irritated ass down on a metal chair right outside the popular yogurt shop and beach hangout, resolving to empty my racing mind and enjoy the ocean view over the raucous Pacific Coast Highway traffic.

My name is Viviana, not the common Vivian nor the obnoxiously trendy Vivienne. Born in the evening hours, I woke up forty-nine years young, but will go to bed at fifty, which is horrifyingly old, unless compared with my tardy friends, Sandi and Katherine, seventy-two and seventy-eight, respectively. Not that I choose my friends according to their chronological age; it simply happens that way. Well, if you bothered to learn what I already have, you wouldn't be surprised. When you are born with the sour-faced planet Saturn in the Eleventh House of your birth horoscope, it means you are most comfortable around friends older than yourself. It also means being able to count on your older sibling for support and acceptance. I guess astrology is like everything else in life: fifty-fifty.

After finishing my cup of carb sin and still not feeling satisfied, I throw in the towel and decide to get more, returning to the yogurt dispensary with my shoulders squared and chin up. I'm self-aware enough to recognize this about my basic nature: Once I get a bite of anything that brings me a hint of pleasure, I simply can't stop.

While I've been trying to maintain my Zen attitude outside, the stampede inside has ended. I'm back outside the store in no time, holding onto my second yogurt cup, this time filled with more unique flavors I haven't tried before, olive oil and lavender. When I was a kid, all we had was vanilla, chocolate, and strawberry.

Luckily, the same little man whose head I practically bit off pretends to ignore what happened during our previous exchange. I can tell he's looking at my legs. Yeah, men are all the same: seventeen or seventy. I recognize I still have great legs, long and shapely, more suited to a much younger woman. This is why I chose my birthday outfit with uncharacteristic care. I'm wearing a well-above-the-knee, high-waisted, denim skirt and a matching denim shirt without a belt. I jazzed up the shirt with my own hands, using pearl buttons and an animal-print velvet fabric along the collar and cuffs. They taught me to sew and fix my clothes instead of turning my spoiled nose up in the air, making an excuse to buy new clothes I can't afford. I save the animal denim for special outings because it also hides my pre-menopausal pouch, the same pouch I'm desperately trying to lose by counting my carbs. Until a year ago, I never had to give my weight a second thought. Dieting is an unfamiliar trip: that's why I'm cranky. I've tried being a vegan and a pescatarian, but it never stopped me from craving sugar-fried dough and chips.

Instead of my usual broken-in ballet flats, I dug out a pair of short, red booties with rhinestones and fringe to cheer myself up. Like me, the booties are showing their years, with some stones sadly dulled or missing, but I've always preferred the vintage vibe anyhow.

"You're staring at me," I say to the barista. "Do I remind you of someone, maybe a retired rock queen? By the way, I like your Sabbath tee." I grin at the kid, attempting to play nice. He bites, returning my smile and complimenting my healing stones and Austrian crystal bracelets; layers upon layers of multicolored beads partially covering the incantations inked into my inner arms.

"Is that a flawless smoky crystal?" he asks, bending over the counter to inspect a large checkerboard-cut stone set in silver. I wear the choker around my neck anytime I'm in public.

"Nice."

"You appreciate smoky?" I'm taken aback.

"Right on. My girl works at the crystal shop across PCH and also reads energy emanations, kind of like tarot cards. Say, I like how you smudged your stone with rosemary and frankincense. We're all about essential oils too. Smoky is great for clearing negative vibes, rosemary is for love, and frankincense for moving Magik. Your tatts are super chill too. Wicca, hey?"

"That's right," I say, now flabbergasted. I didn't guess I was that obvious. Perchance this soul is not a typical OC brat. Perhaps I shouldn't jump to conclusions or down folks' throats either. Could be, I shouldn't have reincarnated as an Aries. Nah. Not going to happen. Aries keep this planet moving.

"Respect." the boy continues, showing a deep dimple on his right cheek. "I'm Adam. Nice to meet you, rocker chick."

Ah, he's a Libra, Sun Moon or Rising. If the dimple were on his chin, most likely he'd be a Taurus. This is the game I love to play, guessing people's birth horoscopes based on their appearances. It's a bit more complicated than you think because your Sun sign shows your inner self and not how you present to the world. It's your Rising, meaning the astrological sign rising over the east the minute you're born that's more accurate. Take me, for instance: I don't have bushy brows or a square chin, a scar or even a mole, more indicative of my April Aries Sun. I'm definitely more of a Scorpio: big eyes, crazy, thick frizz, and full, pale lips. Fun, right?

"Thanks," I say to Adam, my heart softening. "You have an expert eye, Few people around here like hex jewelry or understand ritual tats," I smile, suddenly feeling young and almost beautiful.

"Look, cutie. I'm sorry I lost my shit. I appreciate you being chill, so keep the change." The clerk nods and tells me to enjoy the weather. I realize a couple of quarters and a dime probably make him laugh, but it's the rest of my cash, at least for today.

As I return to my thankfully unoccupied chair, I hear a familiar booming contralto calling out my name. Swinging my head in the general direction of the noise, I see Sandi dropping my birthday gift right on the pavement. Sandi's always lucky to get a perfect parking spot, even in Laguna. As usual, my ditzy BFF forgets to lock the doors of her 1990s faded blue Chevy Lumina. The funky Lumina is forever overflowing with plastic bags, cracker and cookie crumbs, and empty bottles of Diet Coke she's not supposed to drink. She also drives around with a large box stuffed with files and files of astrology charts, given an honorable place on the passenger seat. All are things Sandi insists she can't live without, and she refers to the Chevy as her "office."

Before getting hooked on astrology, I chalked up Sandi's parking luck as a coincidence, but now that I see better, I attribute it to my friend's glorious Neptune placement. As you would expect, Sandi wins whenever she enters any contest, be it bingo or playing video poker for days on end at a local Indian casino. Last year, she won a brand-new Toyota Camry, then sold it online and made a bundle.

"Hey, baby girl," Sandi said, waving energetically; her sparse, pixie-cut brown hair all messed up, black prescription sunglasses askew, upper arms jiggling in the gust of a cool ocean breeze. "Happy Birthday. Oops, I dropped your goodies; lucky for you it's nothing fragile."

Sandi laughs off her own clumsiness, never the one to punish herself for making mistakes. "The gift of being old," she tells anyone who questions her.

Anxious about Sandi tripping, I wave back and get up and walk toward her. When we meet, she gives me one of her special iron-gripped hugs, hugs that instantly lighten up my world.

"Hey, Wicca princess, how's your special day going so far?" she asks, smiling with a lopsided grin. Although she's doing as well as expected, Sandi suffered a stroke last Christmas Day and is still recovering. To be fair, both of us are still recovering; I hadn't been that scared for anyone, including myself, in ages.

"You realize, Mercury Retrograde isn't exactly a favorable position for my birthday Solar Return," I say, trying to justify my visibly sour mood. (We calculate our Solar Return chart according to the exact moment our Sun returns to its original position on our birthday, at the exact time and place where you're celebrating it.)

Unlike the pointless, bogus, general horoscopes you read in the newspapers or nowadays online, this precise moment is as special as each individual, a unique, magical moment that can change your life for the upcoming year or even longer. Here's the crux of the matter: when Mercury, the Jokester planet, retrogrades on one's birthday: its screwy influence can last the entire year, right up to the next birthday. I also notice too well that the time of the dreaded retrograde messes up computers and travel plans and signing documents and shit; plus, it can bring back things one hasn't dealt with in the past, as if I need to deal with more old baggage.

"Mercury is fine; it's your boyfriend who is retrograde," chuckles Sandi, always right. I've been dumped yet again by my on-and-off-guy, Carlos; this time, at a most inopportune moment, immediately before I turn the dreaded fifty.

"I assume, Lady Katherine is late as usual," Sandi affirms rather than asks.

"Not her fault since she lives so far away with all the traffic." I quip sarcastically, finally sensing my tension lift like fog on June afternoons at the beach. I love Sandi's energy and how she can shake me straight out of my foul moods. Sandi only appears like a kindly, Target-shopping, chubby grandma; actually, my silly-looking lady friend is a super brainiac, a retired chemical engineer who worked at NASA in the early '70s. If she were working there now, I'm sure she'd be in charge.

Jupiter the Giant, Earth's Cosmic Santa, sure smiled at me when my friend moved back to Southern California from Washington State. I guess she always went back and forth to take care of her mentally ill son, who was also dealing with addiction. That's how we met, through Danny. When things with Danny got much worse, Sandi assumed she had no choice but to stay put. Sadly, her move was in vain. Poor Danny took his own life about a year ago. No wonder her health took a tumble, that, and her lousy marriage.

Sandi married a younger man whom I trust as far as I can throw. But no matter what Katherine and I say, she refuses to listen. Sandi is financially sound, while Jay, her dickwad of a husband, is, as usual, between jobs. How can she not see what's right under her nose? You don't need to be a great astrologer to predict that he's been chatting up women on dating sites and spending his wife's money on expensive cars and electronics. He's not the one driving an old Chevy, that's for sure.

Of course, I can't compare Sandi with Katherine, who's loaded; still, it's Sandi's generosity that makes it possible for me to remain in insanely expensive South Orange County. She knows too well it would break my heart to leave this place again. I'm a rare find, a fourth- generation local on my mom's side, whose grandfather and dad worked on the old Moulton Ranch raising sheep and cattle. That was before they sold the big ranches off to damn developers who couldn't wait to get their dirty hands on the land, burning down thousands of orange trees in favor of building suburban boxes and then more boxes. As my Orange County-born dad used to say, "what a paradise we lost".

I was born in a three-bedroom, one-and-a-half bath box over ten miles inland from the beach. I started kindergarten at good old Tustin Elementary but was yanked out a short time after my folks split up. I don't remember the details, but I sense it was bad.

My parents' divorce wasn't civilized, that's for sure; neither of them giving a rat's ass about our well-being. No matter how hard I cried, Daddy took me and my older brother to Texas so he could dump us with his folks as Mom explored her newly found sexuality and every chemical known or unknown. Bitch.

"Say, you want me to call Katherine and see what's holding her up? Maybe she flaked on us again?" Sandi asks with more than a hint of irritation, controlling her temper for my sake. Guess she hasn't gotten used to Katherine and her shenanigans. These two old broads are always at each other; I figure

I'm the only thing they have in common. (We got to appreciate Katherine when Sandi was rehabbing after the stroke at the same facility as Katherine's husband, so, she's a pretty recent addition.)

"Nah, why don't I get you an iced tea and we can sit around and gossip before she arrives? And no, they don't sell sodas." I say, hoping she agrees. Sandi is not a fan of acai bowls or probiotic yogurt, but since she shouldn't have soda, she enjoys a little jolt of matcha.

"Sure, it's your birthday, kiddo. Here's a twenty; get yourself something too, but why don't you open up your goodies first? The card's in my purse."

She hands me her beat-up old handbag, filled with a bunch of crap: candy wrappers, two wallets, several pairs of readers, a box of tissue, and a tube of ridiculously expensive Italian hand cream that she buys on some TV shopping channel when she can't sleep.

I stare at my card, open it, and promptly burst into tears. It's beautiful: two small cherubs holding a pastel wreath of pansies and roses connected by English ivy. Inside, Sandi wrote, "Happy Birthday to my lifelong friend. Thank you for being in my life. Your fairy Godmother Sandi, xoxo."

Excited as a little girl at her very first friend's party, she insists I open the sloppily wrapped package held together by plain kitchen string, like those you used to tie a roast or a stuffed chicken. Sandi is nothing but practical. I tear into my gift since there's no reason to save the paper. Inside, I find a trove of treasures: a travel-size pouch filled with lavender-scented skin and body products, a rose quartz crystal pyramid, and two almost impossible-to-find, out-of-print books on astrology.

Sandi is my esteemed star guide and lately my personal teacher/mentor. Ever since she first cast my birth chart, I've been overwhelmed by how the planets have changed, not only how I go about my daily life, but how I see myself. She helps me with so many decisions, especially about what I am supposed to do with the rest of this shit show of an incarnation. When I ask her why, she reassures me I have something special showing up, something that means I can and must learn astrology.

One of the gifted books, a thick, faded paperback, smelling of lazy afternoons spent digging through used bookstores, takes my breath away. It's a 1983 original U.S. edition of Alan Leo's *Astrology for All*. He is our favorite Western astrologer. Alan wasn't an American: He was born in England on August 7, on the exact day Sandi made her appearance. She views Alan as her true twin flame, considering that both of them popped into the Royal Fire sign of Leo, the Lion, at the same exact solar degree. She told me all about his life, how he wrote about New Age subjects, how his father abandoned him when he was a kid, just like hers did. Alan Leo wasn't born into money either; he started working at 16, moving from one shitty job to another. Sometimes he wasn't able to get a job at all. Sandi said he changed his luck when he used numerology, the ancient study of numbers, to change his name. She also gave me hope, explaining that Alan never went to school to study astrology, instead learning from his own teacher, like me. Talking about karma and reincarnation well over 100 years back: what a rebel. Sandi says he was the first truly modern astrologer. And now, I have my very own edition of his book to read and reread. It's like I'm his own personal student through Sandi. It's like we're our own Star family. I've got to stop saying like. What am I a Valley Girl?

"Thank you so much. Where did you find it?" I cry out, impatient to dig in. "Not online, that's for sure."

Sandi smiles, pleased by my reaction. "I was sure you've been looking for Alan's book, but please give the one about karmic relationship a good going over too. It is useful when studying charts of couples. I found the books at a used bookstore in San Clemente, before Danny transitioned," Sandi explains, tearing up as she usually does whenever she mentions her son's name. Some grief never goes away.

"Wow, you've been saving them for my birthday for that long? I will read both of them," I promise her, although after the last go around with Carlos, I'm not sure I want to explore our astrological relationship karma.

As I'm about to go get her tea and use the potty, I recognize Katherine's scratchy, heavily accented voice, *"Liebe.* I'm here. Let the party begin. Sorry, the traffic coming up was murder." Sandi and I glance at each other, make identical funny faces, and dissolve into giggles.

Yep, here she is in all her South Laguna glory: shoulder-length blond hair extensions, freshly healed face-lift, loads of blush, and all the bells and whistles. What's this I see, a new Hermès shopper? The dumb bag is worth thousands. (Before Katherine "educated" me, I couldn't tell the difference between a Hermès and a hermit.) Got to love our Katherine: She started her own fashion blog for "grown-up" women, #seventyisthenewseventeen, gathering hundreds and hundreds of followers, although calling Katherine a "grown-up" is like calling my gun-toting, racist, xenophobic brother a patriot.

Katherine was born in Germany, smack in the middle of the big war, although she never refers to herself as German: "I'm a Berliner. We are nothing like the peasants down south.

They were the ones that let the Nazis screw us. Why everyone makes a big deal of Venice is beyond me? Berlin has more waterways and bridges. Venice is full of messy Italians and pushy Chinese tourists, while Berlin is *das land de dichter und denker*," she switches to German, sometimes forgetting to translate. I've looked it up on Google translator and I guess it means they are famous for poets and people who care too much about nothing that matters to regular people.

Katherine travels to Germany to see her two younger sisters, Berta, and Rosie, every other year, promising to take me along if I can stay clean and get a passport, always pulling strings. Not that I'm planning to use again, but still. It would be nice to get some trust from one of my best friends.

"Where did you park your Rolls?" Sandi asks with that special disapproving click of her tongue she makes whenever she mentions Katherine's silver and royal blue 2015 Rolls Royce Wraith. The swanky car, which Katherine calls the baby, was the last gift from her most recent husband, Hans, that is, before she had to place him into a memory-care facility where he finally croaked, leaving her a bundle after less than a decade of marriage.

Katherine has two planets in her own birth horoscope helping her to marry rich men. Hell, even now, she's dating another one, a widower who lives in Colorado but spends winters in Laguna Beach at his million-dollar mobile home. Katherine's been bragging about spending time on his fancy private yacht, docked nearby in Newport Harbor, not that she'd ever invite me or Sandi. She says it's too early for him to meet her "oddball" girlfriends.

Personally, I could not care less if she drove a Rolls Wraith or a Christmas wreath, but Carlos, a long-haul truck driver, practically wet himself when he first saw it. Boy, oh boy, do I regret asking him to drive me down to help Katherine at the care facility during one of Hans' violent dementia episodes. For days on end, he wouldn't shut up about the damn Rolls and how I should talk Katherine into lending it to me until we had yet another horrible brawl and he stormed off, this time taking his toothbrush with him. To really hurt my feelings, Carlos called me a racist *gringa* who didn't think he was good enough to enjoy a nice car. I told him to go off himself since a Rolls Royce is not exactly my definition of a "nice" car. I can still remember our last exchange.

"Why are you obsessing about the dumb car?"

"I'm not obsessing, I'm only trying to prove my point."

"Bull. What I think is you need the Rolls for some shady deal. I told you, this is one boundary I will not cross. No more drug dealers in my life. I'd had my fill with Glenn."

"And I said you better stop comparing me to your fucking exes. Mama is right: The problem with us is *you* and your too-many exes. Never mind the fucking Rolls. I'm out of here."

Ouch. Not that Carlos's absence was causing me to lose sleep. I was well aware he was about to leave on another job. Several weeks dragged by with no contact until last Sunday, when I saw Carlos's status change on Facebook from in a relationship to single. Was I livid?! (I don't have a profile, too dangerous with my history, but Sandi practically lives on her page and she's friends with Carlos.) Too shaken to drive, I dropped everything and took the #47 bus from my place to his family's house in Santa Ana to give him a piece of my mind. Even though he's never invited me in, I'd dropped him off there plenty of times when he was on his ass, drunk.

Stupidly, I made the mistake of texting the only family member I met, Carlos's sister, whom I considered my friend. Within minutes, even before I got off the bus, Carlos texted me himself. He broke up with me formally, wishing me *buena suerte* with getting laid again now that I'm officially *la viejita*. So instead of being spoiled, getting R & R and sex on a peaceful beach south of Tijuana, I'm spending my birthday trying to keep peace between these two stubborn, old women and obsessing about my latest ex.

"Naturally, I left the baby in expert hands at Montage," Katherine answers Sandi's question about the Rolls with a pout, then clarifies, "I rode the trolley up." (Montage is a crazy-expensive ocean-front hotel and spa that Katherine considers her second home.)

She's not fibbing about the trolley because she prefers to leave her car nice and safe with the valet and get a free ride to anywhere in the village. We three adore the blue and beige rustic little buses with open windows, lots of fresh ocean air, and outgoing drivers. That's one thing I've missed no longer being a resident of Laguna Beach: free in-town transportation. The open- window trolleys used to run only during the summer art festival season, but they became so popular with the locals, the city extended the service, adjusting the hours.

I'd love to rent a trolley for my birthday and ride it up and down the canyon and the coast highway, stopping at all the beaches, but it's too expensive. Before we broke up, I asked Carlos to see into it and he did, but he wasn't about to pay over 300 bucks, since there's a three -hour minimum, and I wasn't about to ask Sandi. She'd done enough. It doesn't matter now, but, hey, anything free is amazing, considering the cost of driving and parking. I only wish we had a free trolley in Costa Mesa.

"I thought you said you got stuck in beach traffic?" Sandi said, poking Katherine and confronting her on one of her most annoying habits: making shit up.

"Did I say that?" Katherine answers, *"Nein,* you're getting hard of hearing, *mausi.* I was sure the traffic would be bad, *albtraum,* since the weather is warm, so I determined I better park at the hotel and take the trolley to grab you girls."

I love the way Katherine equates herself with me, almost thirty years her junior.

"We must leave soon to make lunch precisely on time. You do realize Montage is hard to get into for lunch, especially once the clouds clear up. I called my spa manager a week ago and ordered a special dessert for Viviana's birthday. I told them to decorate it with violets, her favorites." Katherine goes on and on, attempting to distract Sandi from calling her a liar.

"Nonsense," Sandi says. "My hearing is perfect. It's your head that needs checking. You're the one who needs memory care and stop calling me a mouse."

Sandi gives as good as she gets. "Is that what you're giving Viviana for her special birthday: mediocre food, obnoxious service, and overpriced wine she can't drink?" Sandi doesn't let up. Here we go again. "And as the kids say: FYI, she's an Aries, not an Aquarius, but then you'd have to ask for my advice and I'd tell you to order tulips, not violets."

"Ladies," I say, raising my arms as if pretending to break up a fight, trying my best to defuse the conflict. "Let me remind you, this is my birthday and you practically blackmailed me into coming out of my woman-lair, so be nice to each other or I'm leaving."

"Sandra, *der quatsch,* yourself. Excuse me for enjoying spoiling Viviana; inviting her to nice places where she can meet a distinct class of men, not like your gigolo husband. And for your information, I bought her a gift card for the spa boutique too."

Now it's Katherine who revs up, her German accent thickening. "I suppose you got her more of those cheap crystals or stinky used astrology books," she adds, now crossing the line.

Sandi, flabbergasted by Katherine's viciousness, turns red, gets to her feet, doesn't say a word, and after giving me a kiss, storms off. I can't fathom what just happened. Yes, I can. Mercury retrograde—all my plans go to hell.

Chapter 2

"Why do you have to be so rude to Sandi? I love her gifts and, with all due respect, I'd rather get some pizza and no presents at all than see my two best friends in the world fight over me," I say firmly.

"So we're not lunching at Montage?" Katherine says, batting her ridiculously long lash extensions, more suited for an exotic dancer, while she plays with her claws and completely ignores my comments and Sandi's untimely departure.

"Not today," I quickly decide. "I appreciate everything you do for me, but how about a raincheck? I've been here for over an hour and the traffic north is getting worse. Why don't you give me my gift card the next time we have lunch?"

"Are you sure?" Katherine asks, seeming more confused than upset. Sandi was right. There was no gift card. She was going to ask the servers to get it for her once they sat us.

"Sure, I'm sure." I smile to set her mind at ease. Honestly, I'm not sore. How can I be? Kathrine's almost eighty. "Thanks for arranging for the birthday cake, but it's better for me, you know. I had all my carbs here when I ate the frozen yogurt."

"*Toll*, you have your car. Won't you take me to Montage? I'll call my neighbors, you know, the Freeds, to join me. Then there won't be a need for you to feel guilty about cancelling," Katherine says in her best "order, not ask" voice. "The Freeds have been so kind to me since Hansie passed away."

I can't believe my eyes, but she actually pretends to dab away a phony tear, then jumps, realizing her lashes are in the way and they mustn't get wet. I almost laugh out loud. Wow. Here she's ruined my only fiftieth birthday celebration, but she wants *me* to play *her* servant, so she won't miss a chance to get loaded on white wine. These rich people are something, as Sandi says. They will expect and demand without even giving it a second thought. I just smile and say, "Sorry, not going to happen, but give me your phone and I'll order you a driver. Remember, Sandi loaded the ride share app on your phone?"

"Really? All right, *schatzi*," Katherine pouts, then pats me on my shoulder, "but stay with me until the driver gets here," she stresses in her special "'you will do what I say" voice.

"No problem, I can do that. Let me check how soon they can get here." I reach for her phone, make a request, and feel relieved: In four minutes she'll be on her way to my birthday lunch at the fabulous Montage, glamming it up with her own friends.

The ride share car arrives right on time. I lead Katherine down the few slippery concrete steps and after helping her into the back of the older, but spotless sedan, return to my table. I know I should get back home, but if I leave now, I'll find the first skanky bar on the way and lose my hard-fought-for sobriety. So I text my AA sponsor, Dave, and tell him I need to hear his voice. He calls back right away, talking me through a rough moment.

Just as I suspected, the traffic back to Costa Mesa via the Coast Highway is a bumper-to-bumper nightmare. I know I should've taken Laguna Canyon to the Toll Road, but I'm scared to drive it after the last time, which practically ended my troubles for good. I'm still having flashbacks, so I use the excuse of the Toll Road being insanely expensive and avoid it. Well, I'm not lying. They have the gall to charge close to eight dollars for under twenty miles. So here I sit, sweating, stuck on the Coast Highway, starving, irritated, and lonely, in desperate need for a hit or a pill or a lousy vodka and cranberry, anything to take the edge off.

Fuck it, I think. *I'm only 50 once and one drink doesn't mean I'm going to go back to using. Come on, you need to eat. Your blood sugar is low.* I try to reason with my sly addict side. *I bet when you get home, you'll find apology flowers from Carlos. He's a Latin lover, a true romantic who always says he's sorry with a bouquet. Maybe he felt he had no choice but to dump you to teach you a lesson. You know you can be a crazy bitch. Maybe he's cooled off, changed his mind, and wants to get back together? Or maybe one of your Texas nieces left a funny birthday message, or maybe your bro's wife sent a paper card.* That's one thing I learned in therapy: positive self-talk, when you talk to your addict side as if it were a friend.

Okay, that worked. As I crawl through the exclusive Newport Coast and even more ritzy Corona Del Mar, the urge for a drink recedes. The traffic lightens up around Fascist; I mean the Fashion Island outdoor shopping mall, yet another example of the insane excess I have to deal with daily.

Almost forty-five minutes after leaving Laguna Beach, I cross the bridge over the sparkling blue Back Bay, finally making a right turn on Newport Boulevard and driving north. That's where the monkey climbs on my back one more time. Here they are, Carlos's and my old hangouts, one after another, sending out irresistible signals to stop by, at least for a brief visit with my loyal friends who'd sing me a birthday song and buy me a few. Normally, I avoid taking that route, recognizing the threat to my sobriety, but today has been anything but normal. I try once more to call Sandi's cell, but she doesn't pick up. In desperation, I call the house line, but it's Jay who answers, so I hang up without leaving a message since he won't give it to her anyway.

I've been drug-free for twenty-six months and five days, not counting today, but living a totally alcohol-free life is still a daily struggle. When Carlos and I first hooked up, we helped each other stay clean and it worked for the first amazing months when we were in love and having crazy sex. Once we started fighting over, well, let's say, everything, especially about his religion, our families, and my astrology "obsession," partying together seemed to help, though I mostly stayed sober, drinking gallons of Diet Coke with lemon. Now I know that was the beginning of the end: You either use together or sleep alone. Thinking about Carlos and being dumped on Facebook hurts so badly, the familiar choking sensation of an approaching panic attack interferes with my driving. I have to stop somewhere to calm down.

Finally, I admit defeat and pull into the parking lot, right behind my favorite home away from home. The Boulevard is a proper bar, at least it was when I was last there. It's anything but a hipster, twenty-dollar-a-shot gastro pub or the beer tavern next door, polluted by whiny, snotty-nosed babies, looking for a cheap high.

That's right, I'm a fucking addict; there's nothing I haven't tried at least a few times, and that is a fact I've lived with since before I lost my virginity to my uncle Barry, but that's all water under the bridge. I know—more clichés, but it happened under a bridge, not that I remember much. I was stoned. We both were. I also know it sounds creepy having sex with a relative, but he was my dad's distant cousin and barely out of his teens himself; my first taste of what was to come: good drugs and bad dudes. Funny, I haven't thought about Barry in ages, but I'm in trouble and need a reminder about the mess I made of my life when I was using. In those days, I was willing to pay any price to feel better; hell, forget better, simply normal.

My thirtieth birthday is a complete blur: Those were my coke and ecstasy days, when I danced at the local strip club. I had fake tits and way too much money in those days. Forty wasn't fabulous either: I can't think about ten years back without wanting to slash my wrists. This was way before Carlos, who, despite all of our problems, was a prince compared to my last long-term disaster, the drug-fueled marathon with Glenn, now rotting in hell, where he belongs. It makes little sense how and why I survived the Laguna Canyon crash, considering what was left of Glenn's Rover. Of course, I've had not one, but several near-death experiences, one so horrifying I won't even let myself think about it. Scratch that, now that I found astrology of the Fixed Stars or to be more precise, the stars found me; it all makes sense.

I take a few deep breaths, wipe my tears, and feel more in control, except now I have to pee. I can cross my legs for a few blocks until I get home or use the ladies room at the bar. Just to make sure I'm not tempted by all the lovely bottles, I avoid the Boulevard and go into the kiddy tavern. Because it's still early, the bar's pretty slow, so I don't have to wait in line for my bladder to explode; the stalls are empty. I feel relieved and proud of my decision to not take a drink. Maybe Mercury retrograde forcing me to return to the self-destructive old habits won't be that bad after all.

As I'm about to walk out the door, a familiar laugh makes me turn toward the smoking patio and whom do I see? It's my ex, Carlos, playing pool, dressed to impress in his sexy 7 for All Mankind jeans, the same jeans I bought him for Valentine's Day after borrowing money from Sandi, money I still owe her. Carlos's button-down, white-and-blue checkered shirt is freshly pressed, a lit cigarette dangles from his lying mouth. Carlos used my smoking as one of his so-called reasons we're not a suitable match. He looks great: freshly shaven cleft chin, curtesy of his Taurus Rising, his thick, wavy, jet-black hair is styled with extra care. He's slathered on his musky aftershave too. I can smell it even all the way over here by the wall where I'm hiding.

It looks like Carlos has been here a while, drinking his favorite, Tito's vodka chased with Pacifico beer, and cavorting with a petite, hard-body gal in up-the-ass denim shorts and leopard- print boots. The woman's got her back to me, so I can't see her ethnicity, except for her long black hair. Then she turns around and I see she's not Hispanic, but Asian. This is where I lose it: In his fuck-off text, Carlos said another reason he's dumping me was the pressure he gets from his family to settle down and start a family with his own kind. Lies, all lies. It seems everyone is having a great time celebrating my fiftieth birthday, except for me. Not knowing what to do, I ru back into the ladies room and lock myself in a stall. I want to confront him and smash the empty Pacifico bottle on his head, but I also have an overwhelming urge to escape without him seeing me. Instead, I just sit on the cracked, smelly john, unable to move.

Someone opens the restroom door. I hear bits and snippets of Vietnamese. Yes, usually I get my mani-pedi around my birthday; the younger gals tend to pepper the sing-song Vietnamese with English. If you want to live in California, you had better get used to folks speaking their own tongue. They say they print the election ballots not only in Spanish, but also many other languages, not that I've ever voted anywhere in any language. As my dad always says, "Government is not the solution, government is the problem." (Wonder where he heard that? I know he's not that smart.) Looking down at the floor of the stall next to me, I recognize the boots of Carlos's latest soon-to-be ex. The conversation gets louder, loud enough that I can hear the other party's voice. Obviously, I wish I knew as much Vietnamese as Spanish. Lucky for me, they use just enough English that I can get their drift.

"You like?" a female voice asks in the middle of a foreign barrage.

"He handsome, but drinks too much beer," replies Carlos's date. She sure is smarter than me. Beer no good for hard and long," she giggles. They talk back and forth for another minute until I hear more English.

"No dinner?"

"He wants next date. Too drunk, need to go home soon. Tomorrow work."

"*Pok gai*, no food, no next time: too cheap. No good for you. Want I come we go get sushi?"

"*Cám o'n.*"

I don't know what *pok gai* means, but the other words mean "thank you," that much I know. It never hurts to learn a few simple words like thanks; it makes the world a nicer place, at least that's what I think. To hear my family in Texas, you'd think knowing how to say *gracias* is a sin.

Just as I am about to sneak out, I hear my neighbor flush, then running water, and finally the door opens and closes. I wait a few minutes to make sure no one sees me and then rush out, getting into my car, but not before checking for Carlos's silver-gray Toyota Tacoma. Yep, there it is, parked a few rows down the lot, away from the bars, behind a new retail store, just in case the Costa Mesa cops are around.

Unlike the rest of his family, Carlos is too much of a car enthusiast to drive American. I recognize the upgraded tires and the wooden cross hanging from his mirror. On the dash, Carlos has placed a small statue of Mary. Of course, the statue is the Mexican *La Morenita*, the Virgin of Guadalupe. I don't care which version of Mary he prays to; it's all mad-up patriarchal baloney to me. I can't understand why he needs all that religious protection, considering he made me crazy driving around to local dealerships and bugging the sales guys about ratings, reliability, and safety.

Hurt and embarrassed, I'm about to place my tail between my pitiful legs and go home alone when I check a pocket-size daily planetary guide I keep in the car's center column, my growling gut telling me something is wrong in addition to Mercury playing its tricks. As I open the guide to today's planetary positions, I see it. I mean, I'm just a student, Sandi would know more, but this much I do know: Sun in Aries square Pluto in Capricorn is not good for Carlos, born under the sign of Cancer, the Crab. Sun is all about authority and Pluto is power struggles. Okay. Things are looking up. I look at Carlos's Neptune and compare it with the moon position: yes, boozing and trying to hook up with a fresh piece. It's making more sense.

Wipe your tears and stop wearing your Aries Venus on your sleeve, I tell myself. *Remember your Scorpio Rising.*

Sandi says my Ascendant sign, meaning the exact time I was born, is a magical gift from the Fixed Star, Alpha Centauri, at 29 degrees, 29 minutes of Scorpio. (She explained that this is the only fortifying influence responsible for saving my sorry ass in my birth chart, considering my other planetary messes.)

I've been reading everything I can about Alpha Centauri, trying to understand the real me. So far, all I've learned is that AC is the closest star to us, home to an advanced bunch of Higher Beings, who watch over us, afflicted "earthlings," making sure we don't blow ourselves up. You can judge for yourself, but when the government says they've seen UFOs, it's the real deal.

I also read that here's where I get my need for passion, sex, learning about the unusual, and fighting to remake myself. On the not-so-nice side, I'm definitely not the one to live and let live. I'm comfortable with vengeance, but only if I've been wronged. I guess the love/hate nature of my relationships is not my fault. I'm also a huge sci-fi fan. For me, it's all real. Where do you think we get the stories about gods and goddesses?

I look at the guide one more time, feeling the weight lift off my chest for the first time in days, smiling at my own fifty-year-old reflection in the mirror. While I've been going through that high school crap at the bar, the moon has moved into a favorable position to my moon. I don't need a pill, or a hit, or a vodka-cranberry. What I need is revenge, I mean Cosmic Justice: a little of both will do. Happy birthday to me.

Chapter 3

My plan is deliciously Alpha Centauri, but not so easy to execute. Let's see, since it involves Sun and Pluto, what I need is a little help from my friends in local law enforcement who regularly patronize the old-school doughnut and sandwich shop across the residential side street, next to the bar's parking lot. You'd expect it would be easy, making an anonymous call to CHIPs to report a drunk driver, supplying the cops with Carlos's truck's license plate and a vague description, as if I saw him momentarily on the road. I've been around both sides of the law long enough to appreciate how to bend the rules just so it serves my purpose, having spent my entire childhood around cops and their families.

My dad, Howard Sr., retired with a full pension, and my one full-blooded sibling, Howie Jr., still works for ICE, making life miserable for the migrants. No wonder Carlos refused to take a trip to meet my folks, but too late to worry about making nice now. If they detain Carlos based on a 911 call and he gets lawyered up, my phone can be traced even with a blocked ID. Any good DUI attorney, like the guy my family hired when I was busted, can tell you it's all a matter of "constitutional" rights vs. using "an anonymous tipster."

You think it's easy to make a DUI stick? Well, if that won't work, somehow I need for the cops to see him getting into his vehicle coming out of the bar drunk. I don't have time for subtle, careful planning either. Based on what I heard from his date, I don't see that he's getting laid tonight and tomorrow he's off on a job, therefore, time is of the essence. It's now or never. Just in case, I pull a long, blond wig from my glove compartment and quickly put it on to cover my faded maroon-color frizz, topping it with a cotton beanie. Thanks to the Goddess, I left my dance days alter ego, Chrissie, in the car. Years of dealing with crazy dealers and dodgy stalkers taught me the art of disguise. Plus, it saves time and money. Have you ever tried to get a color and a trim around here? I can't afford to spend over a hundred bucks every six weeks.

I turn my engine on and slowly exit the parking lot, but instead of turning left to go home, I drive straight and park in front of the doughnut shop. There they are: two local motorcycle officers and a deputy from the OC Sheriff's Office. I kind of recognize one of the guys, but the other faces are new. So I smile blandly, careful not to make eye contact, and go over to the counter, where an older Asian woman reminds me that I'll need cash to pay for my order. (I keep a few dollars of change for beach parking in my car in case I run out of money.)

"I remember. No problem. I don't use credit cards anyway," I respond without making a fuss.

"You're nice," the woman says. She's obviously used to customers' complaints. I get it: You'd be surprised how many times I had to take out a few bucks to buy a cup of coffee and a madeleine cookie for Katherine, who hasn't seen cash in years. I look down at the case and see that most of my favorite doughnuts, especially the apple fritters, are gone, probably sold by noon. Instead, I order an iced tea and pick up a snack-size bag of salt and vinegar potato chips and find a small, plastic table with a single chair, just far enough away from the cops not to look suspicious or flirty, but close enough for them to hear me, and, more importantly, for me to hear them. I take out my refurbished phone, a gift from Sandi, and text my old, broken phone using voice application. First, I say hi to an imaginary friend and then use short bursts of words telling my nonexistent girlfriend all about running into her wasted boyfriend at the tavern where he is partying with another woman, knowing he is not supposed to drink while on probation.

My family always said I should have been an actress. As the ghost conversation continues, I consider what today has been like and find no need to force a dry sob, no longer needing to pretend. That gets their attention. My daddy always said a good cop can't resist a crying blond; rescue complex is real.

The biggest of the fish looks up. "Excuse me, miss. Is everything all right? Do you need assistance?" asks the impressive, well-armed and vested deputy.

"Oh no, Officer, thank you," I say. It's all good. I just got into a dumb argument with my girlfriend. I need to keep my big mouth shut." I look up at the big guy with a much-practiced deer-in-the headlights expression, my crystal-blue eyes, the one attractive feature I inherited from my mom, swimming with tears.

That should do it. I think.

"Perhaps, in some personal cases we should, but in our business, we need help from the community to keep it safe," the cop says, offering his opinion without a smile.

They heard me!

"It's none of my business, really," I say, refusing to bite. "My friend and her guy will figure it out. I better get going; I live just two blocks down."

"Is that so? Where?" he asks forcefully, trying intimidation. *Ha-ha, hilarious and way too predictable.*

"I live right of Tustin Street, Officer," I answer, looking nervous, just like any other average citizen would be when confronted by a power-wielding asshole. "It's my birthday today, and I had lunch in Laguna with my lady friends. Do you want to see my license?" I ask.

He ponders that for a minute, looks me over with those too-familiar cops' eyes, and wishes me a good night. Whew, that was close! If I'd had to show him my ID, he would've found the discrepancy in my appearance suspicious, except women change their hair color and style all the time.

I finish my stale chips, take my flavorless iced tea, and walk out, careful not to look at the cops who are talking about a slow night. I make a left turn, avoiding the back parking lot, knowing in my gut that Carlos is about to get his. I drive around for a few minutes and then make a turn into the same lot, but from a different direction, turning my lights off and parking by the wall. Shit, the wig! I remove it along with the hat and use my fingers to fluff up my hair, getting ready for the show. Desperate to witness the payback for myself, I take off my ancient moto jacket, exchanging it for a flowery poncho that Sandi left in my car.

Although I'd love for Carlos to see my "resting bitch" face, I exit my car through the passenger side, making sure I stay in the shadows while awaiting the action. The spring sun has just set, but the rusty glow to the west remains. It takes just a few more minutes for my doughnut-shop friends to make their presence known to the entire neighborhood—man, their equipment is loud. The two motorcycle cops are there as is the big guy in the cruiser, but wait. Within sixty seconds, two more cars pull up right behind the tavern, this time they are

Costa Mesa police. I wonder if they're there for someone other than my soon-to-be-sorry ex-boyfriend.

Curious about the police activity, a few young guys who rent the cheaper apartments down the street, cross over to where I'm standing.

"Hey, what's the deal?" one kid asks, yawning and scratching his bald head.

How do you lose your hair at twenty? I ask myself but don't answer, shaking my head no.

"You wanna check it out?" the second, much smaller, Indian-looking kid asks the third guy, his visibly chemically "chilled," muscular buddy, who stands at least a head taller than him. Not getting anywhere with me, they walk toward the bar, but I hang back, letting them do all the work for me. I can see something bigger than I planned is taking place, but I can't tell exactly what it is. Just as I'm about to give up and go home, I see the same three guys, now looking bored, stroll by on their way back to their apartment. This time it's my turn to ask.

"So what happened? I was meeting my girlfriend for a beer," I lie, "but the cops scared me off."

"Yeah, just stay put. There are too many of them in there for my taste," the tall, better- looking of the trio says, offering his sage advice.

"DUI, drugs, or illegal?" I ask, not giving up and trying to sound naturally curious.

"All of it, plus they got him on RA, resisting arrest," the short Indian chimes in. I can tell he's a chatty sort. 'This Mexican dude was out of his mind, screaming about some witch putting a curse on him and threatening a lawsuit and calling the cops racists pigs."

"I bet that didn't go over big. I mean, this side of Newport Boulevard is not Costa Mexico, as the Hispanics call the west side of Costa Mesa, where you can get a better Tacos Carbon than a burger. Wow, I hoped it was going to be a fun night because tonight's my big birthday, but nothing has been going right," I blurt out without thinking, both gratified and just a tad guilty about getting Carlos into bigger trouble than I first intended. Actually, scrap the guilt: The arrest has probably saved his life, Now, he'll have no choice but to get sober.

"Costa Mexico? That's so funny and so true," says the bold kid with a big grin.

Costa Mesa is peculiar that way. Katherine says it's like Berlin before the fall of the Wall: one city, but two different worlds, each one with its own language and rules.

"Big birthday, hey?" asks the good-looking one. "Let me see: I don't mean to offend, but you're forty, right?" he says flirtingly, putting on the charm offensive.

"How d'you guess?" I say, beaming back, feeling so much better about tonight. It's amazing what a compliment from a younger man can do for a gal's bruised ego, especially if she has her Venus, the planet of love, in the sign of the easily infatuated, trusting Aries.

"Say, since it's your big four-o, how'd you like to party with us?"

Aha, this one is ready to get it on. The night is getting even better. Fuck you, Carlos—this *viejita* can still get some anytime she wants it. I enjoy a familiar sensation in my gut, the one that speeds up my pulse.

"We've got some dope pipes, but if you're not into it, we've got some high-end molly," the cutie adds with a sexy wink.

"That sounds great, guys, but my old man is waiting for me at home," I say, making a plausible excuse and coyly touching him on the arm. "And I mean, he's pissed since I've been gone all day."

"Well, happy birthday anyway," he says with increasing confidence. "I'm Nathan— Nate—and this here's my roomie, Raj; just kidding, this is Brandon." He turns to his buddy. "Told you she's too hot to be single." Nathan tries again, turning to his other buddy, the boldie. "This is Ryan. Hope to see you at the tavern sometime."

Wow, this one must be a Fire sign for sure. (Fire signs are Aries, Leo, and the ever- restless Archer.) So I ask, "When's your birthday?"

"December, I'm a Sagittarius," says Nate proudly. "You're into astrology?"

"A little," I say. No reason to get into anything too serious.

"Here, read my palm." Nate turns his long, almost-feminine hand upside and shoves it right under my nose. I just laugh. Why is it whenever I say I'm into astrology, people shove hands into my face? I'm not a freaking palm reader.

"Maybe next time. Thanks for the invite, though." I wave goodbye, open my car door, and immediately lock it. You never can tell when a friendly chat will turn into something sketchy. Nate taps on my window, still smiling, Not wanting to seem rude, I roll it down, but just a few fingers worth.

"What's your name, birthday girl?" he asks with that look they all get when they see something they want to nail. They say a man, I mean any straight man, decides in the first few minutes after meeting a woman whether he wants to go to bed with her and I agree with that assessment. At least it used to be that way. Who knows nowadays with all that fake-profile online dating?

"Chrissie," I answer without hesitation. "Look, I like you, but I'm too old for fun and games and I'm beat. If the stars align, we'll run into each other; if not, thanks for the good wishes and the compliments; you made my birthday." Then I make a mistake and look at him closely. Damn, what a hottie: the rugged jaw, the full lips, and those perfect teeth. Somehow he even looks familiar. Uh-oh, he's just my type: the lethal combo of slim hips and full lips. Here I go again.

"How about a birthday hug?" he asks.

This one doesn't give up easily. I'm suspecting that tonight's stars are aligned. The familiar excitement, the anticipation of the chase is rising in my belly. Hell, if I were forty and using, I'd end up spending one crazy night at his place, getting my heart ripped out of my chest again, but I'm fifty, and although he doesn't recognize it, I do.

Time to grow up, Viviana.

I wipe Chrissie's smile off my face, roll up my window, wave, and drive away.

Chapter 4

It's dark by the time I pull my dinosaur of a black 1983 300 D Mercedes without working air or radio into the back of the cracked, weed-infested driveway that spans the entire length of the astonishingly large (by Orange County standards) property and turn off the rattling engine. The dense fog has rolled in from Newport Bay, causing the temperature to drop by at least ten degrees. Although, I'm well prepared for this crazy climate where it can be 60 degrees in the morning, 98 in the afternoon, and then go back down to 60, I'm shivering from adrenaline withdrawal caused by my encounters with the cops and Nate, not to mention the lack of a proper meal. Now I'm grateful for that high-carb yogurt and bag of stale chips, which turned out to be my only birthday treats.

Removing Sandi's gifts from the car, I don't bother to lock the driver-side door. Let them have the old junker. (I finally have insurance thanks to Sandi, who put me on her policy, telling her agent I'm her full-time caregiver.)

"Damn," I mumble as I try to get my shaking hands around my keys. Finally, I get the front door open and then lock it. When I flip on the lights, a small field mouse, an on-and-off visitor, runs past me, disappearing into the darkness of the overgrown potted-plants-filled yard. The mouse reminds me of Carlos. I used to call him Mr. Macho because he detested anything small and furry, even dogs and cats. The jerk demanded I set a mousetrap or else he'd shoot it with his stupid Ruger, the same Ruger that became a topic of too many fights. Since I grew up around service weapons, I'd come to detest guns.

I take off my scuffed-up ankle boots and Sandi's poncho, dropping both on the small leather recliner in the front room, and go straight into the bathroom to pee and wash my hands, but not before checking for messages on Sandi's last-century answering machine. There are two new messages—most likely birthday wishes from Texas.

"There sure isn't one from that cheater, Carlos," I say out loud, talking to myself, a habit I'd picked up only recently since this is the first time I've lived on my own: no boyfriends, crazy roommates, or unintentional fuck buddies.

Because I don't like being reminded about being fifty, I leave the messages for tomorrow, remembering that I left a bit of a keto-diet-friendly cheese and salami in the fridge. I finish my ruined celebration eating standing in front of it, not even bothering to close the door. Once I'm sort of full, I go to bed, leaving the lamp by the recliner on. It'll take a few minutes before the Seroquel, my last chemical crutch, takes effect. Hey, it's better than benzos and booze.

The place where I'm trying to get it together and put down roots to be more precise is a 669-square-foot, one-bedroom back cottage that belongs to Sandi, making her my "Fairy Goddess Landlady." The cottage hasn't seen a fresh coat of paint since I was a school kid, but the tiled roof, covered by pink bower vines, is sound and I adore the original oak flooring, where the scratches and stains only add to its faded charm.

Since I don't have any furniture of my own, thanks to my last living situation fiasco, I appreciate it being furnished with some delicate pieces, including an authentic French walnut armoire with loads of shelving. However, I sure could use a proper mattress instead of this wreck of a waterbed. One day I'll even buy one of those special beds with cooling gel. One day, if I stay, I'll try to talk Sandi into making a few improvements. She can put in a new toilet and I can find cheap curtain panels, but not until I can pay market rent and not the absurd six hundred a month Sandi insisted I can afford to pay, much to the dismay of her dickhead of a husband, Jay.

The original 1950s front house, with its three bedrooms and two full baths, is now empty and locked up. I try to avoid looking at it since that's where poor Danny died, rest his tortured soul. He was a mess of a guy, but so sweet and such a talented musician. He was always trying to introduce me to what he called "authentic sound," but it was lost on me, the Top 40 gal who still listens to KISS FM.

The first time I met him in group therapy, I noticed something didn't add up. He was clearly down, but not the violent type, and I should know. He also gave out a gay vibe, but Sandi told me he dated women, even getting engaged once or twice. Well, that meant squat. I danced with plenty of girls who slept with men but loved women.

I was inside the front house only once, when Katherine and I helped Sandi clear out his stuff, and let me say, it wasn't one of my favorite moments. Danny had trashed the living room walls, fucked up all the brand-new appliances Sandi had put in just for him, and had stained the carpet badly with his own blood. She hadn't been able to rent the house to anyone else because of the damage. I don't even want to recall what we saw in his bathroom. (A clean bathroom alone is enough of a reason to stay sober; when you're loaded, hygiene needs are not exactly on the top of your to-do list.)

Financially shrewd, Sandi bought the property for practically nothing, paying off the mortgage when she retired from her corporate job. Those were the days when you could buy something nice in one of the older, traditional Newport Beach neighborhoods for around two hundred thousand; I can only imagine how little Sandi paid for this place.

There's a small, remodeled cottage for sale on a nice size lot a few doors down that's listed for nearly a million dollars. I guess the "hipster" millennials see east side Costa Mesa as a bargain compared to Newport, its snooty neighbor. Personally, I could never be comfortable in bigoted, white supremacist Newport. I prefer Costa Mesa because it's down to earth and diverse.

Ever since Danny died, Jay's been pressuring Sandi to sell the house as is. What Jay doesn't suspect because they keep their finances separate, is that Sandi owns three more houses in the same neighborhood, bought with her own money, all mortgage-free. Let's put it this way, she's making more money on rents than she ever made working for NASA. That's why she's my role model and hero. What I pray for is that she can damn well afford to leave Jay's house in Riverside and move down to the beach, closer to me and Katherine, but she won't hear of it.

I worry about her safety; his place is a tri-level monstrosity on tons of land and needs remodeling more than my little cottage. I helped Sandi manage after her stroke, and the place gave me the creeps. She's always falling down the stairs and bumping into piles of junk. Jay, a pack rat, doesn't see the need to pick up. She says we're lucky he doesn't move her into the Palm Desert condo, his mom's place. Then we'd never get to see each other.

Sandi is trying to teach me everything she knows not only about astrology, but also about real estate because she says my birth chart is favorable for working with properties, but as a manager, not as an agent. If only I'd had good karma to get my chart read when I was younger and struggling with job decisions, but no such luck. However, despite my lack of money and sex, overall, I must admit, things are looking up now that I'm sober, although being single is something I'll have to get used to if Carlos is correct about me being an old woman, even if meeting young Nate made me hope all is not lost. Perhaps when Venus moves retrograde in the next few weeks, we will run into each other again. He looks like a guy who works out, and I've been wanting to join the popular gym a few blocks away. I'll run into him on 17th; everybody is hanging out at the chicken place. Heck, per chance, we'll even share a Sidecar doughnut.

I remember him looking at me, practically begging me for a hug and I now regret not going for him, just to spite Carlos and my chronology. No matter how hard I try, I'm not yet sleepy, so I decide to do my astrology "homework" before passing out, hoping to do something useful since nothing else has worked out.

I open my astrology notebook filled with scribbles and random thoughts, once again looking at my birth chart. According to Sandi, this is how you start: learn all about your-self and then try to help others.

Right now, I'm learning all about what happens when a person is born with an important Fixed Star right on their Ascendant, meaning when a baby pops into her latest incar-nation. Because I don't have any of those fancy astrology software programs, Sandi sends me printed copies of charts of famous people and then reviews them with me over the phone. I can't imagine that someone who sucked in school and hated history and science is now spending hours happily pouring over astronomical positions and finding out a bunch of interesting stuff about old cultures. Who would have guessed you can actually understand what's going on with folks just by looking at a few weird symbols? As my Fairy God Mama repeats, "People lie, charts don't." I realize my family and Carlos think I've lost it with the astrology "nonsense" (the only thing they agree about), but I'm used to being judged harshly, and, hey, studying the stars helps to focus my mind on something other than booze and sex.

Would you suspect that three thousand years ago, back in Iran, then Persia, before telescopes and rockets, astrologers wrote about four of the brightest stars they could see with the naked eye, considering them the guardians of heaven, kind of like one of my all-time fav movies, *Guardians of the Galaxy*. Back then, they used the position of these stars to mark the seasons, equinoxes, and solstices. Let me see if I can remember. I can find Aldebaran in the constellation of Taurus, the Bull; Regulus is Leo, the Lion; Fomalhaut, no, Antares is in the constellation of Scorpio; and finally, Fomalhaut, in Pisces, the Fish. Oops, actually the latest notes say (because even the Fixed Stars drift), Regulus is now in Virgo.

I yawn and stretch, savoring the longed-for Seroquel heaviness. The sweet heaviness drifts over my hyperactive mind as I slip under the blanket of nothingness.

Chapter 5

I jerk awake because someone is banging on my door, then the house phone rings, the sound I find as agreeable as what my dad usually plays at home, country music, if you can call that background clatter music.

Drowsy, dizzy, and dry-lipped as usual, I take the silly kitty face eye mask off and slowly move my stiff neck side to side and reach for some oxygen water I have nearby wherever I am. When I look at the clock, the time reads 10:50. I've slept for over twelve hours. Mercifully, the banging stops; clearly whoever it was has given up, but the phone won't stop making that special sound I associate with nothing good. I pull myself up, swinging my naked, unshaven legs to Carlos's side of the bed and stab my little toe on one of his Earl work boots. The hideous, size-12 boots are sticking out from under my bed.

"Damn it, Carlos. You're such *a chancho*. I almost broke my toe. Where the fuck are you? On the toilet again?" I call him out on his rude pig behavior.

Oh shit, he's gone, I remember, a jolt of adrenalin finally waking me up.

The phone stops ringing as I go into the bathroom, but when I'm finished, it starts again.

"*Ola*," I answer slowly, ready to say I'm just a cleaning woman who doesn't speak English, but it's Sandi, calling from a number I don't recognize. We haven't spoken since she stormed off after her asinine scrape with Katherine.

"Good morning, birthday girl," Sandi replies suspiciously cheery.

"What's good about it?" I growl back, still grumpy from yesterday.

"Want to have lunch? I've got something to tell you."

"Not really, I'm in a shitty mood. Someone was banging on my door and woke me up before the meds wore off."

"Poor kid. You must still be tired from your big birthday celebration. How does it feel to be a grown-up?" she asks, daring to make light of my predicament.

"What celebration? Yesterday was the worst day since I stopped using. Why didn't you warn me?" I say bitterly. "On second thought, yeah, let's have lunch and I'll tell you what happened to me. I wasn't partying, that's for sure."

"Calm down, girlie. You will change your mind about your birthday soon enough," Sandi says, trying to cheer me up.

"Fine, if you say so. I pray today will be a better vibe."

"I'm positive it will. The Moon is cheering up your sexy Venus."

"Venus, Moon... sometimes I suspect it's not the stars but you that always makes me appear better." I finally take a deep breath and smile.

"Ah," Sandi sighs, "I love you too, angel."

"Say, were you planning on coming down here or should I meet you halfway? Maybe at the Circle?" The "cuteness overload" shop-and-dine neighborhood, referred to by the locals as the Circle, is about ten miles inland in Old Town Orange. It's Sandi's favorite place for enjoying a cup of proper tea and spending hours upon hours picking through its many antiques establishments. Last time we had a blast, buying embroidered hankies and trying on vintage hats. It's yet another thing we have in common: that nagging sensation of being born in the right place, but at the wrong time.

"Not today. I'm driving down your way," Sandi says, surprising me. "Lots of business to attend to in Costa Mesa. I'm meeting a prospective renter for the front house, and I want the two of you to meet as well, Vivi."

"Really? A renter?" I'm shocked.

"It's time..."

"Of course; whatever you decide, I'm on board." I'm not sure Sandi is being totally honest about moving on after Danny's death, but I approve of her at least trying.

"You want Mexican food?" I ask, knowing well I should probably eat something less greasy, but this morning, I'm missing Carlos like mad. (I can only blame my sore little toe for his gorgeous face and hot bod getting stuck in my head.)

"Sure, but not the new place," Sandi insists, referring to one of the trendy restaurants popping up and down the old 17th Street.

"How about Avilla's?" I offer, reasoning Maria's generously sized portions of home-style cooking will do both of us some good. I'm sure I'll even have some leftovers to solve my dinner dilemma.

"No, too fancy."

"Avilla's? It's not fancy at all; just a little expensive, except on Taco Tuesdays," I say, suddenly craving their guac and guava margaritas.

"I'm thinking Mi Casa."

Well, I'll be. That was her and Danny's favorite hangout.

"Sure, but it'll take me at least an hour to get moving. I can meet you at noon."

"See you then. Love you." Sandi hangs up quickly, before I can tell her I love her back.

By the time I get going, it's way past noon. I've had several dizzy spells and dragged myself out of a liquor store a block away from Mi Casa before I snuck a shot of something to make me normal.

It's nearly 1 p.m. when I finally pull into the strip mall and park a few rows back, full of guilt as usual about leaving her alone in a public place, something she hates. I'm happy this place doesn't hold any memories of Carlos. I associate it more with another ex, Glenn, and his snooty Newport friends, if you can call your buyers friends. Here, even the owners have always been Caucasian. Last time I was there, the bartender told me Mi Casa's been around since the early '70s and let's say their "rustic" darkness agrees with lots of folks looking to tie a few on in the middle of the afternoon. It's been months since I had lunch here with Sandi and Danny. Sadly, I fell off the wagon and sneaked a few shots of Sauza Silver (hey, it's cheap) while she was on the can. (For some dumb reason, Danny was a big fan of George Bush Sr. and the idea of eating in the same place as the former president made him happy.) Too bad you're not supposed to speak ill of the dead, but Danny was always a Tea Party fuckhead, even without the drugs.

I'm amazed I haven't caught shit from Sandi about running late. I'm positive she's here because I saw her car parked right up front in one of the handicapped spots. The hostess is away from the front desk. I wander inside, not paying attention to the dark wood or the brick accents or who's sitting at the red banquet booths.

"I'm looking for my girlfriend," I say when I bump into the hostess who's just finished seating a large group of rich, old dudes, all wearing expensive golf clothes and hats. Not one of them glances at me, as I'm doing the best I can, trying to avoid looking at the bar and all those gorgeous bottles.

"Help yourself," the hostess, a hot, young Newport blond answers with a dismissive smile, barely acknowledging my presence.

Within a few seconds, I spot Sandi. There she is, but she's not alone: My friend is lunching with a man, visibly younger than herself based on the back of his head and those broad, muscled shoulders bulging out of a crisp denim shirt.

Well, I'll be!

That explains the lack of phone calls nagging me about my tardiness. There was no reason to worry since it seems my friend has picked herself up a real hottie. *Dios mio*, as Carlos would say. Just look at all that surfer-boy hair, a perfect shade of Texas wheat, and listen to Sandi's laughter.

As I approach the table, Sandi lifts her eyes and notices me, placing her hand over her lips and blowing me a kiss. Has she been drinking?

"Here she is, our birthday girl. I told you she's coming. Art Russo, meet my dearest friend, Viviana Glover," Sandi says to her male companion, who immediately gets up and extends his hand in my direction. Because her companion is seriously tall, I look up and just gawk, ignoring his handshake offer as my mouth hangs open and my hormones fire up.

Stop.

This glorious creature can't be human. He's an older, crustier version of Thor, the Norse God of Lightning, that is, if gods aged or if he were played by Brad Pitt. I can't help but stare at his chiseled features lit up by crazy-gorgeous, amber-colored eyes. I forget every man, including Carlos, I've ever loved until this very moment.

"Our birthday girl doesn't shake hands with strangers or just hates men, hey?" the God asks without a smile, his gravelly voice oozing sex. "All right, we don't need to get personal," he says, looking down at my head and making me wish I'd fixed my hair. "I thought you said she was friendly," he says to Sandi, withdrawing his hand and sitting his ridiculously hot ass down.

"Viviana, Art is my, I mean, your new renter," Sandi says, snapping me out of my dreamlike stupor.

"Hey, nice to meet you, Art." I squeak out, my voice cracking as if I were a horny teenager. What the heck is wrong with me? I've never had this type of reaction before, even to the best-looking guys.

"Wait, he's my what?" I ask Sandi, who's beaming at me, the lopsided grin making her look like a naughty, little girl.

"Art will live in the front house and yes, he is your renter. I've decided to put you on the deed for your birthday. This way, the house will be a hundred percent yours in case I decide to check out earlier than planned. In the meantime, you'll collect the rent and manage the property. You'll also keep the money, that's after all the property taxes are paid. There's no mortgage, so I need nothing else. I wanted to tell you yesterday, but got sidetracked by Katherine and her crap," Sandi says firmly, suddenly sounding like my fourth-grade homeroom teacher, Miss Dawn, both scary and helpful.

By now, my head is spinning, my mouth is dry, and I'm about to pass out from shock. I burst into tears and jump on Sandi's lap, laughing and crying and hugging her tightly, something I never do.

"Thank you. I can't accept it. I simply can't. I don't deserve it. Tell me I'm dreaming. This is the best birthday gift, like ever. I'll never be homeless again. I'm rich!"

"There, there, my little Aries drama queen, you won't be exactly rich, but there's definitely no need to be afraid of being without a roof over your silly head, plus you'll never have to go back to Texas, I mean, not if you don't want to." Sandi tries to calm me down. "Art, can you pass me a clean napkin, please?" she asks Mr. Thor Pitt.

"No need to sully the restaurant's linen, Miss Sandra," he answers formally, taking me by surprise. "Here's a fresh hand-kerchief. I'm an old-fashioned guy, always prepared to come to the aid of a drama queen. Aries, you say, When's that, in August?"

"April," Sandi and I say in unison, "and you can take your hanky and blow yourself." I jump down his throat for abso-lutely no reason, finally getting off Sandi's lap and finding my seat.

"Suit yourself," the unnervingly hot renter tells me with-out raising his voice. "It's all right. I understand. You've had quite a shock. Sorry, I didn't mean to offend your sensitive feelings." Now he's being a sarcastic dick. I'm about to pull my new rank and ask Sandi to reconsider renting to this arro-gant, self-serving alpha, when I get hit hard on the back of my shoulder.

"Ouch!" I utter, turning around to see who just bumped into me.

"What did you do to my brother, you *gringa* whore, you, evil *bruja*. He was right about you. You are a weirdo witch. And I was sure you loved him. You said you were my friend, more than a friend—a sister. Where is Carlos? *Donde es mi hermano?*"

Before I can react, Art jumps to his feet and steps in between me and my assailant, Carlos's baby sister, Irma. Poor thing; she's no threat to me, all 4-foot-11 inches of her and barely 100 pounds.

"You need to calm down, miss," he orders Irma, using a tone of voice I associate only with the law. The girl is clearly distraught, so she tries to push past him to get to me. People are staring. Sandi grabs Art's cell phone, which he'd placed on the table by his glass of water. I'm sure she's about to call 911.

"It's okay, Art, Sandi, I know her. It's my ex-boyfriend, Carlos's sister. She's terribly upset, but I'm going to talk to her," I assure both of my companions, staying as chill as possible, my Scorpio side taking over. I'm always like that: good in a crisis.

"Not a good idea," Art disagrees. "Let me handle the situation. I'm a professional, Viv."

"No shit, and don't you dare call me Viv, you're not my father," I hiss at him, then turn to Irma. "Come on, *linda*, let's take it outside before this pig takes you in." I smile, reaching for her hand. "I'll tell you everything I know about your *hermano*."

"Fine, it's your head, and for your information, I'm a retired police officer, not a pig," Art barks back, finally showing a hint of humanity. People continue to stare as I take Irma by the hand and lead her out of the restaurant. Some onlookers are openly hostile.

"Fuck them," I whisper to Irma, normally a gentle girl who works full time with the elderly at a local assisted living facility. She also attends nursing school and looks after her mama. I don't understand how she does it. Irma squeezes my hand as tears well up in her sad, drip-coffee-brown eyes.

We walk out into the bright sunshine, neither of us wearing sunglasses, our eyes taking a minute to adjust to going from the dim restaurant to the blinding light. The parking lot is packed, the pavement as hot as a pizza oven. All I want is a drink.

"Where do you want to talk?" I ask Irma softly, trying to keep her from losing it again.

"I don't care."

"Okay, it's too hot to sit and talk in my car without air, so let's walk to the side street, find us a nice tree, and figure out what happened. Do you want me to stop at Jack's across the street and get us a couple of ice teas?"

"No. I told you I don't care about anything. Just tell me now, where is my brother?"

"Irma, listen to me. I know nothing. Sure, I wasn't happy when he dumped me just before my birthday and by text, but I didn't touch a hair on his head, I swear by the Goddess Herself." That is as close to truth as I can come.

"Then what happened to him?"

"Beats me. Why don't you tell me what you believe?"

"I know little, except that he was arrested around dinnertime coming out of the tavern on the east side, but then he texted to say he was being released at 3 in the morning and getting a ride home from a friend, so we didn't worry."

"That's great." I say insincerely, instantly seething with anger. Here I'd assumed they'd keep him for a few days and scare the crap out of his lying, cheating ass, but no, he got away with it again.

"He's missing, I tell you. Mama's sure something terrible has happened because Carlos never made it home. I told her he probably went to your place since it's the closest to the police station. In the morning we called and texted, but he didn't respond so, I went to your place."

"It was you who was pounding on my door?"

"Yes, but you didn't answer. I see how you get when you take your meds. I just waited in my car until I saw you leave and then followed you to Mi Casa. I never believed Carlos when he told Mama he wanted to break up with you for a while now but was afraid you'd do something witchy to him. He said you were so mean to him and jealous because he was totally sober, but you were sneaking booze behind his back."

Now it was my turn to lose it. "Afraid of me? *No mames*! Bullshit! Your brother is a total fraud. He told me he couldn't wait to get out of your mama's house because he was sick of her interfering in his life. FYI: I'm sober, he's the one who went back to using. Fuck him. I don't know where he is and I'm glad we're done and if you don't believe me, then fuck you too, Irma. I've always been good to you, supporting your schooling, defending you to your entire family who just want you to breed and get money for it."

"You really don't have an idea where he is?" Irma asks again, looking defeated I guessed she was hoping for a different answer.

"For the last time, no and no! Why don't you check with his work or with his precious *vatos*?" I spit out, using Carlos's favorite word to describe his "homeboy" associates. This is when Irma dissolves into tears and tries to hug me.

"I'm sorry, Viviana. I'm such a bitch. I should've known better, but now I'm not ready to tell Mama. Can you help me? Maybe you can look at his horoscope or something. Can you read cards or bones?"

"No, I can't do his horoscope and I'm not a psychic. Carlos never wanted to give me his birth time. He said he wasn't sure," I lie, knowing well that Sandi, an experienced astrologer, has rectified his birth chart, meaning she ran a bunch of charts until she found the right fit. I wish she'd done that before we hooked up. Well, I've learned my lesson. Next time I won't go get a cup of coffee with a guy until I triple check every aspect and transit to make 200 percent sure we're compatible.

"Mama said we were all born at home in the morning," Irma says, not giving up.

"That's too general," I say, standing firm. "I tell you what, if he contacts me, you'll be the first I'll call."

"All right, I guess if that's the best you can do for him."

"That's the best I can do for *you*, Irma. *Adios*." With these words, I turn on my heel, forgetting all about Sandi and the former cop, get into my car, and take off. I'm so pissed that Carlos got out without even a slap on the wrist, I can't even see straight. I'm sure he's spending his time at that Vietnamese chick's house, banging, or with his buddies, working on one of his "once-in-a-lifetime" deals to separate some unsuspecting fool from his money.

Just as I pull into the driveway, I notice an unknown older model Expedition pulling in right behind me. Based on my long experience, I suspect it's an unmarked police vehicle. I mean anyone can tell a cop from the tidy shoes and lilly-white hands, not to mention the posture; they hold their arms far away from their bodies, used to carrying regulation weapons. However, not everyone knows they prefer driving Expeditions. I turn off my engine, automatically reaching over for my license and registration, but when I look up, I see its Sandi and Art, so I take a deep breath and slowly get out. They exit the Expedition, but Art hangs back, obviously giving Sandi and me a chance to talk things over.

"Are you all right?" Sandi asks, looking concerned. "We were worried about that crazy girl, Carlos's sister, doing something foolish."

"Calm down, I'm fine. She's not crazy or violent, just upset and worried. How did you know I wasn't coming back?"

"Easy, I could see meeting Art was a bit much for your hormones now," she chuckles. "I told Art, let's wrap it up and go straight to the house. I wanted him to see it again before I called my Tony. You remember Tony, the handyman? We need to fix things up."

"That Art, he's an arrogant male chauvinist, that's for sure." I say without really meaning it. (What I really need to figure out is how to get him to like me.)

"I'll give you a little arrogant but definitely one of the rare good guys."

"Are you sure he's a right fit, I mean, someone you can trust with your house?"

"*Our* house. You don't assume I would bring someone here without checking his chart?"

"Sorry, I'm an idiot. Of course you checked. I can tell, you've decided."

"I double checked; he is the right man for you."

"You mean us? All right, Art it is, but first let me give you a big thank-you hug for being the best part of my life."

Chapter 6

Well, Sandi was right as usual. I'm not rich, at least not just yet. Of course, I'd rather have her with me, safe and sound than inherit the house outright. It's July, and since it took longer to fix the front house than we planned, my nemesis/unattainable lover Art finally moved in as of June 1st.

The sizable deposits and rent (after expenses) allowed me to open up a legit checking account and get a prepaid credit card, something I didn't expect could ever happen again. I've been living off some leftover cash from my bad-girl days and a small inheritance from my paternal grandparents, doled out bit by bit by my brother, Howie Jr.

I've been trying hard to walk the straight line, and so far, Sandi's been pretty impressed with how I've handled the repairs, giving me a generous bonus: five hundred dollars to use for anything I wanted. The "new" grown-up me spent two hundred dollars joining a gym and getting my purple frizz finally under control. But rather than blow through every penny as I usually do, I put the rest in my bank account, just in case Art is late with his rent, though based on his Virgo Sun Sign, that is unlikely. I'm itching to get more birth info on him, like the time he was born, but for no reason I can understand, Sandi won't tell me anything other than Art was born in September, and there's no way I'm going to risk him thinking worse of me than he already does by asking him nutty questions like exactly what time he was born. It's not that he's being mean or rude, not at all, but I can practically smell his disapproval every time we interact. I suppose he could've been born at the end of September under my opposite Sun sign of Libra, but I doubt it. He's way too prickly and not enough of a love bug.

Irma, Carlos's sister, still calls at least once a week to see if I've heard from him, which I haven't. Once, we met up for coffee and a bite at the Gypsy Den, a super-chill, my-kind-of-bohemian-vibe coffee house nearby. She told me *la familia* is afraid that Carlos was murdered by the "dirty" cops. Why else had they let him out without a charge? She didn't accuse me, not directly, but I still got the impression the family blames his arrest on me, though they can't connect the dots. I told her what I figured out was the most obvious explanation: His criminal past caught up with him and he took off for Mexico. Of course, she disagreed, telling me a long, boring story about how he was always too scared of the corrupt Federales and the drug-crazed dealers to return home.

"When I was growing up, he was gone for a long time. I didn't see him much when I was in high school. He returned once a year, for Mama's birthday, not even for Día De Los Muertos or Navidad."

"Is that right? Was he in jail?"

"No, just driving long haul. He is an awfully hard worker, so kind and generous."

"Did he say where he lived?"

"I don't recall exactly; wait, I think he said something about Vegas."

"Makes sense, since he's such a player."

"Don't say that. He is a good man and a wonderful son and brother. I will never get over his loss. How will we live if something bad happened? Mama is heartbroken. She hardly gets out of bed. Are you sure you can't find someone who can tell us if he's all right? *Por favor, mija?*"

I'm aware I'm supposed to take responsibility, but I can't and I won't. Frankly, I could give a rat's ass which hole Carlos has crawled into and I don't fantasize about him either when I take care of business. Falling madly in lust with Art, a guy who barely looks at me, has its pluses. I've been working out every day, resulting in my supposedly old body looking so fit that the guys at the gym are noticing, plus the cravings for sugar, so common to most fellow addicts, have all but disappeared. I bought a couple of cute summer dresses, a nice pair of jeans, and I can now tuck in my shirt. Katherine keeps promising to invite me to meet her beau with the boat and take me to Catalina Island, but I'm not holding my breath.

It's July 14th, the day my birth mom, Gail, was born, and the Orange County Fair is in full swing. This is as patriotic as I get: Driving Sandi and Katherine to the fair because parking is a nightmare. My ladies love the arts and crafts pavilions, the fried pineapple, the pig races, and above all, checking to see if Katherine's latest travel photo won a prize. (I gather she won an honorable mention a few years back for her black-and-white winter scene taken from her apartment window in Berlin.)

For once, Katherine is the one who's on time and not Sandi. Katherine persuaded Efren, the male part of the Philippine caretaking couple who work and live in her house, to drive her up from Laguna to my place in his own car. She doesn't trust us, the low-brow Costa Mesa folks, with the Rolls.

Efren, whom his boss lady calls Effy after one of her favorite jewelers, is a pleasant looking, middle-aged man who used to work as a math teacher. He is also a hyper-nervous driver and a horrible worry wart, who treats Katherine as if she were a ditzy high schooler and not almost eighty years old. Effy's wife, Annie, can be tough; still, she's a kindhearted soul, a former family physician with years and years of experience. At first, I assumed Annie was full of it. Why would an actual doctor take a low-status job as a domestic, i.e., a personal "bitch?" I kind of said something rude to her, but she didn't take offense and explained how difficult it is for foreign-trained doctors to continue their medical careers in the States. I guess they look for young ones who've finished school within the last five years and demand at least a year of local work. To make matters even more difficult, Annie would have to study like mad to pass the exams and get extra high scores to boot. That was impossible because she needed money to live on and to send back home, so Annie had no choice but to take a permanent live-in position with Katherine, who later helped her to bring over her husband, Efren. What I realize is that with all the medical problems in this country, it makes little sense to turn away hard-working, honest people with so much education and experience. But who am I to judge? I barely finished high school.

Katherine is a demanding, fickle employer, but something tells me she'd be lost without Efren and Annie.

I grab Sandi's straw bucket purse, absentmindedly left at my place, along with my vintage velvet crossover pouch and go outside to meet my fancy pants friend at the curb, knowing well, she will not come into my place for an iced tea. She can't breathe in my place. It's claustrophobic, or so she says.

"Hello, *mausi*," Katherine, who's becoming hard of hearing, almost shouts. Sandi says its karma, considering Katherine never listens to us or anyone else.

"Why are you screaming at me?" I demand, still holding a little grudge, not entirely over the events of my birthday. What do you expect from my vengeful Scorpio side?

"Where is that rocket scientist?" Katherine asks, ignoring my question and referring to Sandi's mysterious absence.

"Actually, let me call her: I'm getting worried," I agree without jumping down her throat to defend Sandi.

"Ah, there's that gorgeous creature," Katherine purrs. When I turn my head toward the front house, I see Art bending over the front porch herbal pots, probably checking if they need watering or getting rid of snails. I've never known a man to be so involved with domestic shit or with such a green thumb: definitely a Virgo. When I smile my most alluring smile and wave, he doesn't respond to either. I ignore the cues and walk over. I'm looking as good as I can in an off-the-shoulder, blue-and-white, polka-dot dress and white gladiator sandals that show off my freshly painted toes. My hair is slicked back into a neat bun that I dressed up with hand-decorated crystal pins. I'm a little embarrassed by my Wicca tats, but I can't do anything about those.

"Hey neighbor, can I use your land line to call Sandi?" I ask coolly, even as my stomach jumps up to my throat and back.

"Go right ahead," he replies without enthusiasm; not even looking up. "Help yourself."

I walk past him into the kitchen, smell his cologne, and go weak in the knees. "Seriously," I whisper under my breath. "This has to stop. Of course, he's judging me: I'm an oversexed, desperate asshole." Just as I'm about to dial Sandi's number, the phone rings and I pick it up without a second thought. Shit. Art is correct. I'm a stalker.

When I hear Sandi's voice, I'm relieved.

"Jinx. I was just about to call you."

"Hi, baby girl, I tried to call your cell and then your land number, but you didn't pick up, so I called Art to ask him to go get you. He's usually home on Sundays."

"Makes sense, but why aren't you here?"

"That's why I'm calling, honey. I'm sorry, I can't make it down to the fair after all. I can't even make it downstairs."

"What did he do now? Did he push you?" I ask, jumping to the most likely conclusion.

"No. Goddess, no. It was me just being clumsy me. The cats needed to be let out, and I tripped over that rug. Remember the hooked one I brought from Jerome when I went to the astrology convention in Sedona and remember how you always tell me to be careful when I'm not wearing my laced shoes?"

"Are you in terrible pain?"

"Not too bad, just can't drive. But don't worry, Jay's on his way home."

"That fucker better get there soon and take you to your doctor or something. You should get an X-ray or I'll..."

"Stop. I'm fine, baby girl. Honestly, you can come visit tomorrow and see for yourself."

"I love you and I hate to go to the fair without you." I back off, for now.

"Go, please go; you and Katherine have a good time and I'll join in next time."

"Promise?"

"I promise."

When we hang up, I break into sweat—something tells me she's lying, covering up for Jay.

As if she senses something is not right, Katherine walks into the kitchen, takes one look at me, letting lose a barrage of nothing sounding too nice. In German, of course.

"Not coming? Tripped again?" She guesses correctly. Not knowing what to say, I can only shake my head.

"You want me to take a rain check for the fair?" Katherine offers, sounding sincere.

"Do you mind?" Sometimes, she can be such a dear soul, and that's why she is still my friend. Just like that, all the birthday mess is forgiven as I give her a hug and kiss her on both cheeks, exactly as she likes it.

Katherine hugs me back awkwardly and reassures me, almost sounding maternal. *"Nein, Liebchen,* I don't mind. Don't worry too much—worry gives you wrinkles. Let's see how she is tomorrow and then we'll make alternative plans. I'll have Effy take me to Fashion Island and buy a new Hermès scarf at Neiman's, something pretty to cheer myself up."

"As if you need yet another gaudy four hundred dollar scarf," I say under my breath, quiet enough to make sure she won't hear me.

After a few minutes listening to her gibberish about this or that, mostly her sisters being ungrateful for all the lovely, "gently" used (by her) crap she sends them, I agree to keep her in the loop and see her to the curb, where Effy is waiting inside his car, no doubt listening to Radio Philippines. As soon as he sees us, he drops everything and jumps out of the car, apologizing for not standing outside. Seriously? As he helps Katherine in, she reaches out for my hand and squeezes hard enough to hurt my fingers. I try to smile back, but I'm too upset to pretend.

For some reason, I can't get the mental picture of Sandi being pushed by Jay out of my mind. Lately, my impressions and dreams have been scarily prophetic, stupidly so, but still enough to freak me out. Like, the other night, I dreamt of a strange cat being stuck in a tree and, sure enough, my neighbor woke me up looking for her cat. The woman was so distressed that I asked Art to help us get the cat down. I don't really care about the stupid cat—I'm a dog lover— but still, I got spooked with my powerful insights. I was going to discuss this with Sandi today, but clearly that won't happen.

The rest of the day is a waste because I've already been to the gym and folded the laundry. Too wired to relax, I decide not to sit around like a fool and daydream about seducing my grumpy renter. I guess I probably can use a little fresh air, so I walk a few blocks toward 17th Street, hoping to get a treat since I won't be killing my gut at the fair.

The weather is exactly right: not too windy or hot, and the neighborhood is blooming with roses, always Carlos's favorites. Not paying attention, I turn the corner and run smack into someone.

"Sorry, I didn't see you," I say, offering a rare apology. "Hey there," the man replies, startling me. "It's Chrissy, right? I've been hoping we'd run into each other again."

Shit, this could be bad, I fear. I'm ready to hit whoever it is in the balls and split.

"Come on Chrissy, it's me, Nathan. I met you on your birthday, behind the tavern, remember? I was with my roomies. Remember the funny Indian guy?"

I exhale with relief and look closely. It is the kid I met the night I got Carlos busted, though he looks different by daylight; good, but different. On second look, he's older than I reckoned, definitely not in his twenties. I can see some gray in his stubble and the deep grooves around his luscious lips. He is dressed casually, in khaki shorts and flip-flops, so different from Art the Fart who wears belted and pressed jeans and collared shirts while watering his plants. Again, unlike Art's, Nathan's forearms are heavily inked with tribal symbols. Nice.

Since I can't very well admit I, too, have been hoping to see him again, I do my best to be chill. "Nathan? Say, I remember you."

"Of course, you do. I've been sending you mental vibes. I mean, I've been thinking of you a lot. Can't understand why we didn't run into each other before in the neighborhood. To tell the truth and I hope you don't consider me creepy, but you left an impression, a big one. I haven't dreamt of anyone this much since I met my son's mama."

Son? He is even older than I guessed. This is getting interesting.

"You want to tell me it was you who's been sending me vibes? Hope they're positive ones. I guess I'm flattered," I brush back a wisp of my hair that's fallen out of my bun, half-smiling my Chrissy smile, the one I use to drive men wild, mindlessly reverting to my old, wicked ways.

"Only positive, I'm a Sagittarius, Mr. Positivity himself. Remember? I've been checking out my horoscopes on YouTube. Say, I believe you still owe me that birthday hug."

"I owe nothing to no one." I finally relax and go into my old professional flirt mode, tapping Nate lightly on his shoulder and taking my hair down, grateful it looks thicker after being freshly washed.

"No problem. I can wait on that hug, but I will not let you disappear again. How about we get some coffee and see if I can change your mind?"

"Hmm. You can?" I flirt back after taking a few minutes to fuss with my curls, flipping them over my nude shoulder, savoring his reaction.

Usually, quick to decide when it comes to guys attracted to me, I continue to fiddle with my hair without giving him a definitive answer. I'm trying to remind myself that I swore I'd take my time poking around the guy's astrology chart before I do anything stupid. I also notice a funny buzz in my head that Sandi calls my "warning bell."

"Do you always make guys beg for a coffee?" Nate asks, taking off his cheap-looking surfer dude sunglasses, looking directly into my eyes but without losing his temper or sounding frustrated. "Then how about a smoothie or an adult beverage?" he offers an alternative with an adorable little-boy smirk, his eyes squinting in the sun. I can't tell if they're blue or gray but, again, a comforting sensation of familiarity washes over me. Is he the one? Now I understand why I took him for a much younger man. Yep, he's an Archer all right—they don't age like other signs. I suddenly remember my dad's favorite Frank Sinatra song, something about fairy tales and being young at heart. I'm pretty confident the old cat was born in December too.

"I'm an addict," I blurt out, shocking myself.

"I see nothing wrong with that. At least you're honest. We all have our demons. I can't drink much either, not anymore. In the spirit of full disclosure, at the moment, I'm without a driver's license. So we either walk or take an Uber. Or is a guy without wheels a deal breaker?"

"Not at all. Look, I'm older than forty."

"I'm not trying to sell life insurance, but just in case, you're hung up on something as superficial as chronology, I'm thirty-six, meaning, I'm almost forty."

"And I lied about my name too..."

"Good, I hate girl names that start with *C*. My ex is Carla and the woman I lived with before I moved to OC was Carol, whom I bet was a lot older than you."

"Look, you seem normal, but..." I try feebly.

"Thanks. At least you didn't say I am a nice kid. This is progress." he laughs, and it's the sweetest sound I've heard in months.

That does it. I like him. I'm keeping him. My fifty-year-old scrooge can take a hike. I don't care about his horoscope, and what if it goes south? I've survived worse, plus my obsession with Art the Cop must end or one crazy night I'm going to lose it and show up at his door wearing nothing but a thong and five-inch fuck-me pumps. Something tells me, being rejected by someone like Art would hurt a lot worse. As my dad says, "Damn the torpedoes. Full speed ahead"

"I have a better idea," I pronounce in my own, suddenly confident voice, lifting my chin up to the punishing heavens in defiance.

"Nate, meet Viviana Glover. How about I take you to the fair? I've got free passes."

Chapter 7

I was expecting my sacred place of peace wouldn't last. With me, it never does. I have zero stability in my horoscope: all fire and water elements, no earth to bring in some common sense. No wonder no matter how hard I try; I always find myself in hot water. It's past Samhain, All Hallows Eve, coming up on Thanksgiving, a "clean," family holiday I hate with a passion, usually reserved for the hypocritical, know-it-all churchgoers I grew up around.

It's the dead of night. I'm alone and can't sleep because I'm jacked up on adrenaline. Let's just say, I don't get scared easily, but someone broke into the backhouse and butchered my next-door neighbor's cat in my kitchen sink, the same dumb cat Art helped save weeks ago. Just for shits and giggles, they left the body on my bed with a note in Spanish, stapled to the cat's tail: *la próxima vez, será alguien a quieres ames.*

Marleen, my neighbor and the cat's owner, a bitch of a white supremacist, had a fit, blaming me, since according to her, "I'm the only one on our street who's whoring with the illegal criminals from the westside." I told her to go off herself, but I must admit, my suspicion is that the harassing message must've come from Carlos's side. Hell, perhaps the vanished hombre himself. I understood what the note said: Next time it'll be someone you love. Well, I don't love anyone. I'm in lust with Art, but love? Too late for that unless they meant Sandi. Carlos better be hiding far away in some shit hole in Mexico because I am well aware where *his* family lives.

I just had an awful image, more of a clairvoyant flash. What if it's someone even closer to me who knows about my cat story? I must remember who I told about my past-life regression and cats. I'm sure I told Sandi and Katherine, but who else?

Basically, several years back, my sister-in-law, Lori, talked me into seeing a past-life therapist to help me understand my addictions. She paid big bucks to this quack of a hypnotist who apparently took me back, way back, before I was born, and asked me a bunch of questions I don't remember. The only thing that came of it is that I got hysterical because I was entrusted with the care of cats at what the guy said must've been an ancient Egyptian temple and a rival group of people broke in and killed them in front of me. All I did after the session is yell at Lori and then got drunk. Pretty traumatic, right? Ever since then, I get the creeps just looking at a cat.

It took me hours to straighten out the mess, so by the time I sit down, it was too late to take my nighttime friend, Seroquel. Why am I alone? Because, as usual, everyone is dealing with their own crap, especially all the men in my life.

Nate and I've been dating since July 14th, the day I literally ran into him, and in all fairness, we've been getting along. I mean, he still can't drive. Rooming with a pair of twenty-something IT geeks who get stoned pretty much three times a week hasn't been great for my sobriety either. Then there is Hunter, his six-year-old son with ADHD and the fact that Nate's dealing with being able to see his kid only when the social workers can supervise, thanks to the false spousal abuse report filed by his ex. That means, if we're not hanging at my place, he goes back and forth over a hundred miles north each way, to fucking Lancaster. Easygoing, he mostly takes the bus, but several times, I've offered to drive, hoping we could have some fun on the way back. All that happened is I put extra mileage on my old Benz, now in desperate need of an expensive service, and wore out the tires I can't afford to replace; so now I'm without transportation, yet again depending on Sandi's kindness and the local bus system. There's no way I'm using ride share services—not safe in this part of town.

Nate is nice to be around. He never criticizes my astrology studies or considers me weird. When I need some space, he is always happy to back off. Sex is fine too; nothing intense, but relaxed and steady, almost familiar. Everyone, including us, jokes that we're like a pair of vintage cowboy boots, already broken in. Unlike Carlos and I, we don't argue about politics or gender equality. In fact, we see the world in much the same way. He never asks about my Texas family and I don't ask him about his. He never pushes pics of his kid on me either or asks if I want to get to meet his son, and that's fine by me. When we went to Lancaster, I dropped him off a block away in case his crazy jealous ex was watching and had a great time hanging outside a super-cute local coffee place on Avenue K with my Alan Leo astrology book and several cups of caramel java. (Hey, it's cheaper than anything around here in Orange County and the folks are a lot friendlier.) If not for Sandi and my little back house, I wouldn't mind moving up here, I told Nate, hoping he'd appreciate me being thoughtful about his need to be near his son, but he surprised me by telling me in no uncertain terms, that that will never happen. Whatever.

Nate doesn't drink alcohol around me and I don't tell him how to run his life or give him astrological advice. If we go out, we each pay for ourselves. I've never been so bored or so desperately obsessed with Art.

Art hasn't been around much as he is going back and forth to his place in Utah every other week. Sandi told me he's having trouble with his daughter who goes to high school in Kamas, a small town outside Salt Lake City, where he left her with his folks. The fact that he abandoned his kid makes me mad because it reminds me about being left with my own grandparents after the divorce. My grandad was a pill, always yelling and screaming at grandma and us. I mean, Dad got us as soon as he remarried. Still, I've never forgiven him or trusted my heart to a man.

I guess the girl's mom isn't in the picture. Around Labor Day, Art informed me that he may bring his daughter to stay with him permanently. I got pissed off with his attitude and we exchanged words. I told him I didn't need any horny, adolescent females bringing drugs, booze, and boy trouble to my finally peaceful world. He got silent and walked off. I went after him and he called me a selfish libtard. Really? Who says that? Well, I need not have worried. The little chickadee came to visit just for a few days and hated Costa Mesa and, I assume me, on sight. I was taken a back when I realize that the girl was definitely biracial. I mean I didn't take Art for a guy who likes to push the envelope, especially in Utah, but there she was before my eyes: a tall, skinny, milk chocolate-colored African American with super-kinky hair-I bet that goes over big in her milk-toast school. No wonder the kid has problems. I mentioned something about that to

Sandi, who promptly put me in my place, telling me that Emery was a star athlete and a popular A student, just not happy with living away from her dad, whom she apparently adores. It makes little sense; if they're so close, why did he move away?

Based on what I've seen with my own eyes, I'm glad I've never had my own brats, that, and climate change. There're too many of us polluting the air and the seas already. Mother Goddess Gaia has cried enough.

Life is full of ironies. Here, both Art and Nate, the two guys in my life are having problems with their sperm donations. Must be a transit to their fifth astrological houses, the fifth, having to do with kids and love affairs. I mean, I still hope Art is a little interested in me. At first, I imagined a spark in his eyes whenever he saw me with Nate, as I made sure we held hands or were sucking face, but most likely it's just my Aries wishful thinking. He sure lights up whenever Sandi comes over. I don't see what they have in common. He's an openly conservative, chauvinistic alpha male. I do recognize she is genuinely fond of him and, in return, he treats her with so much care that I'm jealous.

And then there's Lady Katarina, the old, spoiled Katherine. As long as we've been friends, Katherine has always been away for the entire holiday season, first taking some sort of fancy Christmas markets river cruise, then visiting with her sisters in Berlin, followed by spending at least a month somewhere warm, like South Florida. I guess she has lots of Berliner friends who settled there. It must be nice to be her. She made some noise about taking me along, but I was a hundred percent sure she wasn't serious. Plus, I didn't want to leave Sandi's—I mean—my place for too long, even if Art is a stand-up guy. That's the problem with him, I chuckle, I need him to lie down.

Not being able to shut off my stupid head, I open my eyes for good, deciding to get some studying done and then take a long nap in the afternoon. The clock reads 5 a.m. Just as I'm about to get up and make myself a matcha latte, I hear broken glass, then smell something like smoke coming from a wooden fireplace. Crap, we don't have a working fireplace.

Accustomed to the reality of California fires, I jump up and run into the bathroom, twisting on scorching water to make some steam to raise the humidity. Within minutes, I hear the sirens from the fire trucks and decide to crawl out of the bathroom window just in case the fire is at my front door. Of course, I scrape my elbow, landing in one of the out-of-control rosemary bushes I've been planning to trim.

The rancid stench is making me nauseous. I'm panicking and in a sweat. I should've taken my meds, just to take the edge off. The fire is licking the entrance to the front house. My intuition or my experience with the sound of broken glass is that someone threw a stink bomb onto the porch. As I hurry toward the street, I can see the ignited wooden herb boxes Art built with his own hands, planting the seeds when he moved in. I suspect the house is empty. What if Sandi had a fight with Jay and spent the night? My stomach turns at the thought as I rush over to the porch to talk to the firefighters, who are blasting the now almost extinguished flames with a full stream of water, gallons and gallons pouring into the living room. Shit, what a mess, and here we just finished fixing things so nice.

"Hey, guys, chill on all that water. It's a stink bomb. You're causing more damage. We've just put in the new carpet. To hell with the planters," I say.

The older firefighter, a nice looking Hispanic who's holding the hose looks me straight in the eye and tells me to move back, something I'm not about to do.

"I'm the property owner and I'm telling you to be more respectful of my property. The fire is out. Can't you stop?"

"Step aside, ma'am," the second firefighter barks. "Let us do our job. Why don't you go check on your husband? He's being treated for minor burns; over there, by the truck."

"What husband?" I ask and then almost pass out, realizing the house wasn't empty after all. Art must have returned from Utah without me knowing. Before I have time to check on him, I see Art walking toward me, his hand is bandaged but he looks all right, better than all right. He's wearing sleep shorts and nothing on top. Be still my heart. What a gorgeous set of pecs. I can't help but respond.

"Oh my God, babe. are you okay?" I practically attack him, losing control, hugging him tightly to my sweaty boobs.

"All's good. Guess I burnt my hand and singed the eyebrows," he answers calmly as he attempts to pull my hands away from his neck. Nope, not going to let this opportunity pass without making my move, making it hard on him.

"I was freaking out, horrified you were crisped alive in the house."

"Crisped?" He gives me a curious look and then chuckles, the grin taking off years. "I'm fine, truly. You can let go of my neck, Viv."

"Sorry," I mutter, not at all sorry for the opportunity to get closer nor jumping down his throat about calling me Viv.

"What happened?" I ask Art, continuing to stand so close I can smell smoke mixing with something amazing. Not cologne or soap, just his skin. Before he can say a word, I rattle on, as my anxiety and sexual anticipation take over. "You know, babe, I'm usually dead to the world. I sleep at least until ten or eleven, but I was dealing with that fucking, I mean poor, dead cat, and I didn't take my meds on time, so I was up. Then I heard some noise that sounded like glass breaking, so, I say to myself, this is no biggie, probably some bum throwing wine bottles around. But then I smelled something stinky. I put two and two together and crawled out of my bathroom window. Just in case it was a fire. Look, I scraped myself raw. And then they told me you were hurt and then I really freaked and here you are, all gorgeous, cool, and calm. I suspect it's the same maniacs who killed the cat and left me a threatening note about next time they'll kill someone I love. It's got to be my ex-boyfriend Carlos's *familia* or his *vatos*. In case you don't understand, *la familia* is family and *vatos* are his buddies, you know, the homeboys who always get him in trouble. I learned a lot of Spanish when we were dating. My family hates it and calls me a traitor. Did I tell you about Carlos? He's been missing since my birthday in April and I'm sure they blame me. I'm an Aries; Aries always lead with their heart. Art? You're not saying anything? Are you even human?"

I erupt into genuine tears that both Carlos and Glenn told me I wasn't capable of shedding—not since I was raped at gunpoint by my now dead ex, Glenn's "business" partners. Then I do something completely weird. I get a hold of Art's face, twisting it just so, and kiss him on the mouth, rubbing my face against his stubble, putting my heart on the line. But no matter how desperately I try to get him to respond, he doesn't kiss me back. He stands still, arms at his sides. Hurt and confused, I finally let go of him, but he still says nothing and that makes me even madder, more desperate to clear the air.

"What's wrong with you? Can't you see I was terrified? What if something bad happened to you because of me? Don't you care that I like you?"

He still says nothing; he just shakes his head and walks away, leaving me standing like the old fool that I am. So much for being a grown-up, authentic and honest. Screw Art. Moving on. Later I'll have to call Sandi and give her the bad news about the property damage, but first I'm going to get me a few drinks.

Chapter 8

The next day is a stinking blur. I feel like the crap I am as I suffer through another useless AA meeting held in a church on the east side. Since my car is still at the shop and I don't want to drive Sandi's loaner, I force myself to walk to the church even though it's over two miles away.

If the transits are right, my luck will turn and I'll get hit by a speeding car, I tell myself, illegally strolling across the insanely busy Irvine Boulevard. Finally, all my troubles would be over.

After years of bouncing in and out of various rehabs, I'm self-aware enough to admit I'm being a drama queen, but this is how it is. I want to lie and tell myself that I didn't enjoy the booze, that I was overwhelmed with guilt, that I stopped. I didn't. I drank at least a half-gallon of vodka diluted with cranberry juice, followed by a six pack of cheap beer, along with a Costco-size bag of ranch-flavored Sun Chips, all alone, in the dark, ignoring Sandi's calls.

After blacking out for a few hours, I woke up in my dried-up vomit. Even the cool shower didn't help, as I threw up again and again. Barely able to keep some peppermint tea down, I made a few calls to the homeowners insurance company, to Nate, and finally to Sandi. Relieved that no one picked up, I left messages.

By the early evening, I texted Dave, asking my sponsor to join me at the AA meeting. He said sure, but here I sit alone. I deserve the "baseball to the back of my skull" headache and nausea. I even deserve everything bad that's coming to me, but I don't deserve to be dissed by my sponsor, who I'm sure has been in the same place too.

Over the years of meetings, I've learned to tune out the noise. I'm not interested in why we use, nor in all the fucking excuses why we continue to fall off the wagon. For a while there, I entertained myself by trying to guess everyone's birthdays by how they talk, but even that has become boring.

Today's meeting is no different from the last time I attended, months ago, when Carlos and I were still together. The usual circus of hard-luck characters are going on and on about nothing that makes sense. Most everyone is white, old, and male. A good number of these losers can't or won't work; everyone has been through the mill. Up front, staring at the wooden cross above him, sits Mark, a painfully thin ex-bank manager suffering from Parkinson's. He is always whining about his ex stealing the house and his business and turning the kids against him. He spent some time inside for what he calls a slight misappropriation, but according to the DA, he was in for big-time embezzlement.

Two rows back I recognize Kenny, the roadie who still dresses like an '80s teenager, his waist-long hair dyed the color of eggplant and divided into two skinny braids. Kenny was doing really well until he married one of those barely-out-of-her-teens foreign mail-order hotties, who thought he was an actual American rock star. The fairy tale didn't work out. I could've told him that even without knowing her birth information. The hottie took off with as much loot as she could carry. When Kenny's bedridden mama, whom he cared for, passed away, his sobriety passed along with her. I sympathize with his situation. It wasn't his fault the music biz is full of creeps and users, and his taste in chicks was, well, not helpful. He still has a kind heart and reminds me of Danny. We're friends.

On my left sits another Mark, the window washer and his buddy, Christopher, two gnarly, old, surfer dudes from Huntington Beach. I've partied with them; they're pretty cool guys. (I even slept with one of them, which one I don't recall.)

Finally, my absent sponsor, Dave, texts, but doesn't apologize for not coming. I text back, "Screw you." I can tell he's annoyed with me. At the moment, I'm not my own biggest fan either. I get up and spill my usual BS about my parent's divorce, my abandonment issues, Glenn, my rape, and having a setback, but I keep my mouth shut about what's really going on.

The meeting is about to be over and since I don't like guzzling gallons of shitty, black coffee and no longer smoke, I leave before the self-righteous, pathetically horny men can get to me.

I ought to take a ride share back to the house, but I don't feel it's safe here and don't want to spend the extra money, in case Sandi asks me to pay for some repairs.

Walking back is probably the best decision I've made ever since I practically attacked Art with my unrequited longings. The fresh air and exercise clear my head. I think I'm getting out of the fog, except that now I'm starving. I place my hand on my gut, trying to contain all the rumbling. What if I had a few? I was scared and rejected. I can forgive myself and move on. I'll glance at my chart and find a good day to start over. All

I have to do is find the right combo of planets, like Saturn being in a good contact with the Moon. Let's see, Saturn is all about sorrow, misery, and self-loathing and the Moon is emotions and my family legacy of substance abuse, so maybe when Saturn trines my Moon? Well, that would be difficult: Saturn moves slowly. Okay. What if I just hope I locate Saturn's trine to the Moon right now? That should work too. The moon would have to be in Virgo or Taurus. Finally, my mood is lifting as I walk faster, almost running home so I can check my daily planetary guide. No matter what I do, the stars never let me down. I hate myself for not checking the transits before I laid myself open to Art's ridicule. Well, live and learn. Before heading home, I stop at Nate's apartment, hoping he's home. I knock several times, but no one is there. Perhaps I'm getting my mojo back or most likely looking to Nate to make me feel wanted.

After stopping at the juice bar to grab a 16-ounce Green Monster for some much-needed nutritional detox, I pick up an order of Vietnamese soup and head home; the rice noodles are full of carbs, but at least they're gluten-free.

When I get back to my place, I see Jay's fancy Lexus SUV. Uh-oh. That ass better keep away from me because I'm still convinced Sandi's "accidents" aren't accidental. plus, I'm in no mood for conversations about whose fault it is that the house got damaged. I decide to sneak into the back house through the side, but no such luck. Jay, Sandi, and Art are sitting on green plastic chairs right by my front door, the chairs I usually keep covered by old sheets in the moldy garage.

"Hey, what's this? Another intervention?" I greet the unsmiling trio, heading off the attack.

"Hey yourself. Trying to sneak past the main house? Get a load of who finally got what's coming to her?" says Jay, all snarky and slimy and perfectly turned out in his usual no-iron khakis and Polo pullover. I don't know what Sandi sees in him. He's bald, overweight, and his face is always covered with red spots from the dermatologist frying his face because he's paranoid of getting skin cancer.

Both Sandi and Art remain silent, looking like someone other than the dumb cat is dead.

"Come here, dear," Sandi says, lifting her arms, signaling her desire for a hug. "Art has something to tell you."

"With all due respect, Sandi, I don't need a hug. I appreciate the porch is a mess and we probably need new carpet, but it wasn't anyone's fault. I told the firefighters to knock off the water, but they wouldn't listen."

"It's not the fire damage," Art says gravely, getting up. "Here, you best sit. I've got some new information about your missing boyfriend."

"Ex-boyfriend, and why should I care if he's back?" I spit out. "I'm done with that loser and his family, blaming me for him taking off."

"Viviana, this is important," Sandi speaks up in an odd tone of voice. "You need to hear Art out. Sit."

"Fine." I realize I sound like a spoiled teenage brat, but that's how they're treating me, with no respect for what I've suffered.

"Let me put my takeout pho in the kitchen and I'll be right back."

"We'll wait," Sandi says, looking at her feet.

I go inside and exchange my sweaty walking sandals for a pair of flip-flops and taking my time transferring the still-hot lemongrass-scented broth out of the plastic and into a glass container (much safer that way). I place the rice noodles and the garnishes (cilantro, jalapenos, and bean sprouts) into individual tea saucers. Then I use the potty, splashing some cold water on my face, combing out the tangles in my hair, and applying a touch of copper-red organic lip gloss to my dry lips. All in all, I must admit, I don't look half bad, considering what I put my body through just hours ago. Eventually, running out of things to do, I join Sandi and the silent men.

"Go on." I turn to Art without emotion, sitting my ass down, trying to pretend that nothing weird took place between us.

"I have bad news. After the last several events, I made some inquiries. I don't know if you're aware of it, but I've taken a job as a private contractor, helping the ADA, the assistant district attorney."

"Seriously? No need to lecture me about the ADA. I'm a cop's daughter, for Christ's sake," I say, interrupting him impatiently.

"All right. Anyway, I figured it would be a good idea to see into the cat and the fire incidents, especially since I'm directly involved."

"Sorry for the bother, your highness," I mumble sarcastically.

Art winces but goes on without responding to my provocation. "Well, I heard from my contacts a couple of hours ago."

"Spill."

"Two days ago, a mutilated body without a head or extremities was found at a new home construction site in Newport Coast. This is a large site because the house footprint is for 10,000 square feet, plus property. The owners live abroad and the project GC, general contractor, told the investigators there was a prolonged break in construction because of issues with city inspectors."

"And?"

"The police suspect the body is Carlos."

"Bullshit, how would they know without visual identification or prints? Unless they found the head, they can't very well check his dental records, either" I say, jumping down his throat and showing off.

"It was an anonymous tip. A man, or someone sounding like one, called Carlos's family and told them where they could find his body. The family called us, I mean the force, and they identified Carlos by his clothing and his truck that was parked nearby. I suppose that's why you've been targeted. I was told, the family pointed to you as a potential suspect. They sure hate you. I suggest you go down to Superior Court and file a CHR order ASAP, but not on the weekend. If you need help, I'll go down with you. I looked up the address on Jamboree."

"I don't accept it. He didn't have his truck with him because when he was busted, the truck was left at the parking lot." I ignore Art and his suggestions. I've filed enough civilian harassment orders in my time to paper a bathroom.

"How would you know that?" Jay asks maliciously. "I'll be. You setup that Mexican with the cops, didn't you?. Now you understand what I've been saying all this time?" He turns to Sandi, practically oozing hate. "I told you not to trust druggie whores, you dumb, old bitch. I'm putting my foot down and kicking her to the curb and as far as I'm concerned, the loser ex-cop goes too."

Art narrows his eyes but remains silent. Poor Sandi says nothing in her own defense, let alone standing up for me. She refuses to look up, but her hand is shaking. Ever since the last stroke, every time she gets upset, her hand shakes uncontrollably as if she's got Parkinson's. I took her in and asked the nurses, who explained it's a side effect of her meds. (I wish she used CBD, but she won't.)

That does it. "Fuck you, Jay. I may be a druggie whore, but I don't push disabled old ladies down the stairs hoping to kill them to get their money. And you can't kick me out of my own house. Apologize to your wife now."

"What did you say, bitch? Your house? Jay jumps up, raising his hand to strike me. Before I have time to kick him in the balls, Art grabs Jay in a choke hold and pushes him to the ground, everything taking place in the blink of eye. The weasel tries to struggle, but he eventually gives up. I want to join in so badly and scratch out his eyes, but Sandi screams and then faints.

Art lets go of Jay, who drops to all fours and tries to get up while holding his left side. I hope he has a heart attack and dies. I get on my knees near Sandi, lift her head up, and turn to Art for help. I'm worried sick that I'm responsible for killing my best friend.

"I'm so sorry. Sandi, open your eyes, Sandi." I gently rock her body back and forth. She moans but won't open her eyes. "Please dial 911," I plead, turning to Art, who joins me on the ground.

"I already did, hon. Please stay calm. She'll be fine. It's just stress—I'm positive." I stare into his eyes and see a genuine concern for the both of us.

"Thanks. I agree with Jay. I'm a shit, but I love her."

Art reaches for my hand, squeezes it, and gives me a reassuring smile. I smile back gratefully. For a second, all is right in my world as he holds my gaze. Then I hear the sirens. The paramedics arrive just ahead of the ambulance. It's the same crew from the nearest station a few blocks away. They tell me to stand back and ask Art questions. I want to talk, but he motions for me to stay quiet and I comply.

Jay is sitting up, moaning and groaning and demanding the paramedics call the police since he is the injured party. Art approaches Jay and whispers something in his ear. Whatever he says shuts Jay up immediately. Sandi finally comes around but is so confused that both Art and I agree that she needs to be transported to the hospital since she has a history of strokes.

Jay disagrees, telling the paramedics that he's her husband and has a medical directive. The guys have him sign some papers and leave. Art and I have no choice but to load Sandi into Jay's car, although not before I tell Jay that if he doesn't take Sandi to the ER immediately, I'll call the cops myself and tell them he's trying to kill her. He doesn't reply, just gives me a dirty glance and nods acknowledgment.

Now, it's me who's sick. I guess I never recovered from my hangover after all. I'm so dizzy, I'm about to barf.

"Here's the deal, Art," I say. "Thanks for everything, but I need to go inside and lie down."

"Yeah, you best take care of yourself," he says. "You look green. Sorry, I'm not trying to insult you, but did you take a drink or something?"

I say nothing.

Chapter 9

Thanksgiving morning arrives whether I like it or not, and I don't like it. Two time zones away, in single saccharine-quaints, public square Granbury, Texas, my family is gathered around the TV, waiting for some football action and any excuse to pound down booze. My stepmom, Judi Anne, assisted by my sister-in-law, Lori, is fixing traditional Tex-Mex sides—jalapeno corn bread and blackberry pie, while my brother, Howie Jr., is obsessing over his only contribution, a massive deep fried turkey. He argues with Dad about exactly how long the bird should stay in the fryer. Dad's a stickler for anything and everything about safety, so I'm sure the fire extinguisher is handy.

Junior's in-laws, Lori's parents, will stop by for a slice of pie and a nightcap after spending the day with her sister, who owns a small ranch in Grapevine, by DFW airport. I don't give a rat's ass for Lori's folks because they don't make a secret of looking down on me. From where I stand, they're just small-town hicks with money.

My stepmom Judi's kids live in New York, refusing to spend holidays with my red neck family. I can't say I rightfully blame them. They come from a completely opposite background.

(Judi's an Italian Catholic who's originally from Long Island.) I met her three married sons only once at the wedding almost fifteen years back when I embarrassed everyone by making a play for one of them, which one I still can't remember. Judi is dad's third wife and, this time, he got it right.

I can imagine Howie's girls, my nieces, Becca and Bre, moping around and making faces, hoping to sneak out to party it up with their crew. They're nice girls, actually, much better behaved than I was at their age. It's been a while since I've seen everyone, and based on how we left things off, they're not missing me.

I miss Judi, my stepmom, probably because she's never been one to pass judgement. I suspect, though, she says nothing in front of Dad. When there's a fight, she agrees with me more often than not. Let's put it this way, she's the only one I've called Mom.

The family doesn't have a clue about me and Carlos breaking up, let alone about what happened to him. What can I tell them? I still can't make sense of it myself. I recognize I should poke around his chart for clues, but I'm too afraid to find bad news. What if he's really dead and I'm the one responsible, just like I was with Glenn? If my sobriety is a priority, I can't think about my past with men, at least not now.

Considering all the trouble with the cat and the stink bomb, not to mention the ongoing hang up calls, I'm lucky to be hiding out in South Laguna at Katherine's place, what I call her "palace."

In between rich husbands, Katherine used to live in a cute condo above Victoria Beach. I'd be more comfortable there, but she has it rented out. Victoria is one of my favorite places to enjoy the sunset. It's still pretty quiet, few tourists or the hordes of Nine-o-niners. That's what we who live in coastal cities call folks from inland who invade our beaches, bringing in traffic, noise and garbage. A lot of them come from the 909 area code. (I'm probably being a bitch, but, hey, it's kind of like expecting everyone from Beverly Hills 90210 to be loaded and most of the time, they are.)

Unlike some of its neighboring, tiny, cove-like beaches, Victoria is a nice, long stretch of soft, white sand that hardly ever burns your feet. It's not boring either. There are lots of shells to pick and cool rock formations to explore. It's also known for its tide pools, the pounding surf, and a weird sixty-foot-tall stone turret structure we locals call the Pirate Tower.

My ex, Glenn, was obsessed with pirates, so he'd tell me about the tower after a few puffs of weed before we'd move on to the more serious stuff. I still have a few pics of the tower and its creepy-looking windows lying around. Oddly, I remember the name of the dude who first built it only because Brown is my bio mom's maiden name. I wish we were related. Bill Brown was working in government, but once he got to Laguna, he fell in love with the art colony and turned to painting. Word was, he was surprisingly good with a paint-brush. Glenn said he sold the house to some old navy captain who was also obsessed with pirates. The captain, whose name I don't remember, was a nut who loved dressing up in full pirate gear and holding scavenger hunts for kids. I thought that wasn't normal, but Glenn accused me of having a dirty mind. I told him that from where I stood, one can never be too sure about men dressing up and playing with kids.

But back to Katherine, who bought the Victoria beach condo for practically nothing years back. That's one thing she has in common with Sandi: a deep belief that a woman can't count on a man for money. I wish I met my ladies before I fucked up my life.

Katherine lives in a tri-level in what she calls an eclectic style (what the heck?) waterfront estate. The house rises high above Thousand Steps Beach, hidden from the street by a long driveway and a security gate. Folks sure like to stretch the truth. There're no thousand steps, just a little over two hundred, but while it may be a breeze to go down the narrow stairway, coming up is a bitch of a climb because the steps are high and worn by the wind and humidity, meaning I've stubbed my toes plenty of times in the cracks. (What's a little unusual for California is that a part of the beach on your right is private.) It's worth the climb back, though: sandstone cliffs, clean, blue-green water, and tons of private space to spread out your towel. You don't want to drag a bunch of gear back up to the Coast Highway though I love taking my time discovering the cave on its south end, but once I was so drunk that I didn't notice the tide coming in. Luckily, I was able to swim back but swallowed enough saltwater to cause my lungs to seize and sending me to the ER across the highway, where I spent several hours.

The beach house is enormous, but the driveway, along with the clapboard and shingles, needs major repairs. It's work Katherine keeps postponing, not because of money, but because she travels so damn much. When I question her priorities, she laughs at me and makes fun of Americans who don't travel abroad. She says only four in ten even have a passport and even those mostly just go to Canada or Mexico. As if that's a sin. People who are struggling just to pay the bills are not obsessed with old foreign buildings.

"What is life without moving around, exploring, learning something different?" Katharine asks. "I want to die on a cruise ship. Let them deal with my body."

"But I worry about your health," I say, trying to reason with her. "You're getting older. If you miss your sisters, why don't you bring Berta and Rosie here? You've got plenty of room."

"I'm not getting older, just sexier," she says, giggling. "*Nein.* No way. I can only stand them for a quick visit. They're the ones who got old."

I give up trying to reason with her, accepting her stubborn Taurus the Bull nature. I guess I get her point. She's had her troubles, survived the big C more than once.

Katherine moved to her "forever" home when she married Hans. Before finally crossing over, he promised her that she would never have to move again. You'd expect that he'd had her sign a prenup, but he didn't. Katherine told me Hans's entire family was gone and his only living relative, a son in his sixties, is some super-loaded dude who lives in Europe. Since the son also owns a private island in the Caribbean, he couldn't care less about a decrepit "beach shack" halfway around the world. I take it that Hans and his son were on the outs. From what I gathered, Hans didn't strike me as the generous, romantic type. (Because Katherine never had her own kids, the house will revert to his son upon her death.)

Katherine keeps talking about dumping the property as is and moving back to her Victoria condo, but every time someone gives her an offer, she makes the sale contingent on not tearing it down, a common practice. Up to this point, no one has agreed to her asinine conditions.

Years back, after Glenn and I moved down to Laguna from Costa Rica, I couldn't believe how big the homes were once you got down to the beach level or how modest they looked from the street when you drove by. I guess that was the point.

In the past, the old money didn't need to show what they had and hid their wealth. It's so different nowadays. You drive just a few miles north and you'll be floored by the in-your-face ostentatiousness of Newport Coast. Twenty- million-dollar monstrosities are the norm. Who are these people and where did they get all this money? What happened to my laid-back Orange County? I guess you can't go home again.

When I was born, the entire county only had a little more than a million people. There were orange groves and straw-berry fields and an old man with wild hair and beard who stood on the corner in Laguna Beach, greeting locals, tourists, and especially us little kids. Once he shook my hand, com-plimenting the color of my eyes, and got me free ice cream. I remember him vaguely because I was about five, just start-ing kindergarten. After Gail split, Dad moved away from our family home: too many memories, not to mention the nosy neighbors. He found a small mobile home park in Laguna Beach, practically on the sand: one bedroom and a cute front room where my brother and I shared a fold-out sofa. I'd never been so happy, running wild, playing in the surf, chasing sand crabs, and building castles.

I was small, but I still remember my dad telling me he was acquainted with the friendly Laguna Beach Greeter. The Greeter must have been in his eighties when he passed, a crusty, old guy from Denmark, a gardener and a bum but so sweet and friendly that people let him live rent-free and fed him. I looked up his horoscope and sure enough, he had a cool chart, Aries with Venus in Aries, just like me.

Later on I found out there was another old dude called the Greeter, a Portuguese immigrant who greeted stagecoach visitors carrying a trident fishing spear, just like Neptune. Wierdo. No wonder I feel at home.

If I count those few short months with Dad, this is the third time I'm living at the beach. I just wish the circumstances were different.

After I told Katherine what had been going on with Carlos's family, she said I could do her a favor by keeping an "eye" on Annie and Efren, logic I find hilarious. I'm the one who's always in trouble. Contrary to what Art assumes, there's no way I can get a protective order against Carlos' folks since there's zero proof that they're the ones harassing me. What if they blame me for his disappearance? I had nothing to do with him being whacked, if, in fact, the body they found was Carlos'. I have an iron-clad alibi, and no one from the police or the sheriff's office has contacted me, at least not yet. It's not like *I'm* going to contact *them*. After all I've been through, you bet I do my best to stay away from anything to do with the authorities—too much baggage.

While I'm her houseguest, Katherine's away traveling, but this time she didn't go to Europe, deciding to shake it up a bit. She said yes to an invitation to spend the holidays with a Dutch couple she met while on her last river cruise. I was a little worried, but she reassured me that this is a common practice in their social set. Besides a house near Amsterdam and an apartment in London, her new jet-set friends own a compound in Costa Rica, growing the local cacao bean on their plantation around Puerto Jimenez. For once, I'm not green-eyed. That's one promise I've kept, after swearing to my family that I'll never go back to that hellhole—way too many memories of my days with Glenn and serious drugs. Yeah, it's all bird-friendly, ecologically clean, and Zen, however, being dangled by your feet over a creek full of crocs by a couple of seriously polluted hombres is not something one repeats.

I don't miss Katherine, but it would be nice to spend some time playing Rummikub and talking celebrity astrological charts with Sandi. After she spent a night at the hospital, Jay insisted they celebrate Thanksgiving "privately" down in the desert, far away from me, since according to Jay, "I'm the selfish bitch responsible for the stress that landed Sandi in the hospital." The nerve of that guy.

As I expected, both Nate and Art are spending Turkey Day near their kids, so here I am, stuck on the California Riviera, sulking in my ten-million-dollar beach residence, enjoying a practically private beach and daily sunshine, as I'm waited on by Katherine's staff: a doctor and a teacher, yet. Such sacrifice.

I appreciate that I should make my personal safety a priority, but I'm still kicking myself for making an outright play for Art. I thought it would hurt to be rejected, just not this much, so I've committed to giving my relationship with Nate 100 percent of my attention as soon as he gets back from Lancaster. It could be that predictability and being comfortable with a normal guy is precisely what I need.

The yellow-and-blue overstuffed guest room where I'm staying is on the small side, if you compare it with Katherine's master, but it has two wide windows facing the ocean. When it's sunny, I keep at least one window open to get rid of the smell of mildew and stale perfume. Ever since I sobered up, my sense of smell has returned stronger than ever. Based on the lack of morning clouds, I can see it's going to be another perfect beach day, even though it's almost December. Still, I woke up in a mood. I guess I'm still trying to get used to being away from the comfort of my cozy Costa Mesa cottage. It's small, but it is all mine.

Just now, I told the reflection of my pinched but already tanned face in the gaudy bathroom mirror: *You're not safe, be thankful you get to stay here. Get your shit together or else.*

Still, I can't stop myself from having an antsy, creepy vibe as if someone were watching me, and no, I haven't taken a drink since my freak-out with Art. I wish I could talk with Sandi about what I'm feeling, but she won't answer her phone. I'm going to let it slide until the holiday is over and then try again.

There's something wrong, but I can't put my finger on it. I'm back having nightmares about the Laguna Canyon accident and Glenn's broken body. It's as if the sounds of the waves crashing against the rocks are bringing up some repressed memories of the crash that killed him.

Yesterday afternoon, I was tortured by Carlos's presence. When I went down to the beach, bringing my astrology homework along, I couldn't concentrate, so I took a quarter of a pill and dozed off. I could swear I wasn't dreaming; it was so real. I felt like I was pulled out of my body and taken to a dark, small space, kind of like a basement, but it wasn't. I saw a man who reminded me of Carlos, but in my dream, he wasn't at all like himself: dirty, bearded, and incredibly sad. I suffered with him. The man cradled his hand close to his heart, the hand wrapped in a small red towel. He looked at me with Carlos's eyes, but the expression was odd, not at all like his. I must've cried in my sleep, because when I opened my eyes, my lids were burning from the sunblock I applied before laying down. The experience freaked me out and I headed back to the house, spending the rest of the day in a daze, locked in my guest bedroom. I even had Efren bring me up supper.

"Miss Vivi, are you awake?" I hear Annie's melodic voice ask.

"Yes, I'm up, just getting dressed for the beach," I yell through the closed door. I know Annie won't open the door unless I give her my permission.

"Efren and I are going to church. You want to come with us? We're friends with the minister."

"No thanks, no church. I'll just hang at the house."

"We'll be back before you miss us, but if you're hungry, I've made plenty of balut and rice."

"Thank you. I'm fine." I continue to shout through the door like an idiot. Exactly what I've always wanted for my Thanksgiving meal: Asian food. Shockingly, I did like a few dishes Annie cooked for the three of us since I've been staying here, especially seafood kinilaw, a Philippine version of limy, salty ceviche. The rest of it had way too much pork with garlic and it gave me gas.

"She made chicken adobo too. Special for you." Efren says, joining in.

"Okay." Now I'm getting annoyed. I wish they'd get lost, pray, or do whatever they do in their church. I assumed they were Catholic, but apparently, they go to a cultlike evangelical church a distance away. Katherine told me she's worried that they're being used. She suspects after sending money back home, they donate the rest to the preacher's orphan fund. I told her it sounds like a scam and promised to talk to them, considering my experience with my bio mom's cult in Northern California. Damn, my life would make a crazy-ass movie. I finally smile.

When I was fourteen, my dad's second wife was on me for doing badly in school and not going to church and not picking up after myself and not letting her fucking son lift my skirt, so I ran off to California to be with Gail. I never considered telling my dad, who'd lock me in the barn. Well, that didn't last long either. One thing you can say about Daddy, he's no pushover, and since he had legal custody of me, he and Grandmom showed up, accompanied by sheriffs, and removed me by force. Not that living with Mom would've worked. Gail's a freak. She's the one that taught me how to use a pipe. Hell, she even got me to try 'shrooms with her. We haven't heard a word from her in years, but based on my astrological transits, she's still around somewhere. It's not like I'm about to look on social media either. I'm sure if Dad didn't show up and get me, I'd be dead, not that it'd be such a tragedy.

"Whatever shall we do this fine holiday afternoon; eh, Milady? Watch a show? Expand our gray matter, or grow a pair and study Carlos's chart?" I ask Annie and Effron's cat, Missy, using my best imitation of an English lady's voice. "I'm not exactly sure where to look at what could've possibly gone wrong, but it's worth a try. We can always run it by Lady Sandi later. You two haven't met, not just yet. But trust me, you'll love her. But at the moment, I'm in dire need of fresh air, so let's also indulge in a healthy snack. What do you think about spending a peaceful holiday at the beach before the weather turns?"

Annie and I've been bingeing on "Father Brown's Mysteries" on YouTube, and my ability to imitate different voices is getting progressively better. Now I'm glad Katherine doesn't have cable TV. YouTube is so much better and it's so simple to use and without having to deal with all sorts of strangers coming in and out of the house to fix the service. For once, Katherine's cheapness is paying off. Annie hooks the TV set to her laptop, and we don't have to pay for anything. She's a true Scorpio, just like the sign on my Ascendant. We get each other.

Missy, a spoiled Birman, a breed I never even heard of, is a mutt, at least that's what I call her when she's being a brat.

Poor Annie gets as offended as if I'd called her child a moron. I'm only kidding. Missy is the most gorgeous, clever creature, a cross between a Siamese and a Persian. Efren bought her for Annie when she was in a major funk after losing her mom. Katherine loaned him the money, then after falling in love with the cat, made it a Christmas bonus, as if she couldn't just give him the money outright. She's always pulling the purse strings; that's our Katherine.

I swear that cat is obsessed with me. Since I've been staying at the house, Missy adopted my bed as her own, as if sensing how much it would piss me off because of her hair shedding all over my things. For whatever reason, today Missy is ignoring my efforts to make nice, looking at me suspiciously with different-colored eyes and hissing when I try to cuddle her. Maybe she too is suspecting something is not right with my energy field? Oh well, I'll just let her be. Even the cat won't give me what I need... Happy, crappy Thanksgiving indeed.

Chapter 10

oday is Sunday, the end of the holiday weekend. I can't wait until I can try to get a hold of Sandi. On Black Friday, Annie talked me into doing some Christmas shopping with her, bribing me with a quick stop at Sidecar Doughnuts. With all the stress, I'm eating carbs again, but my weight is still down. Unfortunately for Annie, the bargain-hunting crowds were too much for my sober nerves and I had a panic attack right in the middle of the Container Store. After over an hour of trying to calm down, I gave up. Off we went, back to the beach. Annie, the doctor, understood what was happening. Despite being told not to, she felt bad enough that I scored a half a Xanax from her. That did it. I stopped hyperventilating and carrying on, finally able to take a full breath in and out. I didn't argue when she sent me straight to bed for the rest of the day.

Since I'm alone and antsy again, I decide to return to my studies at the beach, looking at anything and everything to do with the astrological causes of death. Some folks don't want to find out the details of their transition from the earth plane to the cosmic, while others fear if they know it, they'll bring it on sooner—a sort of self-fulfilling prophecy. Personally, I've been sucked into the light tunnel more than once and I am no longer afraid, especially since I brought back a few unexpected gifts.

When I shared my near-check-out experiences with Sandi without a freak-out, she said I was ready to study an old astrological technique. This particular method uses Fixed Stars to predict if not the timing, but at least the method of transition each soul chooses for itself. I told Sandi I still don't get the concept of whacking yourself on purpose. (Hey, I don't judge. I've been there myself.) I've also seen plenty of friends leave this world, not because they wanted to go. Right now, I save my skepticism for another lesson and just try to pack as much info as I can into my dense head. One thing is certain: I need to find out what happened to Carlos one way or the other if I'm to stay safe.

Not having a fancy laptop loaded with expensive astrological software stops me from learning fast. I have to study the old-fashioned way: Read a book, take notes, and try to memorize as much as possible. I must admit, I feel myself getting smarter. It's as if my brain is stretching, kind of like when I up my weights at the gym. Last year when I first started studying astrology, I couldn't even recall the names of the different signs, let alone understand what they meant. Look at me now, learning a whole novel way to figure out how a person can actually die. Sadly, no one except for Sandi sees what a miracle this is and how much better I feel about myself.

Studying astrology online with others is way too much pressure. Because of my dyslexia, I must write everything down several times, then call Sandi with tons of questions. So far, she's been able to explain most of what I don't get. Then comes my favorite part, spending hours practicing what I learned by looking at charts of famous people, those whose deaths are well documented. This way I can tell I'm not wrong.

My two latest homework charts are those of Anna Nicole Smith and Heath Ledger. Sandi gave me the assignment because she considered their death charts were so different although both were Fire signs, like me, and both died thanks to drugs.

Anna Nicole was born under two unfortunate stars, Marfic and Mufrid. Her Sagittarius Sun came way too close to Marfic. That made her a sweetie with a big heart, but she was also ruled by her passions and easily seduced. Her Libra Moon and Venus sat with Mufrid and that didn't help matters either. Mufrid is all about powerful desires and excess. Too bad: Did you ever see such a gorgeous body? All honey and cream.

Heath was an April Aries, just like me. This kid was born under the lucky star Alpheratz, (seriously weird name, so I call it Alfie). It's Alfie that made him so popular at such a young age. This is a glorious star! I wish I was born under it. The books say that Alpheratz makes you motivated and brings you honor. On top of it, he was such a gifted actor, thanks to the Fixed Star Aldermin. Of course, Aldi brings on trials, sadness, and moodiness too; he was way too serious. (He should have stayed away from drugs since I don't see how he used them for fun.) I can't find a proper explanation except that his death was an accident, a dumb accident, but I'm sure Sandi will help me find it.

I'm so proud of myself when I get the concepts. The addictive side of my brain gets a jolt of pleasure and satisfaction, apparently because of my Lunar North Node position. My North Node makes me susceptible to loads of dangerous crap, I guess because I haven't yet learned my karmic lessons. Imagine all of this time, my battles with addiction were because of my unstable childhood, weak nature, not to mention poor choices. Just knowing this info really helped me to deal with all the anger I've always felt toward my family, especially my dad, who should've kept his pants zipped, at the very least staying unmarried until I was a little more grown.

Okay. Let's go, genius. No more procrastinating by looking at dead celebs. You're ready to get to the bottom of what really happened to Carlos.

Yep, here comes the rush. I had Sandi print his birth horoscope. Although the copy is all crumpled and stained, I can still read my notes, scribbled inside each one of the twelve pie segments that make up the astrological wheel.

So for this to work, all I have to do is organize Carlos's birth chart info, this time inside my notebook, starting with the sign, the exact degree, down to the minute placement of his planets. Then I must examine his Ascending sign and the other three angles, meaning the signs on the cusp of his 4th, 7th, and 10th houses. The stars' position can be important when our planets move by progression, but Sandi says the idea of progressions is way too advanced for me to understand, at least for now.

Let's keep moving. Step two would be to study my list of the Fixed Stars with the probable cause of death. If there's an exact match between his chart and a particular star. Bingo! Sounds pretty easy, right? I haven't even started yet and my head is already throbbing.

Today, simply concentrating on my notes takes some effort because my mind isn't settled. I keep going back and forth between the last time I saw Art, how much his rejection hurt me, being worried sick about Sandi, and feeling sorry for myself for having to spend another holiday season alone. Then there's that odd vibe of being, if not followed, at least watched. I'm nervous as fuck, constantly looking around the beach and behind my back, up the steep stairs leading to the PCH.

I wish Annie left a few Xanax behind, but she knows all about me, so she keeps the prescription bottle hidden and I'm not yet desperate enough to tear Katherine's place apart looking for it. Not that I haven't done that before.

Time is dragging along as I put down my Dollar Tree-bought high school notebook and gaze over the silvery surf toward Catalina Island. Today the Island's barely visible in the afternoon haze. I've never visited there, even though it's only twenty-six miles from Newport. Dumb fantasies crowd out astrology. "What would it feel like to have Art take me on a boat ride date?" I wonder out loud. He probably has never been there either. Perhaps we'll drive south to the marina in Dana Point and get on one of those catamarans. I hope he likes the sea. We'll find us a private place somewhere on the deck, the brisk sea wind forcing us to cuddle. Then we'll walk around the tiny main street, buy a few trinkets, have a meal and a swim and return closer than ever. Damn, who am I kidding? Art can't stand the sight of me, let along take me to Catalina on a date.

Snap out of it, Viv, and get back to Carlos's chart.

I stare at my notes again, shaking my head. What was I thinking? I can't do any of this alone. I need Sandi. She's the one who writes questions and answers. I only read the information, copy it by hand, and read it again and again so I can remember something. I'm way too stupid to be a real astrologer.

Because it's been a while before I could even consider learning something new, I need to reread the notes from our last lesson. Not exactly known for being patient, I get frustrated really quickly. It's so hard to read what she wrote... poor Sandi. Ever since the stroke, her usually neat, up-and-down handwriting is all over the place, looking more like my own scribbles.

The day is getting away from me. By the time I got down to the sand, it was way past two. Unlike during the morning hours, the beach was mostly deserted, outside of the few neighbors walking their fur babies. I moved closer to the surf today, finding the hypnotic sound both soothing and energizing. Instead of using the public stairs, I came down along the private pathway separating Katherine's house from the neighboring estate, lugging a few beach items, the bits and pieces that Efren found in the storage room to make me more comfortable: a green-and-brown lounge chair, a small, yellow-and-blue pillow, and an old TV tray, just like the one we used when I was a kid. I've had my snack and enough of the caffeine-loaded Diet Coke to keep my mind nice and focused. If only I can stop daydreaming.

I force myself to pay attention to Sandi's questions. I do my best to organize everything nice and neatly so I can refer to my notes in the future. I sure like to talk to myself when no one's around.

Question: "If everything in space is in the constant state of motion, why do we call the stars Fixed?"

Answer: They aren't actually fixed in the same place, but because they're not a part of our solar system, we have a hard time seeing their motion. They move exactly 50.2 seconds per year. That makes a Star move a full astrological degree every seventy-two years.

And? I don't understand.

Question: How did the ancient astrologers use the Fixed Stars?

Answer: They kept observing with their own eyes and testing the meaning, finally telling us that the most important stars only had influence when they came close to the planets and angels and made an exact conjunction.

I assume by conjunction Sandi means the Fixed Star is within about one degree of our own planets: pretty exact if you ask me. That helps to narrow it down. If even one of Carlos's important planets has a Fixed Star sitting on top of it, I should be able to figure out the most probable way he died. Digging for secrets makes me excited. Am I my father's girl, after all?

Question: Who were the two most important Greek astronomers who came up with the Fixed Stars' meanings, and when did they practice?

Answer: Hipparchus of Nicea (130 B.C.) and Ptolemy (140 A.D.).

Question: Who were the most important modern astrologers who developed the system even further?

Answer: William Lilly, Vivian Robson, Rene Dumont, Andre Boudineau, Andre Volquine.

Seriously? What's with the foreign names? I can't even pronounce them, let alone remember. Give me a break.

As I put my notebook down, I can't help but crave a nice tall glass of ice with a couple of shots of Absolute, but I get myself together and continue on my sleuthing mission. A gust of chilly wind stirs up a handful of sand, getting in my eyes and forcing me to get up to move my chair to the left so it looks south toward the cave where I almost drowned. I see a familiar figure in the distance and assume its Katherine's neighbor, Mr. Freed. I wave and he waves back.

Based on the sun's slow slide toward the horizon and the color change of the surf, it's probably past four. I should probably gather my stuff and continue inside. Nah, I enjoy studying by the water too much. I'll give myself a little more time, not more than half an hour, because based on the gray clouds now completely covering Catalina, there may be a front coming in.

I continue my excursion by looking at my list of the Fixed Stars, copied from Sandi's computer. I made the list when I was helping after her stroke because Jay was away who knows where. I wish he'd stayed away. I must admit, it was sort of nice to get access to both her astrological software and have her all to myself.

For starters, I need to find a match for Carlos's Taurus Ascendant (sexy), Cancer Sun (for sure mama's boy), Sagittarius Moon (he'll never settle down), Venus in Gemini (shit, no wonder he cheats), and Mars in Leo (selfish peacock). If there's no match, I'll examine the angles.

The chart Sandi came up with shows that Carlos was born on July 3, 1974, most likely at 3:05 a.m. in Guadalajara, Jalisco State. Now I write everything down carefully using my best fourth-grade printing technique.

Ascendant: Taurus. 23 degrees.

The Stars close: Zaurak: 23 degrees 52 minutes. Influence is 1 degree, 40 minutes.

My notes say Zaurak shows a fear of death or death by suicide. No way Carlos would off himself; he loves himself way too much.

Capulus: 24 degrees 12 minutes. Influence is 1 degree 30 minutes.

Oh no, it says this star has to do with murder or execution, most commonly by hanging or beheading. Wait, it also says it causes poor eyesight or even blindness. The man in my dream had something wrong with his eyes, but he wasn't dead, at least I don't assume so.

Algol: 26 degrees 10 minutes. Influence is 2 degrees.

I remember this star. Sandi told me the ancients called it the "Blinking Demon." The worst star ever. Again, my notes say Ptolemy wrote cause of death is decapitation, hanging, lightning (now it would be electrocution). This is horrible. The English astrologer William Lilly determined it was the most cursed position, a star that for sure brings a violent ending.

Oh, no, Carlos is DEAD! That's enough. I hate astrology. Why did I have to poke the snake? I'm upset and need to talk to Sandi right now. I'm panicking as I recognize well the funny metallic smell and feel my heart pounding right out of my chest. Here it comes. I can't breathe.

Breathe, Viv, just breathe. 1-2-3-4-5 in, 1-2-3-4-5-6 out.

Fuck, it's not working. I need a Xanax. No, I need to cool off. I jump up and run over to the edge of the surf, getting down on my knees. With badly shaking hands, I scoop up cold, sandy sea water and try to splash my face. But before I get a chance, something hits me from behind and everything goes black.

Chapter 11

"As a psychiatrist, I am chiefly interested in the particular light the horoscope sheds on certain complications in the character... I must say that I very often found that astrological data elucidated certain points which I otherwise would have been unable to understand."— Carl G. Jung

First-time visitors to Southern California beaches arriving during the late fall or early winter make the mistake of assuming that if the air temperature is mild and the water is temperate, they are safe. They're wrong, dead wrong.

As the low, thick, drizzle-filled fog coming from the west raced toward the shore, the dim sun slid into the agitated ocean. By 5:10, the Thousand Steps beach, now eerily empty, was concealed even from the mansions rising right above the sand.

If you could clearly see what was taking place at the edge of a small cave, you would probably consider dialing 911 in a hurry. A nondescript figure wearing a dark hoodie was up to no good. He was bending over a human body, half-immersed in rising water, his back turned to the home built right into the cliff. At first glance, not listening to your gut, thinking you're being paranoid, you may hope he was helping, but if you'd grow a pair of *cojones* and approached, you'd see he was actually holding a head under water, keeping the unfortunate soul from taking a lifesaving breath. Just as the assault seemed close to its inevitable end, the man stopped and pulled the body out of the water, turning his victim on his or her back. He took off on foot, first climbing over the rocks and then sauntering north, toward the next strand of beach casually leaving the scene of the crime without looking back.

If he'd turned around, he'd see the rising tide pushing the body onto the slippery black rocks covered with mussels and seaweed. The body remained motionless until it was spotted by a man running down a private path. The man held a cell phone to his ear, screaming something, something lost in the fog.

Uh-oh. Back again, but this time without the bright, warm light or the tunnel. My lungs are on fire. My head's exploding. I recognize this feeling because it happened before, but what's with all the noise? I try to open my eyes, but the pain is too intense. Did I slip on the rocks and fall into the rising surf, swallowing saltwater again? Wait. I recall I was sitting on the sand, away from the rocks. Wait, yes, right on the sand. Did I pass out? Did I sneak some Xanax? I can't remember what happened and forcing myself to recall details is making my headache worse. I better sleep it off.

"Viv, are you okay?" I hear a familiar man's voice say. "Wake up, hon. You can't sleep. Viv?"

"Leave me alone," I whisper back, my lips cracked dry. "I'm tired. Got to get some shuteye."

"You can't. I'm sorry, babe. I appreciate you're sleepy, but you have to stay awake."

"Go away, Daddy. There's no school. Its Thanksgiving. I did all my chores. Sorry about the beer."

"Why are you laughing at me, Daddy?" I force one eye to open. Oh, my... I guess I am dead after all and by some sort of mix-up, in heaven, because the laughter belongs to Art. Art's holding my arm pierced by an IV needle, looking at me like I'm a warm slice of lemon cake on a keto diet.

"Well, I am a daddy, just not yours," he chuckles good-naturedly and runs his hand through that gorgeous head of hair, exposing his forehead, deeply lined with years spent outdoors. Finally, a man who wouldn't dream of hiding his age.

"Hey there, you gave us a scare. Annie's about to have a stroke. And her husband, don't remember his name, was on FaceTime with your friend Katherine, acting as if he's killed you," he goes on, gently dropping my hand, then placing his palm on my forehead as if to check for fever.

"Hey, yourself. Sorry for the trouble. I'll tell Katherine it wasn't anything they did. Where am I?" I ask, the jolt of adrenalin I get just being near him making me feel so much better.

"You're in the ER across the street from your friend Katherine's. I found you on the rocks and called for help. You've been out for a bit. They did a C-scan and X-rayed your lungs. Good news, nothing serious outside of a mild concussion. You'll live. They just have to keep an eye on your lungs in case you swallowed too much water. Do you remember how you fell and bumped your head?"

"No, that's the thing. When I try to remember, it's like I was sitting on the sand in front of the steps, studying astrology. I'm quite sure I was drinking a Diet Coke. I remember the clouds over Catalina. Say, have you ever been there?"

"Are you sure you didn't go into the water? What about Catalina?"

"I'm not sure about anything right now, but someone must have sneaked up behind me and whacked me on the head.. I'm trying to remember more, but my head hurts like a mother F."

"It's okay, just rest, we'll figure it out later, but keep talking to me."

"Listen, you need to get me out of here. I don't have insurance. I'm an Aries, remember? I've had a shitload of head injuries over the years. I can take care of myself at the house."

"Again, with the gibberish. You're not going anywhere. Try to rest and definitely stop worrying about insurance; I've got it covered."

"You don't understand. I can't afford to stay. I don't have the money."

"I do understand, and I'm telling you, I'm the responsible party. Sandi asked me to take care of the bill instead of rent."

"Sandi? Where is she? Please ask her to come in. I've been trying to reach her since the fight with Jay, but she's been off the grid. Tell her I need to talk to her. It's a matter of life and death." I can't help but tear up.

"Sandi isn't here. She's still in the desert. She's the one who called me in, but I'll explain later. Listen, don't get angry, but I have to ask. Were you drinking again?"

"You mean drinking booze? Hell, no. I told you I was drinking a soda. Can't study astrology if I'm not clear-headed. I've never been good at remembering what I read as it is. Why are you asking about what I was drinking?"

"Well, we're still waiting on your blood results, but I have to tell you, I smelled something on your clothes."

I can't accept what I'm hearing. I wasn't even close to booze. Guess this ain't heaven after all. "I've got zero idea what you smelled, but I'm sober now and planning to stay that way. And why is it any of your fucking business anyway?"

"Hey, hey," Art says, putting his hands up. "Don't get upset. It's not good for your health. You realize, a cop is a cop, even a retired one. It's just that they pulled your records and apparently the last time they saw you, you were also pretty banged up—and high."

"That was then, and this is now."

"I'm sorry, Viviana, but I had to ask."

"Yah, whatever," I say without meaning it. Then a terrifying notion hits me. "Where's my homework? My notebook and my printed charts? What if there's another spill and all my notes are ruined? Didn't you see my chair and a little tray? You know, a TV tray, like the ones we used to eat on when we were kids?"

"What spill?"

"A fucking leak from the hospital generator. They don't care about our beaches or the environment, just how much money they can make."

"Sorry you're upset about the leak, but there was nothing around you on the rocks. I'm not a beach guy, but it looked like the tide was pretty high. Could be your things were swept out to sea ."

"It can't be. I had everything Sandi and I've been working on with me at the beach. Oh, no, Art," I plead, trying to make him understand my desperation. "I beg you, please go down to the sand and search again. I can't lose all my homework. It took months to put it together. I'm a terrible student. Really stupid. I'll never recover."

"I don't want to leave you, not until I'm convinced you're okay." He cringes, shaking his head, clearly uncomfortable with what I just admitted about myself being stupid and all.

"I am okay; nice and safe: I'm here with the staff, aren't I? Can't exactly go anywhere." I smile, his unexpected kindness making me foolishly giddy. "Please try."

"All right, but I'll be back ASAP. Don't you dare close your eyes. Here, play Candy Crush on my phone," Art compromises with me and steps out of the cubical. He returns a minute or two later with a warm blanket, wrapping it around my lower body without a word, then leaves.

Has he just handed over his phone? No man I've ever been with would give up his precious damn privacy. I've always had to snoop. Art really has nothing to hide from me. What a prince. No wonder I'm crazy in love with the guy. And just like that, all those good intentions of making my relationship with Nate work dissolve as fast as those god-awful Alka Seltzer pills my dad used to give me for hangovers.

Candy Crush, hmm? I've heard of it, but never was into playing phone games myself. Could I actually learn it? An older, friendly-looking male nurse with military tats stops by to check on me, so I ask him if he knows how to play. He shows me the beginner level and I actually get into it until my eyes close, despite my best intentions to stay awake.

I guess I stay dead to the world for more than a few minutes. When my sore eyes half open, I find myself face to face with a doctor who looks like an Asian teenager. She's accompanied by the guy nurse who taught me to play Candy Crush.

"Am I going to be okay, doc?" I ask as respectively as I can.

"Yes, you're doing well. We're getting your paperwork together, so you can go home tonight, provided someone can monitor you for a day or so. If not, I recommend we admit you."

"I don't want to be admitted if I don't have to be."

"That's fine. You may still suffer from headaches, but if they get worse or your vision changes, come back immediately. Although, you swallowed some water, your lungs appear in decent shape. I'll still prescribe a few days of antibiotics and a mild steroid, just to be on the safe side. Otherwise, you should follow up with your own physician and your neurologist. I'm sure you've seen a neurologist based on your brain scan. Car accident?"

"Something like that," I mumble, avoiding my checkered medical history. Too complicated. "What about by blood work?" I ask her, again avoiding the neurologist recommendation. I don't need more expenses, considering I've been banged up a lot worse than this.

"Well, everything is in range, but your drug test wasn't clean. Blood alcohol: point one; pretty high for an older woman, even if you're not driving."

"What do you mean, point one? This is bullshit. Run it again. I'm sober, and it'd take a lot more than point one for me to get this fucked up. I've been a point three and lived. Oh my God, Carlos's family IS trying to get me. Hey, who you're calling old, little chickadee?" My temper flairs. The headache returns with a vengeance and I scream. The doctor ignores me, turns on her heels, and walks out without a word.

"Don't you dare discount me. Who the hell do you think you are? What kind of service is this? Are you serious? You expect me to pay for this? You millennial snowflake!" Now I'm really getting worked up.

"Ma'am, there's no reason to raise your voice at the doctor. We have a zero-tolerance policy for staff abuse. You either calm down or we'll have no choice and put you on a 72-hour psych hold." The asshole nurse gets in my face, close enough that I can smell food on his breath. No compassion for everything I've been through. That's why men shouldn't be nurses, I judge, but keep my mouth shut. I've been through plenty of psych holds and let me tell you, it's not an experience I'd wish on my worst enemy, well, maybe Carlos.

"Do you want us to call someone to stay with you until you're released?" asks the nurse, now cold as a dead fish. "Or do you need to make a statement to the police?"

"I have no one," I spit out and close my eyes. "No cops," I add more forcefully, keeping my eyes closed. "Say, my head is worse. Can I get some meds?" I open my eyes and rub my forehead despite the pinching IV sticking out of my hand.

"I'll check with the doctor. Right now, I have to work on your release paperwork. I'll be back. Oh, and Dr. Bernstein wants me to include the number for our drug and alcohol program. Behave." He shakes his head, looking at me with all-too-familiar disgust and leaves the cubicle. Bernstein? That Asian doctor doesn't look like any Bernstein I've ever seen. Makes little sense.

"Fuck you and fuck your program," I screech at his back. "Who are you to judge?"

"What in the world is going on?" Art demands, walking in with Annie tagging along. Her hair's in curlers, eyes puffy and red, and she's pulling along my Walmart overnighter.

"Nothing is going on. They won't give me anything for my head, so I'm pissed. That bitch doctor hates me. I don't even consider her license to be real. Supposedly her name is Bernstein. Does she look like a Bernstein to you? More like Chen or Park."

"What are you saying? Knock it off! Just stop your racist rant!" Art insists. "That's not what I just overheard. Viviana, so help me, tell me what's been going on. I can't help you if you keep lying. I was told about your blood test coming in as point one. It's time you come clean. We can get you the help you need."

"Fuck you too, Art the Cop!" I scream. "I'm clean! I've been clean! Ask Annie. I've had half a Xanax in all this time I've been at the beach. Ask her. I'm telling you I haven't got back on the juice since that day I told you how I felt about you and you rejected me. I'm not the one lying. They are. Why won't you trust me? *La familia* is trying to get me because Carlos is really dead, and it's all my fault."

Chapter 12

By the time they wheel me out of the ER, the drizzle has turned into a light rain. It's way past two in the morning. After dropping off my bag, Art leaves again, insisting on taking Annie home, even though she could've easily walked. What a fucking dinosaur: I'm sure she would've been perfectly safe. It's South Laguna, not South LA.

Because my blood pressure went sky high and they had to give me a pill, it took longer than I hoped for them to discharge me. Eventually, the shift changed and a new nurse, this time a sympathetic African American woman, helped me get dressed. Annie had brought me a pair of sweats and Katherine's musty, moth-eaten cashmere sweater, and she lets me use a pair of her UGG slippers. I guess most of my clothes were dirty. Lisa, the nurse, even brushed out the tangled mess on my head. Still angry about the unfair alcohol accusations, I refused to call Art, so Annie texted him to come and get me.

"I hope you get better, Miss Glover," the nurse says as Art pulls up in his truck.

"Thank you, Lisa. Goddess's blessings on you for treating me like a human, and I wasn't drinking."

"Of course. I'm only glad you're going home. I'm sure you'll rest up and feel better in the morning. Make sure you come back if you're getting worse," she adds, sounding genuinely concerned. Then she winks, motioning with her head toward Art, who parks right in front of the wheelchair.

"Lucky for you, you have a champion, and a looker at that."

"He's just my renter," I try to explain for no reason at all. "I'll be fine, hon, and thank you for remembering my name." I turn to Lisa, extending my sore arms for an impulsive hug. You never can tell where a little kindness will come from, so just be grateful and take it.

Art helps me get into the truck, but I'm so dizzy, I almost pass out as a wave of nausea hits my gut, then moves up my throat. I'm getting worse. My entire body aches horribly, but not enough to tell the nurse and risk being readmitted. Used to faking it, I smile at Lisa, wave, and pretend I'm fine. As soon as she goes back inside, I lose it and start to cry.

"I can't work the seat belt," I whisper, frustrated and humiliated.

"It's okay. Let me," Art says, pulling the belt over to buckle me in, accidentally touching my breasts. The electricity of his touch makes me jump.

"Sorry," he apologizes, wincing.

"It's fine. Men have done worse," I whisper, crossing over into utter despair.

"I'm not men."

"Yeah, we both learned that didn't we?" Even now, I manage to get snarky.

"Knock it off.," he says. "You're going to get your blood pressure up again and this time, I'll make sure they keep you."

"Fine, but I need a drink," I say. "Don't worry, not booze." I continue to bait him. "Do you have a soda or something to eat, like chips? They starved me."

"It's protocol. They wanted to make sure your gut was empty in case they needed to go in. Dr. Bernstein was worried about a brain bleed. She's an excellent emergency physician. You got lucky there. Sorry about the food. I have nothing on me, but I can stop at the 24-hour mini-mart on the way."

Art ignores my provocations. "Never mind. Annie always has some leftovers in the fridge. Did I tell you I had Philippine food for Thanksgiving? No turkey with fixings and no pie."

"You didn't, but we're not going to Katherine's place. I'm taking you back to Costa Mesa."

"Like hell you are. It's not safe. Let me out, you hear me? I'll walk."

"That would be a negative," he says, making his decision clear.

"Art? Why are you doing this to me?" I ask, now panicking.

"Calm down and listen. I'm not leaving you alone, not for a moment. Whoever attacked you knows your location. You'll be safer at the house with me."

"So now you trust me? I told you I wasn't drinking."

"Yes."

"Yes, what?"

"Yes, I trust what you said is what took place."

"How about saying, 'I'm sorry I didn't believe you?'"

"Yeah, what you said, but give me a break, Viv. You are an addict and lying is part of the disease. So how about we put this away and see what we can do to protect you."

I realize he's right. Still, the injustice of no one trusting me, especially someone like him, hurts worse than my head. For once, I'm all talked out. As I rub my eyes, the truck stops at a light. It looks like the corner of Bluebird Canyon, but I can't be sure. Even as a kid, I wanted to live up the steep part of the street in a little ivy-covered cottage with a couple of white-washed rooms. I guess they called the cottages Olympic Village, because the cottages were moved from LA, right after the 1932 Olympics. Even the streets were named after the medal winners. I've always loved Laguna stories.

The dense beach fog changes the color of the light from red to light pink, obscuring the front of the truck. I'd be afraid to drive in this weather, but Art doesn't seem to be bothered. Without a warning, Art reaches out, picks up my hand and gives it a firm, reassuring squeeze, his hand rough, but oddly warm. I say nothing, holding my breath. He doesn't stop there, lifting my sore, needle-bruised hand to his lips, he turns it over and kisses my palm. I must not be that sick, as all of my nerve endings come to life like the desert flowers in Borrego Springs after a rainy year.

Just before the fateful accident, Glenn and I took a bus to Borrego from Tijuana for one of his "special" meetups. It took us over five hours to get there, but once I saw the place, I didn't mind. For a split second, I recall the quilt-like patches of purple and orange wildflowers that would soon be burned crisp by the punishing heat—just like my heart.

Art says, "I am sorry, Viviana. I truly am."

"It's okay. I get it. I am an addict and a liar and an ungrateful bitch for not thanking you for saving my life. So here goes: thank you," I say gravely.

"Why, it was my pleasure, young lady." Art says, pretending to tip his imaginary hat, suspiciously sounding like my dad, the original old-school alpha male. "I was scared I wouldn't be in time," he admits to my delight. "Sandi was two hundred percent positive you were in serious danger. I still don't understand most of her explanations about Mars squares and something to do with a Disney character, but because I have so much respect for her, my gut told me to listen. Can you explain why she was talking about Pluto? And I'm not the sort of person who considers a strong-willed woman a bitch. Well, sometimes you can be a handful, but mostly I find you honest to a fault, even if it's not always comfortable." He takes a deep breath and then goes on as if he were holding his tongue for a long time.

"I don't know how to talk to you, Viv. You can be so weird, and you talk nonsense. Maybe it's my problem, but I'm not used to women telling me how they feel about me from the get-go. I'm a regular guy. When I like a gal well enough, I ask her out on a date and see if we have something in common and like to do the same things. Sometimes she's a single mom who dates other single parents. But here you are, and you're already seeing someone, and he's younger than me, and then you stare at me with those baby blues, and bite those lips, and you're always in trouble, and you're right, I am a cop, I can't resist a damsel in distress. Yeah, I get it. In your eyes, I'm a throwback, but that's just who I am, Viv. An old-fashioned guy who was raised to take the initiative and I'm way too old to change. Sorry."

That's the most the man has said to me in months. Now I'm the one who's tongue-tied. Not knowing how to respond, I nod, confused, thrilled, and terrified. Did he just tell me he likes me, despite my weirdness? I'm not sleepy anymore because I'm feeling too many emotions. I stare out the window at sleepy, traffic-free Laguna as we continue to drive north, wishing for once that there were thousands of cars on the road, so the drive would take hours.

We drive past the historic Hotel Laguna. Sadly, it's boarded up because of some asinine business deal gone south. When I was a kid, it used to have an enormous neon sign, which is also gone. The grand, old girl is dark. Paper the color of cheap, red wine covers the front door. Just get a load of the shuttered windows. What's wrong with the rich? Why can't they get together for one of those parties and fix it up? I asked Katherine, who's always coming and going to one party or another, and she said no one gives a rat's ass for history. Guess everybody wants a new, shiny toy.

The last time my dad and stepmom, Judi Ann, came to visit California, my crazy ex, Glenn, took us for a super-expensive Sunday seafood brunch there, with freshly made omelets and a Bloody Mary bar. We all got loaded, but I was the one to take a long snooze, sitting in the rose garden gazebo while the staff was setting up for another swanky wedding. It was a day of rare, wonderful memories, one of those bright January days without a cloud drifting off the water. That's the thing with my little overcast Laguna. More often than not, January is prettier than June. A master manipulator, always pulling on my heartstrings, Glenn formally asked my dad for my hand, telling him he'd pay for everything. What a creep! When I pressed him for a date, he just laughed it off, telling me he's still legally married, plus I wasn't exactly his "dream" wife material. Brokenhearted, I got high and hit him. He hit back, landing me back in the hospital with a broken nose and my last concussion. This is yet another "friendly" reminder of why I must stay clean.

Art mercifully interrupts my dark thoughts. "Hang on, I'm going to stop to get you something right now."

"It's okay. I can wait."

"Nope, I need to pick up a few things anyway: some creamer for coffee and some bread to make you toast. I'm sure you're still pretty nauseous. My fridge is empty because I drove straight from Saint George to Laguna when Sandi called me yesterday morning."

"What? You were still in Utah?"

"I was, but already on my way back after Thanksgiving with my folks. I left just ahead of the snow coming in. I'm sure glad I didn't bring Emery along. Remember Emery, my daughter? Definitely not safe. You're right. Something stinks. I'll go back home to Utah for Christmas, and then we'll all fly to Florida together. I booked a little holiday cruise for the family to thank my parents and make up to Emery for me being away."

Damn my Scorpio side. I'm already jealous of his family. I must get a hold of my feelings if I ever get a chance to make a go of it with him.

Don't question him or make nasty remarks, Viv, I whisper under my breath. You can't expect him to spend Christmas with you, right?

A few tense minutes go by. Since we just left Laguna, another twenty minutes is all I get. The ocean is on our left. I pick up the sound of the angry surf but can't see anything. No matter how badly I try to stay chill, I can't help myself. I need to touch him so much. I can't breathe, but no risk, no reward. This time I'm the one to reach out by laying my head on his upper arm. He inhales deeply but, shockingly, doesn't reject my move. Art bends his head to the right, closer to mine. I take a hint and move mine closer. We drive on, heads touching, afraid to break the spell.

"You're going to be okay, babe," he promises, his voice firm and sure.

"Damn right," I echo, not trusting either of us. "I don't eat bread," I lie, for no reason at all.

"You will now," he orders.

I surprise myself by not bristling at his command and, offering a compromise, say, "Some stores carry English muffins; they have fewer carbs."

"Listen, I get that everyone's crazy thin here in Orange County, but I'm telling you, you look good. Better than good. You certainly don't need to lose weight. At least, not for me."

I should jump down his throat with, "Don't tell me what to do," or "I'm not losing weight to be more attractive to hook up with a man," or whatever crap I would normally say, but I don't. I just mumble "Thanks," and leave it at that.

Chapter 13

O nce we get some distance away from the water, the fog isn't as dense. I can now make out Costa Mesa's streets signs, actually feeling excited in seeing my place again. I'm glad I'm going back to my little house, despite my Scorpio obsession with the water element. We pull into our driveway and for a while sit in the truck, our heads still touching, still not talking. The heat coming off his body along with the soft music and his measured breathing finally takes their toll. No matter how much I want this moment to last, there's nothing I can do as my body takes over. My eyes close, pushing me under as I plunge into lifeless blackness.

I'm floating. My head doesn't hurt and I can breathe without coughing. I should feel good, but I don't. I find myself in a room, the same room I've seen before. I'm cold. Is it a basement? No. I can see light coming through a window. I'm overcome by the familiar smell of blood and vomit and I'm about to will myself into a waking state. Then I hear his voice crying out.

"Mi amore. Finalmente. Me encontraste. Salvame."

It's the same man I've seen before, the one who looks a little like Carlos, but is not. Carlos is dead. I examined Carlos's Fixed Star death chart. He's gone. It was his truck and his severed head and hands that the cops found in Newport Coast. A bolt of clarity strikes my heart. This man is somehow related to Carlos. He must be one of his brothers from back home.

But who exactly is he, and why is he calling for me? Why does he say I finally found him and I can help? I can't do anything to save anyone, especially him. Someone just tried to kill me, I finally admit to myself, oddly detached.

The man is sitting on the filthy stone floor, barely dressed. His hair is long and matted, a beard covers half of his face. It's wild and more than a little gray. He is barefoot. I peer down in horror to see his toenails missing and his left hand is a bloody stump.

Oh no, poor soul.

He looks straight through me and smiles. "*Gracias a Dios.* I trusted you'd find me. *No confíes en el. No confíes en el,*" he repeats over and over. I don't understand what that means, but I'm convinced it is something important. Two short entities, male, I sense, appear. They laugh at the bearded man. I sense another presence right behind them, but I can't see who it is. I'm afraid they'll see me. They approach their prisoner and begin to pound him to a pulp. I've seen this show before, but last time, I was high. It's the cartel. This man pissed off the cartel. I can't stand his pain and I can't help.

When I return to the land of the living, it's still on the dark side, and for a moment I'm all mixed up. As I rub my eyes, I realize I'm in the front house, sleeping on Art's dark grey L-shaped leather sectional. My head is supported by a spongy neck pillow and someone has covered me with a familiar hand-knitted gray-and-red blanket, the blanket that smells of Sandi's aromatherapy concoctions. The thought that Art carried me inside and made sure I was comfortable brings tears to my eyes.

"Good morning, Sleeping Beauty." I get a buzz from Art's sexy drawl. "How's my mermaid this morning?"

I try to sit up too fast and the dizziness returns, so I lay back, this time slowly, putting my hand to my throbbing forehead. I've had plenty of these "the day after" mornings, but in the past, I could at least say I deserved them. That's right, the doctor said I'll still have a whopper of a headache. Then I recall how close I came to crossing over permanently and I'm suddenly gripped with fear.

"Damn," I whisper, then, shocked, I notice I haven't been sleeping alone. Not quite awake, I see my rescuer, his shower-damp hair brushed back, sitting on the other side of the coach, grinning at me. He's wearing yellow-and-white-striped pajama bottoms and his long feet are bare. Art's holding, based on the aroma, a cup of freshly brewed coffee. Does that man ever get cold?

"What's good about it? Speak for yourself. How did I get here?" I squeak out, hypnotized by his chest and arms, now almost glad I stayed on this plane.

"It was the magical dragon who brought you inside and tucked you in," he jokes, jumping up. "I need to grab a shirt before I get your meds and some food. Still nauseous?"

"You should've woken me. The last thing I remember, I was in your truck. You didn't have to carry me; I'm heavy. I could've walked."

"I told you, it was the dragon, or do you prefer the fairies, those garden fairies you're always talking about? Emery loves all that magical gobbledygook too," he chuckles, now crossing the line. No one makes fun of Magik.

Not even noticing the changed expression on my face, he rattles on. "I made coffee and toast. I expect you can keep both down. Sure, you still feel like crap. I mean, you don't look so hot. Sorry, I don't have eggs, but I'll go to the store later, if it's all right with you."

"I'm not hungry and you can go anytime you like, but first I need to use the potty. Can you stay close to make sure I don't pass out?" I hate asking, but I have no choice.

"Please?" Art corrects me, as if I were a child. When I don't respond, he adds, "Of course. What's the matter with me? I just haven't had the pleasure of a lady's company for a while. Don't be shy. I've been taking care of my baby girl since she was a toddler, so I can help you with the personal stuff without looking. I can even braid your hair." He grins.

"I'll be fine," I answer curtly, acting awkwardly, like a girl waking up at her boyfriend's place for the first time. What in the world has this guy done to me, and why is he suddenly so nice? I'm getting annoyed for no reason, except for that gut gurgle that tells me there's something he's keeping from me. I've been through enough crap and all, including several heart-crushing betrayals, not to question peoples' motives. Plus, if I listen to my Capricorn Moon sign, I can pick up what people really mean, not what they say. The trick is to put my feelings away and allow the hidden information to bubble up, despite risking getting hurt. And my Moon is screaming he's not who he says he is. If even fifty percent is true, he's perfect, and I'm not a complete fool. No one is.

I sit up, taking my time, and swing my legs off the couch and allow him to help me stand up on my wobbly legs. He tries to hold me close to his still-shirtless, freshly showered, lemon- soap-scented chest, but I move away, keeping myself upright by holding onto the back of the sectional. The leather's cool and smooth to the touch.

I could get used to this, I finally admit, terrified of the consequences of my hopeless romantic Venus in Aries clashing with my logical Moon in Capricorn, not to mention paranoid but life-saving Alpha Centauri.

"Listen, I'm grateful you went above and beyond to help me, but I need some space to process last night. After I get clean, we have to talk. I have to ask you some questions," I add, sounding harsher than I probably needed to.

"No problem, Viviana. You can have as much space as you need. First, let me walk you to my bathroom. You're welcome to my en-suite. I'm still fixing the guest bath. Don't lock the door in case you fall. I'll be outside." He nods, this time in his all-too-familiar impersonal voice.

Oh-oh. I hurt his feelings.

"Thanks again," I say, faking a smile as I slowly enter his bedroom, the same room where Danny took his last breath. Who am I kidding? Me, a druggie-slash-former dancer and a single dad, an ex-cop do-gooder who works for the DA. This is a recipe for disaster I won't survive. Plus, he'll never accept my Wicca side, let alone astrology.

I try not to stare at Art's bed or any of his personal items. Mercifully, I no longer endure Danny's energy. Art asks me again if I'm dizzy. I lie, telling him I'm fine, so he opens the bathroom door and helps me in, leaving me on my own. I take forever to empty my bladder. When I wipe myself, I see blood. I've restarted my period. It's been a while since I've had to deal with crap like hormones. This is bad news. It must be the shock of getting attacked or the concussion or, most likely, getting hot and bothered over Art. I'm ticked off. When I get off the toilet and see myself in the mirror, I almost faint from disgust. Art said I didn't look that hot, but what I see is truly hideous. I'm so embarrassed that he's seen me in this state. I want to howl.

"Hey, can you hear me?" I call out to him.

"I'm here. You need help?"

"No, but can I take a shower here? I think I'm too weak to go to my place, plus, my tub hasn't been cleaned since I left."

"Help yourself. I'll check on you soon. The fresh towels are in the cupboard and you're welcome to use Emery's robe; it's clean."

I don't respond, hoping he'll just let me be until I can put myself together. I pull back the oddly feminine curtain decorated with shells and crabs, suspecting that he got it for his kid because the guest room only has a shower. The tub and shower combo is sparkling clean. He is OCD for sure or has a lady friend, one of those single moms who likes what he likes.

At first, the water doesn't seem comforting as I soap and scrub my battered and bruised body until my skin turns blotchy red. In my Magik voice, I whisper healing incantations, directing the energy up and down my body. Some believe it's just self-hypnosis, but my experience tells me otherwise.

I recite the most common elemental spell, evoking the Earth, Water, Air, and Fire elementals and I ask for them to heal my mind and body. I'll have to wait until later to make my special ginger, lavender, and peppermint pouch. This herbal combination has worked for me many times. What I really could use, though, is some Balm of Gilead oil for my sore muscles.

Balm of Gilead oil remedy comes from my dad's mother, who was part Greek. She was good with herbs and especially those mentioned in the only book she ever read, the Bible. I find it so funny that Gram, who swore up and down the street that all psychic stuff was Satan's own handiwork, used herbs for just about everything that ailed her, as long as it was mentioned in Christ's own manual. I still remember her showing me the exact place in the book of Jeremiah. Chapter 22, verse 8, or was it the other way around? I can't rightly remember. (Knowing my terrible memory, probably the other way around.) I guess even the Queen of Sheba used Balm of Gilead oil. She recognized it as a most special substance, gifting it to King Solomon. And what did she get for her healing generosity: a broken promise and his bastard. Well, at least that's what my crazy gram said.

Finally, feeling more like myself, I use Art's shampoo and conditioner, inhaling his scent. My thoughts drift back to my vision/dream, to the man being tortured by what I suspect is the drug cartel. The poor man was desperately trying to warn me about something. I resolve to look up the few words I didn't understand, but right now, my mind is as foggy as a night on the coast. I guess I've been in the shower too long and don't hear Art's knocking because when I finally turn off the water and step out of the tub, I run smack into Art, who's sitting on the toilet, holding a towel and a robe.

"Fuck! You're going to give me a heart attack!" I scream, grabbing the towel.

"I didn't mean to scare you. I knocked and called your name, but you didn't answer. I was worried about the heat making you faint," he explains without an apology, using his usual, it's-nothing-personal voice, looking away as if I'm damaged goods.

"I'm fine. Please go away. I'm a mess and I started my period. Damn, sorry. TMI. I get it."

"You okay?"

"Yeah, I'm a big girl. I just expected to be done with it."

"Should we call the hospital?"

"Why? What are they going to do about cramps?"

"Do you need a pad or something? I have a box there. He points to the cabinet beneath the sink."

"Are you kidding me? You have Midol too?"

"Yep."

"You *are* a do-gooder."

"It's for my daughter. She's growing up," Art explains, still avoiding my eyes. "I'll see you in the kitchen. Take your anti-biotics and get ready to make a follow-up appointment with your own doctor." He adds in his you-will-do-what-I-say voice.

"Fine," I snap. "I'll be there when I'll be there." I don't understand why I'm being a bitch to him. Still avoiding eye contact, he walks out, leaving the door ajar.

I decide to blow-dry my hair to get my natural frizz under control, but my right arm is too sore from the IV, so I give up on trying to make myself appear if not attractive, at least presentable. I wrap myself in Emery's short, French terry robe, which barely covers my boobs and ass and go into the kitchen. Feeling somewhat guilty, I sit down at the little counter, vowing to say nothing else rude.

Art points to the pills. I see he's got a glass of water and a pretty porcelain plate with buttered toast and a mini bottle of jam, like the ones you get from room service at fru-fru hotels. My breakfast is arranged on a white linen matt with a match-ing cloth napkin, tied together by a spring of rosemary. Now I'm choking on guilt. Without a word, he pours me a fresh cup of coffee and again walks away.

Why is he being a dick? I'm the one who almost died. Did I ask him to take care of me? I try to excuse my bad behav-ior by shifting the blame to him, something I do well. What a baby! So I barked. Considering everything I've suffered, what's the big deal?

"Hey, aren't we going to talk?" I call after him.

"I'll be back in a few," he answers without turning around.

I swallow my pills and stuff myself with as much of the buttered toast and jam as I can. More than a few minutes go by before Art returns, all tucked in, his hair dry, everything back in place. Aside from the bags under his eyes, you wouldn't imagine he'd been up for two days straight. I'm all done with breakfast and antibiotics, but I decide to pass on the steroids until I really need them. I always gain at least eight pounds whenever I take them. I need no more doctors judging and poking me. What I need is Sandi. Once I've worked things out with Art and get a few answers, I'll take my own meds and go back to bed and sleep it off. Goddess, I hope I don't have scary dreams, not just yet.

My aching head has cleared as much as it will until I get more rest. I should probably go back to the back house without jumping down Art's throat, but, as usual, my fiery Mercury can't be stopped and I'm too beat up to try. Mercury in Aries, the God of War, isn't known for being exactly diplomatic. (On the positive side, my notes say, I express myself honestly and as Daddy puts it, with lots of verve. On the not-so-good side, I've been called argumentative and mean. I'm also prone to lay it on thick and to throw a fit or two. To make things even more complicated, I have a hard time keeping my thoughts to myself, but only when I feel unfairly accused or judged.) Yeah, I could've told you that in first grade. The difference is now that I learned a thing or two about my horoscope, I don't consider myself "evil incarnate," and if I'm not worthy of happiness, at least I'm deserving of peace.

"Where did you put my beach stuff?" I demand, assuming Art found my notebook and charts. I prepare myself for the worst-case scenario: water damage. But I'm prepared to do whatever's necessary to recoup my work, even though it'll take forever to copy everything into a new notebook.

"Nowhere. I found your chair and a tray, but nothing else."

"Are you kidding me? Why didn't you tell me that last night?" I ask, almost in pain.

"Perhaps you don't recall, but you weren't exactly yourself, and I didn't want to upset you."

"Well, I *am* upset. Hell, I'm more than upset. I'm furious. Are you sure you saw nothing other than the chair?" Men! Why do they always use the excuse about not wanting to upset us when all we really want is the truth.

"I'm positive. In fact, I found the chair and the tray floating in the water, right by the steps where you told me you were sitting, nowhere near the rocks. This is when I got it. You weren't crawling around the cave. Do you remember the tide coming in?"

"I don't," I sigh, placing my head on the counter in utter defeat.

Art tries to reason with me, only making me madder. "Listen, I'm sorry about your notebook, but I'm sure you can fix everything later when you recover."

"Oh please, don't even go there." I say, raising my voice. "You don't get it. No one but Sandi understands how hard it is for me to learn anything new or how studying the planets and the Fixed Stars has changed my life. It took her forever to talk me into learning anything new. I've never had enough confidence to even try." Feeling sorry for myself, I sob, "Everything is lost and I'll never get it back. Jay will keep Sandi away from me forever."

"You're right," Art says, looking perplexed and changing his tone. "I don't understand. Please explain," He comes closer and massages my shoulders.

"I'm too old and tired to explain anything to anyone," I say, shaking my head, stubborn as usual. Even his touch is no longer comforting.

"Get a hold of yourself, hon. Things are not that bad. You could've been seriously injured, or God forbid, worse."

"I wish I was," I mutter bitterly. "Who'd even notice if I was gone?"

"I would. Sandi would, and your family too. What about your boyfriend? Come on, you don't mean it. Could be I can't relate to what you've been dealing with, but I do understand one thing: You're smart enough to realize you're overreacting. I'll talk to Jay and make sure you can see Sandi again."

I know Art is trying once again to make me feel better, but his calm, logical voice is grating on my nerves. "What did Sandi say about me when she called you?" I wipe my eyes, ignoring his attempts to make nice.

"That's the thing I don't get. How did she guess something was off with you? Did you leave her a message? I gather you haven't been able to talk with her. Did you see something or someone suspicious?"

"No, I couldn't reach her. He's been keeping her away from me. You're just like the cops, asking the same thing over and over, hoping to trip me up. How many times do I have to tell you the same thing. We haven't spoken since the fight. You think I'm lying? Obviously, she looked at my horoscope and saw danger. Even when we're not together, she always keeps one eye on my transits." Beyond annoyed, I raise my voice again. "Didn't you hear anything I've been telling you? She looked at my horoscope."

"Listen, enough with the fucking horoscopes," Art says. "This is serious. You best tell me everything you have—now."

Oh brother. I'm getting to him. He's never used foul language before.

"I have nothing, except that Carlos won't be back. Poof, he's kaput as Katherine would say, and his family wants me to pay for it."

"I thought you didn't believe it was his body they found," Art says, probingly, raising one eyebrow and rubbing his forehead.

"I didn't until I saw his Fixed Stars chart," I insist. "That's what I was looking at that day on the beach. It happened so fast, I freaked out. I mean, all I did was to line up the Stars with his Ascendant, something we refer to as the Rising sign. It's the time when you're born," I add. Excited to share, I force myself to slow down and explain what I found and since Art doesn't interrupt me, I continue. "I didn't even have to go further to his Sun or Mars or the Moon. And what do you think I saw? Everything I didn't want to see: Capulus and Algol—bam. The two most horrifying Fixed Stars, sitting right on his Taurus Ascendant. Capulus brings death by execution, mostly by hanging or having one's head chopped off, right? And as if that wasn't enough, Algol, we astrologers call the Demon, means the most likely cause of death is also decapitation or electrocution. Electrocution can refer to being burned. Didn't you say, the body was found without the head and it was burned?"

I'm so darn proud of myself for remembering everything I learned. Despite the concussion, I can hardly stand it. "Aren't you impressed by how I put it all together? Like a real detective. So there you go: Carlos is truly dead."

Art looks at me like I was one of those little gray-skinned aliens, says nothing, and walks off in disgust.

Chapter 14

everal days go by without a word from Sandi or Nate. In fact, all I get from my "boyfriend"—at least that's what Art calls him—was a terse text telling me his kid got food poisoning at Thanksgiving dinner, meaning he was staying up north longer than planned. No "I miss you" or "how was your holiday?" Nada. What did I expect from a Sagittarius, guilt for leaving me alone? It's not in his DNA. Sagittarius can be all fun, open, and enthusiastic until you cross them and they turn on you. This is one sign that will not respond to anyone who has expectations. You best don't cramp their freewheeling style or else.

Knowing this info only too well, I wait to respond, just to see if Nate calls me. When he doesn't, I text him back, "whatever," and that was that. (I don't get why I didn't tell Nate about my near checkout or being back in Costa Mesa. I guess I didn't feel like explaining myself to yet another guy, plus, I have a notion that bringing up Art, who probably saved my life, wouldn't be one of my brightest ideas.) There's honesty and there's being stupid. (Daddy would scold me and tell me I'm hedging my bets in case I change my mind about permanently breaking it off with Nate and he'd be right. I guess I'm not one to stay single for long, no matter my goal of being independent of men.)

I haven't seen my rescuer either. After we quarreled, I picked up my shit and went to the back house, where I've done nothing but sleep, take my meds, and eat delivered junk food, barely able to use the bathroom. I get a call from the hospital checking up on me. Naturally, I fib, telling the nurse I am fine. I also promise to make an appointment to meet with my neurologist. I tell them everything they want to hear, so they will leave me alone. Like I have money for a specialist! I still haven't picked up my car from the mechanic's. Sooner or later, I'll have no choice but to ask Sandi to loan me a few hundred bucks so I can get it out of hock.

Finally, this morning, I feel more like myself and I decide to venture out. I fix my hair, carefully gloss my lips, squeeze my butt into a cute pair of dark-wash jeans, and put on my boots. Luckily, I find a clean sweater, one of Katherine's hand-me-down Neiman Marcus silver cashmere V-necks in the back of the armoire. The yarn's so fine, it seems more like silk. Hey, I've never been one to complain about free stuff. Because it's the holidays, I top the entire outfit with a vintage red leather biker jacket, the one I've had for ages. I ought to call Dave and get myself to an AA meeting. I could use a little support or, at the very least, listen to others' woes. I grab my scratched-up but still serviceable Coach shopper and open the door and running smack into Art.

"Hey, there," he says with a cheerful grin as if nothing happened. "Wow. You look so much better."

"Hey," I answer, suddenly wide awake, my heart doing its usual annoying flip-flopping bit whenever I get close enough to smell him.

"I have a surprise for you. You could say, it's kind of an early Christmas present," Art announces, clearly not bothered by my cool greeting. He looks amazing in a navy blazer, white shirt, and a gaudy, holiday-red tie held together by an American flag tie pin.

"I don't need any presents, and I hate surprises," I say, pursing my lips, still angry about him bailing on me the other day.

"Well, you'll love this one, I guarantee." He continues to smile. "Ta-da! Look who's here," Art sings out and moves out of my way. Because I keep my place nice and dark, the sudden bright light makes me squint.

"Merry Christmas. How's my fairy goddaughter?" I hear a familiar voice. It's Sandi! Art brought Sandi to visit me. I can't trust my eyes, but here she is.

"Sandi!" I cry out and jump on her like a stray dog who's gotten his first meal in days. "I missed you so much!" She hugs me back and we stand there for the longest time without letting each other go. Is it my imagination or has she gotten smaller?

"Did you buy new clothes?" I gasp, noticing her billowy flowery and dotted blouse, a size or two large for her torso and a pair of navy knit slacks. Even her wool sweater is unfamiliar. This is weird: She never wears slacks, only pull-on jeans.

"I bought a few items and guess what? I'm a size 16 for the first time since I don't remember when," she replies with pride.

"All right, ladies. I assume I've done my good deed for today," Art chimes in. "Got to run. There's a holiday work lunch I can't miss. You need anything, you call me. You understand?" Art puts his arms around Sandi, shocking the heck out of me and making me a little jealous. He gives her a kiss on the cheek, turns around, and walks off before I have time to react.

"Art? Wait a sec," I call after him. "Can you hang on for a moment?" I turn to Sandi. "I have to say something to him."

"Go on. I'll be inside. How about I make us some tea? No rush. I'm not going anywhere." Sandi winks.

"I love you."

"Love you more," she answers.

When I get to Art, I don't know what to say, so I move toward him, reaching out to touch his arm. "Thank you," I blurt out, the first thing that comes to my mind.

"You are very welcome," he responds warmly, taking my hand in his, which causes my stomach to lurch up and down.

"Look, I mean, I don't know how to say it, but..." For once I try to consider what to say before once again screwing things up by revealing what I really feel.

"Well, that would be a first," he chuckles, clearly making fun of me. But then he does something I couldn't have imagined just a few minutes ago: He opens his arms and draws me close to his chest, laying his chin over my head. He sighs. I almost pass out from the sheer pleasure of being held by a man who brings me a feeling of peace I've never experienced.

"So what were you trying to tell me?" he whispers.

"I forget." This time it's me who sighs.

"Mustn't have been important."

"Everything I have to say is important," I say, trying to get a grip on my emotions.

"Every word," he agrees, cracking me up.

"Is that so? What I wanted to say was thanks for everything."

"You already did. That's all?"

"Not exactly. Why did you walk out on our conversation? Remember when I told you about me looking at Carlos's horoscope?" I ask slowly, looking up at his face, terrified I inadvertently ruined a perfect moment.

"I'm sorry about that, Viviana, I truly am. I don't under-stand myself why I took off. I suspect I didn't comprehend it or refused to get what you were saying. It's outside of my com-fort zone. Too woo-woo California for me," he jokes, making a funny face. "Everyone knows I can be a kind of pigheaded about things I don't get."

When I'm taken aback by his apology and don't respond, he adds. "I was taking a few minutes to walk around the block. Ever since I was a kid, running off helps me to process, but when I returned, you were gone, so I figured you needed space. You probably called your boyfriend. Ned? Right? Don't worry, though, I've been keeping an eye on your place. You were safe, and when I couldn't, a friend of mine from the department was there. I bet you're spending Christmas with Ned."

"I don't need space from you." Oops, I realize I actually said that aloud. "Thank you for keeping me safe and for bring-ing Sandi down. I've been worried sick about her." I push my hair out of my face, trying to hide my embarrassment, not bothering to correct him over Nate's name.

"And that's why I can't help but like you. With all your own issues, you're still concerned about someone else's well-being."

"She's my best, my only friend," I say, trying to explain, feeling almost giddy that he likes me. Then going out on the limb, I blurt out, "Actually, I don't think I'm going to be seeing Nate. I mean not in that way."

"Oops, sorry. I said Ned, but it's Nate. Anyway, you can stop thanking me now. I get it now why you were upset. I had a nice, long chat with Miss Sandi. She really opened up my eyes on a lot of things I never even realized. What? No boyfriend?"

"She did? Yes. I mean, no, not at the moment. I mean, not him anyway. Nate hasn't been around lately. The thing is he's way too young for me. He has a little kid with special needs and a crazy baby mama he must deal with, not me and my shit. Sorry, issues."

"Wow! Well, I can't say I'm unhappy about it. Listen, I want to talk, answer your questions, and ask a few of my own, but I'm running behind. Tell you what," Art says, grinning, showing his beautiful white teeth made imperfect by a slight gap. "I have a great idea. Say, what's your middle name?"

"Iris. For my dad's mom. Why?"

"I want to ask you something."

"Ask away."

"Viviana Iris Glover, would you do me the honor of accompanying me on a date?"

"What?"

"A date. With me. This Saturday night. You see: two single people, hopefully having some fun, getting to appreciate each other. I don't know about you, but I'd like to see if we can become friends. I want to try. No dead cats or stink bombs or near drownings. No talking about ex-boyfriends, dead or otherwise. Maybe getting to first base? Kind of a regular date? Viv? Am I moving too fast? Are you turning me down?"

"Turning you down? Are you kidding me?"

"So yes?"

"Yes. What's your middle name?"

"Howard."

"Hell, no."

"You have something against my name?"

"My dad is Howard Sr. and my brother, Howie Jr. "

"And?"

"Well, I'm not exactly their favorite."

"That's their problem. So we're on?"

"Yes, Arthur Howard Russo. I'll be honored to spend my Saturday night with you." I finally answer gravely.

"That's my girl. I'll come calling at six sharp and don't bother to stand me up. I know where you live." Art kisses me soundly on both cheeks and takes off.

Wait. What just happened? Did my crazy life take another U-turn? I need to check my transits. Has the Moon aligned with Venus? Or is it Jupiter? Crap. Sandi. I forgot about Sandi. She's been waiting inside.

I go back inside in a hurry. Sandi's in the kitchen, making tea, our favorite, the loose-leaf kind. I see she did my dishes too. I hate guilt. I was right to be concerned. That weight loss doesn't flatter. Sandi takes one peek at me and chuckles.

"What?"

"Nothing."

"You won't ask about him?"

"Nope. Not if you don't want to share."

"Fine," I sulk at first, but then burst into an uncharacteristically wide smile, quickly grabbing the four-cup English porcelain tea pot out of her hands. I can't help but worry about her shaking. (It's funny, how she always picks the things I'd pick for us.)

"What's today's magic brew?" I inquire.

"Wild sweet orange with licorice," she explains. "Orange to boost your cranky mood and licorice for your sore throat. I'm sure you have a sore throat from swallowing all that saltwater. I didn't expect you were up to going out, so I brought along a few goodies." With those words, she opens her magic bag and pulls out an unwrapped package with my all-time favorite peach scones, a small log of goat cheese, and two Almond Joy candy bars. When I sneak a peek inside her purse, I'm not happy to find a half-empty bottle of regular Coke but decide to ignore it.

"That's wonderful. I'll drink at least two cups." I reassure Sandi, despite my lifelong distaste for anything licorice. Poor Judi Ann could never get me to even try her signature sausage and peppers because of the licorice Italian spice mix.

"Oh goodness, I forgot your Thanksgiving gift," Sandi says, looking disappointed and smacking herself on the forehead.

"You didn't need to get me another gift."

"Not need, want. Wait until you see it. Would you mind getting it? It's in my car in a green plastic bag. Sorry, I didn't have time to wrap it."

"Your car? I thought you came with Art. Sorry, I'm a little confused." What the heck has been going on since her last episode with Jay?

"I did?"

"Do you want me to check?"

"Hmm...are you sure?" She is getting that expression I don't like, the expression I've seen plenty of times on my grandparents' faces. "Ah, yes. He drove me down. I forgot. Guess you'll have to wait to see it," Sandi concedes, contemplating her teacup, as if the tea leaves held answers.

"Do you want me to tell you what happened to me at Katherine's?" I ask, trying to engage her by changing the subject, worrying about her mental state.

"Sure, honey, but can we have our scones and tea first? Do you figure it's warm enough for us to sit outside on the front porch? I'm sure, Art wouldn't mind. I love what he did with it. The rocking chairs and the herbal pots. You realize I wanted to do something exactly like that, something special... for Danny." She tears up. "Do you still have the French decoupage tray we found at the Circle, the one with the black-and-white checkers?"

I don't dig sitting outside. We're having one of our December heat waves, but I don't want to be contrarian, so I return to the kitchen and dig for the damn tray.

"Why don't I wait for you on the porch?" I hear Sandi say.

I disagree firmly. "Not a good idea. I'll walk you over."

"Don't be silly. I'll be perfectly fine. I'm not a cripple. I can walk all by myself to my own darn porch," she snaps. "You're not my mother."

I stand firm. "Not on my watch, you don't. It's windy and the yard is full of junk. You'll trip. Do you want to cut our visit short?" I bargain with her. "Don't be stubborn."

Okay. Something is wrong. She's never this testy with me.

"I found the tray. Let me take it over to the front house and I'll be back for you. Stay!" I raise my voice to be sure she hears me.

"Fine." she says, giving in, "but I'm eating some candy first."

Within a few minutes, we're sitting down on Art's repaired, freshly painted front porch, munching on our scones. (I left the candy bars in my kitchen on purpose, hoping our conversation would distract her from eating sugar, something she's not supposed to have.)

"Why didn't you return my calls?" I ask, being careful not to sound accusatory.

"I was too busy."

"Busy? I assumed you were down in the desert. What's there to do? You're not exactly the outdoor type and you've got no friends who live there. Wasn't Jay golfing?" (Personally, I've never been one for the insane 118 degrees of breath-taking heat, annoying old drivers, or the petty crime. For a good part of the year, there's nothing to do but sit indoors and eat yourself silly. And don't even get me started on the architectural tours of ugly, overpriced, '50s houses and the same hipsters who make my blood boil with their "craft" concoctions called midcentury modern. I'm not a fan.)

"Jay was golfing every day," Sandi mumbles, moving on to her third scone. He's been starving her. A scary prospect crosses my mind and my gut agrees. Her blood sugar is low, that's why she's loopy.

"Are you telling me that that jerk left you alone every-day?" I ask.

"I slept a lot. Jay got some extra meds. He told me my doctors want me to get more rest. If I rest, I can get stronger. He promised to take me to our timeshare in Maui."

"Did he now?" I say sarcastically, but she doesn't notice.

"Yes. He's so good to me."

I'll be damned. He's got my friend exactly where he wants her: drugged out and in his claws. I'm starting to get the picture and it's not a pretty one.

"Can you explain one thing? Why did you call Art for help?" I ask her, trying to reel her back into reality and hoping to switch the topic to astrology.

"Let me try to focus," Sandi says, again examining her teacup. "Ah yes, I remember. I was studying your charts."

"What did you look at?" I ask.

"I drew a horary chart to make sure you were alright and I identified a nasty hit. Plus, you understand your Mars causes troubles with your head. On top of it, your Lunar return had Neptune right on the cusp of your first house. Not good, considering Neptune is an indicator of drownings and many problems with addiction. Need I say more? At first I thought you'd taken a drink, but Mars is Mars, so I feared you'd hit your head again."

I take a deep breath of relief because she's sounding like my Sandi. "That figures. I did almost drown and I had a concussion. The thing is—and I don't want to scare you—but I'm fairly sure it wasn't an accident."

"Aha. Yes, I noticed it. Remember what we learned about the horary technique?" she asks, ignoring what I told her about my incident not being accidental.

"Not exactly."

"Go get your notebook and I'll explain again. It looks like we have plenty of time. Write this down because I want you to get proficient in the horary. This is the best technique for a beginner such as yourself. I want you to learn how to answer a specific question without even looking at the natal positions. Sometimes the natal charts are missing information, like the exact birth time or someone is lying altogether about their birth date. People lie. This way, you can make sure you're in control. Actually, it's pretty easy: Simply calculate a chart for the precise time and place when you ask something and you'll get a simple answer provided you're clear about the rules."

I raise one eyebrow. "Really? That sounds too easy to be true."

"Well, I wouldn't say easy, but definitely something you can learn. For example, when someone asks me about a missing person. I can tell that a missing person is dead if I find that the person's 8th house is in the 8th house of the horary, especially if it's malefic. If only afflicted, then there's a danger of death. Of course, there're many rules. But you can start with a few well-studied ones. By the way, who was the great astrologer using this technique? Come on. Can you remember his name? I'll give you a hint: It has something to do with a flower."

Now I'm the one to tear up "That's the thing. I lost everything at the beach. My notebook, the charts, everything ended up in the water. All our work is gone. I'm so sorry. I screwed up. I should've been more careful." Now I'm so upset, the tears are dripping down on my leather jacket like water from a leaky faucet. "And you would have been so proud of me," I sniff. "I totally figured out what happened to Carlos by lining up his chart with the Fixed Stars list. He was kidnapped, murdered, burned, and dismembered. When I realized what happened, I got freaked out, and after, I don't really remember much, that is until I woke up in the hospital with Art acting all gooey and emotional."

"Carlos is not dead."

"Yes, he is."

"Nope. I can't tell where he is, but he's positively not dead," she insists.

"I'll prove it to you. For once, I remembered the names of the Stars. I'm telling you; I documented every conjunction. It's as clear as day. He had a hit from both Capulus and Algol. Bam. Double whammy."

"And I'm telling you, you're wrong. You are mistaken."

"Not this time," I say not understanding what was going on.

"He's alive as you and me!" she screams, her head and left hand shaking, scaring the crap out of me.

"Okay, okay, you're right and I'm wrong. I must've made a mistake." I say, putting up my hands. "Such a dummy. Learning impaired. Can't get anything straight."

A hollow ache settles in my throat. I failed miserably to take care of Sandi and she's paying a high price for my self-ishness. I'm beyond panicking. Even if I'm not positive about what Jay did to her during the last few weeks, whatever abuse he's been perpetrating it's bad. My poor friend has lost it.

Chapter 15

andi's cell chimes Crosby, Still, Nash and Young's *Déjà Vu*. Crosby's unearthly voice haunts, "I feel like I've been here before..." I'm too young to appreciate what this meant to the previous generation, but Sandi told me this was the song she was listening to in 1970, the year I was born. Well, that figures. She's chosen to obsess over a song about reincarnation. Of course, Crosby could've had a bad out-of-body trip and not a past-life memory considering the times, not to underestimate his attraction for mind-blowing substances. My time came in the late '80s, when metal ruled and my eardrums buzzed like a swarm of killer bees. I never did like pasty grunge or sugar pop boy bands.

"It's your cell, honey," I gently tell Sandi. Can I grab it for you? It's in your purse." She's still shaking, so I reach inside and answer it. It's Art.

"Hey, it's me," I tell him, trying to stay chill. "Can I call you right back on my cell in a few? Sandi got a little upset and her shaking returned. So I want to calm her down. Is that all right?"

"You can call me anytime, babe. She'll be fine. These shakes come and go," he answers, clearly in a jolly mood, dismissing my concerns. I can tell he's buzzed and I'm instantly pissed for no logical reason, except for being insanely bitter that he can drink and I can't.

"Talk to you soon," I tell him, proud of myself for not jumping down his throat, considering he's probably right.

"Why don't we finish up inside? The Santa Anas are picking up again," I propose to Sandi. The shaking has stopped and she's resumed sipping her tea, seemingly oblivious to our disagreement about Carlos's state of being or the gusting winds.

"Yes, I best take my afternoon pill and lie down for a bit. Do you mind?" Sandi looks past me, putting the teacup down on the little whitewashed side table Art found among the garage junk. "I always liked this table, but the iron got too rusty. That man is sure good with his hands," she snorts out loud and pokes me in the arm with her index finger.

"Ouch, that hurts," I say, rubbing my arm and ignoring her double meaning. "Of course I don't mind if you lie down. Let me help you get settled on the sofa. Sorry, but my bed sheets need washing." I'm happy to do this because then I can make a call to Art in private.

"And afterward, you'll drive me home and stay a few days, right?" Sandi asks. "I probably could manage on my own, but since you already left Laguna, I don't mind asking you to help. Maybe we can bake a pie or cook up a pot of vegan lentils? I should teach you the horary technique. I'll let you use my laptop. I downloaded a new program. Didn't you say, you weren't careful with your astrology notebook?" That, she remembers.

"Stay with you? I'd love to, but what about Jay? Did you forget we're on the outs?" Now, I'm the one who's confused. "There's no way he's going to let me stay without a major brawl, that is, and I'll be damned if I let him verbally abuse you because of me."

"Silly girl. You don't need to worry. He's not there. Jay and a few of his buddies went in together and bought a fishing boat. He left for Mexico this morning and should be fishing for an entire week. It was his early Christmas present from *moi*."

"You bought him a boat? A tie and a sweater wouldn't have done it?" I say, shaking my head in both wonderment and disgust. "All right, since he's not there, I'll come. Let me check if I can find a few clean pairs of jeans." Then I remember about my car. "Crap," say, slapping my forehead with my palm. "Sorry, I can't do it. My Benz is still at the mechanics. It's ready to be picked up, but I haven't been able to get to it."

"Oh, that?" Sandi says, undisturbed. "I asked Art to call the shop with my credit card this morning. It's ready to be picked up. Oscar and his father have been fixing my cars for years. I had a sense you might run short this month," Sandi informs me, sounding completely lucid.

I don't know whether to be mad that she went behind my back or grateful for yet another gift. I settle on giving her a tight hug and a sincere thank you.

I take two trips to get everything inside from the front porch, escort Sandi and get her comfy on my sofa. I can't wait to find out what she's been taking, but her pills are neatly arranged in a small plastic pill box, and I don't want to get her upset by asking.

Sure enough, by the time I clean up, she's fast asleep. I'd like to get me some of what she's having. I make a clicking noise with my tongue, finally exhaling in relief. She seems to be okay, at least for now. It's time I call Art and pick his brain about Sandi.

I text ahead, "Is this a good time?" and within a few seconds he calls me.

"Hello, pretty lady."

"Hello again. How are you doing?"

"Me? Never better. Why?"

"You sound lit."

"Lit?" Art laughs. "You sure have a way with words. Not at all. I'm pretty sober, less than .08. I always check before getting into the car. We had a few beers and lots of gluten-free pizza, that's about it." He chuckles again. "Oh, yeah, and loads of Christmas cookies. Sugar high."

"I understand. Well, clearly there's no need to worry. Why did you call Sandi earlier?"

"No particular reason. Could be I wanted to check on how everything was going and to see if you've picked up your car. If not, I was going to offer you gals my ridiculously cheap Uber services. PS, I can pick you up at Sandi's Saturday night for our date. Would you like to hang out in Riverside? Sandi told me about this pretty nice Italian restaurant and lounge near a place called the Mission Inn?"

I don't get it. Is this guy for real?

"No need to drive us and I don't do lounges or booze. Thanks, anyhow. I haven't got my car, but if you don't mind, I'll take a lift to the shop. It's pretty close, off 16th, a block off the Great Divide, on the Costa Mexico side. Sandi took some kind of new medication and has passed out on my sofa. I figure by the time I return, she'll be up and we'll get going. The traffic inland is murder."

"Sure, no problem. I can get you in about thirty. Costa Mexico? What's that?"

That's right, he's not from around here.

"I'll explain on Saturday," I promise coyly. "Got to have something neutral to talk about."

"I'll be looking forward to you educating me."

"Listen, there's something on my mind," I say tentatively. "It's about Sandi. You've been talking to her more than I. Have you noticed some changes? I'm not sure, but she doesn't seem like herself. I mean, sometimes she's perfectly clearheaded and normal, but then she'll say something that doesn't add up."

"In what way?" Art asks, suddenly serious.

"For one, she got pretty testy with me and that never happens, even after her stroke. Also, there's the astrology stuff. You wouldn't understand, but trust me, she's definitely not being rational. On top of that, there's the weight loss. I'm worried that Jay's been starving her. Did she tell you she's down to the size she hasn't been in years?"

"Hmm, well, that could be it. My parents are older and when my mom's dehydrated or forgets to eat, her blood sugar drops and it makes her loopy."

"Yeah, that's probably it, you're right. I'm overreacting, again. You must understand that she means the world to me and I couldn't handle losing her."

"No, no. I get it. I'm glad you feel comfortable enough with me to ask for my input because I care about her too. I'll tell you what: I'll keep an eye on her. You could be right. I wouldn't be shocked if something isn't kosher with Jay. I agree that his behavior doesn't fill me with confidence. Okay?"

"Thank you for that, for not dismissing my worries. I'll hang out on your porch until you get here?"

"You bet. I trust your intuition."

"Thanks. I guess, I'll see you soon."

"Count on it."

After we hang up, I go inside to grab my bag for the second time today. Sandi's still asleep, her breathing is nice and even. I cover her with a shawl and go out front.

My phone reads a missed call. I guess I turned my ringer off. It's Oscar, my mechanic, offering to drop off my car at the house. No charge. Weird. Everyone seems to be way too accommodating. I call him and say I've got a ride. He asks about Sandi, something about her being mad at him. I reassure him that that's not the case and tell him I'll catch up with him within the hour.

 Right on time, Art pulls into the driveway, leaves the car running so he can play the old-fashioned gent opening the passenger-side door for me. The truck has major ground clearance, but I've been climbing into monster trucks since I was seven without being helped. I take his hand, anyway, keeping my big mouth shut and thanking him for the ride. He's in a good mood. I crinkle my nose, somewhat annoyed, not looking forward to a two-hour freeway nightmare, but within ten minutes we're past Newport Boulevard. He offers to go in with me to check my car and drive it back to the house if I don't mind driving his truck.

Okay, now he's gone too far.

I tell him no and leave it at that. I can manage my own damn car. He tries to kiss me, but I jump out, blowing him an air kiss, back to my old flirty ways. I decide to maintain a bit of mystery before going on our big date.

Since the mechanic's bill has been taken care of, I get into my freshly washed junker and drive home, enjoying the new tires making the ride ever so smooth, despite the rattling sound of the diesel engine. The annoying mix of gas and air, compressed by the pistons, seems louder than usual, but I ignore it. As Daddy describes it, it's "a magical blend of ignition and pressure, like good sex." I probably appreciate more about cars than some. The day is getting away from me because by the time I walk into my cottage Sandi is up and ready to go. It's almost 4 p.m., what I call the freeway "witching hour."

It takes a few minutes to get onto the 55 North. It's only forty miles to Riverside, but it'll take some time and plenty of stamina because the Costa Mesa Freeway, the only way to connect the beach cities with the Inland Empire, is a parking lot. Great planning, folks. Pack them in without rhyme or reason.

I'm inching past Orange, then Anaheim, Disneyland, and Angel's Stadium all the way on the way. I haven't been to a game in years, since Carlos is a Dodgers fan, I mean, was a Dodger's fan. One more thing we didn't have in common. That's the thing about sitting on the freeway with no one talking. You have plenty of time to reflect.

We pass tidy, green Yorba Linda. I notice the sign pointing toward the Richard Nixon Presidential Library, one of my dad's favorite go-to local spots. Though I'm not a fan, I still like the rose gardens and the simple citrus-ranch farmhouse where Nixon was born. Sandi had me study Nixon's Natal chart carefully, since we can clearly observe how the Fixed Stars caused his downfall. Sandi, a huge fan of the English royal family, told me that although the family was dirt poor, they were related to one of the medieval kings. I don't remember which one, but she went on and on about the possibility that it was he who was reincarnated as Richard Nixon. Edward, his name was Edward! Excellent. My memory is improving. I wouldn't mind showing it to Art, the cottage, not the chart, *he-he*. I suspect he'd appreciate it more than Carlos ever did. Then I stop myself. I'm at that scary place when I start making plans. That's a red flag.

My sleepy friend closes her eyes as we make a painful transition to the 91 East. The 91 will take us through overcrowded, overbuilt Corona all the way to Riverside. As I drive East, my mood is going south. Over a billion dollars spent for nothing. All these so-called freeway improvement projects have only made the commute worse. Someone made a bundle of money, though.

Sandi's still groggy from the meds, and her reaction is worrying me. She's probably dehydrated too, like Art said. I told her to drink before we left, but she refused because she's afraid her bladder will be too full to handle the drive. One more lovely thing about getting old. We're not talking, and that is another red flag. "Be careful what you wish for," I whisper, quietly enough not to wake her. I recognize I'm being an ungrateful bitch and I missed her, but I'm not in the mood for caregiving or fighting about Carlos being a goner.

Sandi wakes up and asks, "Are we there yet?" She sounds like an impatient kid. "I've got to tinkle."

"Not yet, but getting closer," I reply as calmly as I can, gritting my teeth. "I'll get off once we pass the interchange. It's too crazy here. People are crossing four lanes at a shot. Can you hold it?"

"I guess. I wish I'd listened to Jay and wore my Pull-ups," she whines.

Here, I agree with him. Damn.

"Try to hold it."

"I'm trying."

I study her face and change my mind. She's clearly distressed and about to have an accident. "I'm getting off at University. We can stop at the Mission Inn for a potty break and we better get some dinner. You love the patio. Remember the nice birthday tea party the girls from the Dragon store gave you last summer? And after the girls went back to work, we walked over to that cute Casey's cupcakes. Remember, I threw a fit about a cupcake costing five bucks and not even tasting fresh?" I try to distract her. (Why a very Catholic Riverside is also home to several metaphysical bookstores patronized by herbalists, a various species of psychic readers, including from the Wicca community I don't get. Probably because the rents are cheaper.)

"I remember," she says. "We should go there." She nods and smiles. My plot to distract her is working. As I turn around and signal to the right, I notice a surprising break in the traffic and aggressively speed up. The odometer reads a whooping forty-five mph: well, it's better than five miles a century. Diesels are not exactly known for their pickup, but I can still make this old girl move.

"We'll be there in a bit," I reassure my passenger. I make a quick lane change without signaling, being careful to crank my traffic-stiff neck both ways to check for the traffic flow.

"Doing good."

Without a warning, the engine makes a booming sound and the front of my Benz starts to smoke. "You've got to be kidding me. What did the fuckers do to my car?" I yell at Sandi, a jolt of adrenalin triggering a painful thump in my chest. "Hang on, I'm pulling over."

I change lanes and slam on the breaks, hoping no one rear-ends me, pumping the brakes once, twice, one more time. I take my foot off, count to five, and try again. Nothing. I've lost control. I put the emergency brake on and shift into neutral. Thanks, bro. Me, the panic attack queen, moves over in an instant, letting the badass bumper car driver take charge.

The strong winds are blowing the billowing smoke from the engine backward. I can't see the flames, not yet, but I'm sure they're coming.

Now grateful for the construction and Sandi's sedatives, I make my move. "I'm going to use the barrier to slow down." Sandi, in shock, says nothing, probably close to stroking out. One more victim of my rotten luck.

I maneuver furiously, barely dodging a landscaping pickup and a Harley Fat Boy, sweat pouring down my face, obscuring my sight. The barrier on my right is coming close. It's happening too fast. I careen down the off-ramp. Luckily, other cars move out of my way. On instinct, I extend my arm in front of Sandi as we crash. The car bounces off the short concrete wall several times before coming to a stop. The seatbelts have kept us fairly in place. Mercifully, my diesel's built like a tank. The car finally stops, but my body doesn't. I hit the steering wheel hard and black out.

Chapter 16

For the third time in only one crazy week, I open my eyes, not in my bed. "Sandi..." my first thought is of her. What if she's hurt? I'm too afraid to face that reality, then I hear her laughing. What the hell?

"That was fun! Exactly like the demolition derby at last year's fair."

"What? Are you okay?"

"Never better. Finally awake. Now I appreciate why you insist on keeping this junker: What a rush!"

"Can you get you get your seat belt off?"

"Let me try. Yep."

"Okay, I'll get out first and then I'll help you." The pain in my sternum and ribs hasn't hit yet because I'm probably in shock. I've got to get us out safely before the car bursts into flame or we get hit by another vehicle. I tug on my seat belt several times before it comes loose and try the door. It's stuck, of course.

Why me, God, I mean Goddess?

"Sorry, I'm stuck." I turn toward Sandi. But she's already out, standing on the side of the concrete barrier, holding on to her purse for dear life.

"Hurry up and get out," she shouts loud enough that I can hear her, even with the freeway noise.

I climb over the middle column, hitting my hip on the shift and exit on the passenger side. Sandi helps me by holding the banged-up door open the best she can, pulling me in for a painful hug.

"Thanks for saving my life."

"Don't thank me yet," I caution her and glance over to the still-smoking front of my seriously messed up car, hoping it won't burst into flames and praying that it's not totaled. Although, the body damage to the right front is substantial, if it wasn't a 300CD, we'd be in a lot worse shape. As Daddy, considering my history with accidents, taught me: safety first,. My Dino-diesel may not be sexy or quick, but I'll take the odds of walking on my own two feet from a head-on collision any day. Hell, I'm even grateful for traffic. If I hit the concrete at full speed... well, I won't let myself to go there. Because no other vehicle is involved, I'm not about to call the cops. Guess it's going to be Triple A, if I remembered the card.

"Don't move; it's not safe," I order Sandi, impressed by her calm demeanor. "Those are some special meds you're on," I say under my breath.

"We're going to be all right now," she says. "I'm sorry about the car, and here you just picked it up and got it washed. I'm afraid the wash dissolved the protection bonds I placed over it. You should've kept it dirty." If Sandi is attempting to lighten my mood, she's failing.

"What else is new? If I didn't have bad luck, I'd have no luck at all. You better cancel your payment right away. You paid for the repairs with a card, right?"

"Oh, I'm not sure about canceling the charges. It wouldn't be fair. It could be a coincidence. It's an old car and probably needed more intensive work. Let's not jump to conclusions before we figure out exactly what happened. That family's been working on my cars for years. They're good guys and I trust them."

"I don't. perhaps if it was only the engine. Say, do you have your automobile club card on you?"

Not wanting to get into another argument, but suspicious about the repair shop, I vow to examine the dead brakes if it's the last thing I do, which it may be. No way I'm having the car dragged back to Costa Mesa. The nausea hits like a tsunami and I vomit up the entire contents of my stomach, barely missing my boots. Sandi reaches into her magic bag and takes out a tissue and a pack of gum, handing both to me without a word.

"Guess I'm still not completely over the concussion," I explain, adding, "I hit my gut crawling over the middle column."

Sandi looks at her feet, a sign that something's off, then shocks me with, "I always have my card, but there's no need. Art will be here in a minute. He's right behind us. He'll take care of everything. Don't worry."

"That's good—wait! What do you mean Art's coming? When did you have time to call him?" Now she's delusional.

"I haven't gone round the bend, darling," Sandi says in a fake English accent, as if she's read my mind. "He'll be here in a few," she insists.

Frustrated and pissed off, I hold my head, now throbbing as if I'd spent an entire evening at a U2 concert. Not that they could ever come close to Deep Purple's eardrum-busting rock, but that was before my time. (Just one of the bits of useless trivia I keep buried somewhere deep in my damaged brain.)

I hear David Crosby again. Sandi picks up her phone. "Hello, young man." she greets whom I assume is Art. Why does she sound almost cheerful, ludicrously so? A burst of what I've come to recognize as psychic messages hits my jumbled circuits: Did Sandi's mechanic friends have something to do with the accident? Did Art? I can't wrap my head around it, despite having been betrayed by everyone I've loved in the past. My paranoia is hitting a record high. It can't be, can it? Have I been so blinded by my gratitude that I've missed something? And what about the house? I still have seen no papers. Is this a cruel joke or a setup? What if it isn't Carlos's family who's after me, after all?

Sandi continues her conversation. "Yes, one exit before University. Off the ramp by the concrete barrier. We're fine. Vivi threw up. See you in a sec."

"Okay, that's enough. What's been going on behind my back?" I scream. "Spill, and I mean it, Ms. Sandra." I'm both livid and scared.

"You're getting worked up over nothing, baby girl. I'll explain everything when we get to my place. You'll be a little surprised, but I promise: it's simple."

"Don't you dare dismiss me. So help me if you don't come clean, and I mean this minute, we're done. Give me your phone. I'll call an Uber and a tow truck myself." I shriek, even though I feel faint.

"You don't look so hot, hon. Are you going to pass out again?" Sandi continues to stonewall. "Here, lean on me."

"No. I'm too pissed off with the both of you and the fuckers who messed up my car. What were you thinking? We could've been killed." The fainting spell passes.

"You're overreacting as usual. Obviously, your Moon is afflicted by Mars and..."

I interrupt Sandi, having had enough "Stop hiding behind the stars. No more excuses. You're always telling me what's right and wrong and what I should or shouldn't do. Who's a pathological liar now?"

"I'm not lying. I'm only trying to keep you from hurting yourself. You still don't realize how often you've sabotaged your progress."

"Bull! I'm not in self-sabotage mode. You've been lying to me for months. I can't stomach the deceit, even if it is coming from you." Something deep inside me breaks. I'm a hundred percent positive I've been played by Sandi and Art. Time stops and I'm back in my dream. It's the dark room and I'm facing the poor, bloodied man being held hostage. My higher self or the Angels sent him because I've been blind. He's been trying to warn me. *"No confíes"* means don't trust anyone.

"I don't want to argue with you anymore right now. We'll talk about this later, after we deal with the car," I say. Now that I finally see clearly, an icy calm drifts over my heart. I straighten up and pretend she got through to me. "Clearly, I'm too upset to hear you out and my head is exploding."

"Poor baby. You'll be fine as soon as Jupiter offers his Divine protection. Jupiter will help everything."

"When's that going to happen? When I'm too old to care?" I ask with sarcasm. (Sometimes, I have a hard time wrapping my head around how some planet on the other side of the solar system can make such a difference in my life or why the good stuff always takes its damn time, but the bad hits right away. I guess that's why I'm the village idiot.)

"You'll have to be patient until January; it's only a few months away. Until that time, we've got Art," Sandi says, seemingly oblivious to my bitter tone.

"Well, where is he then, your Savior, the cop?" I demand, determined to get to the bottom of what's been happening to me.

I'm here to help you in. Already called the tow truck.

Of course, he did.

"Ladies, is everyone all right? Ms. Sandra? I best take you both to the hospital. Viv? You're still recovering from your concussion. I'm convinced it would be a prudent thing to do."

Art sounds cool and unflappable with his oh-so-special, irritating-the-crap-out-of-me tone; that special zing that everyone uses to let me know I'm a loser who can't manage her own shit.

"No need for another pointless, overpriced visit to the hospital. I'm fine. It looks worse than it is. Look, my car stopped smoking." I motion to the front. "I didn't even hit my head. I'll just have a few sore ribs probably, but nothing serious, that is, except for a little body damage to my Benz's right side," I say, keeping my tone nice and even. I'll show you.

"Really? Are you sure?" Art asks, sounding doubtful. "You seem calmer than normal. If it were me, I'd be a lot more upset, considering the car was just worked on."

"Well, I'm not jumping for joy or about to write them a five-star review, but we're both in one piece. Your friend Ms. Sandi here was still high on her pills. She thought it was fun, kind of like our own demolition derby. Ask her. She needed to pee. Speeding up, did something to the engine. I wanted to get off before she wet her pants." I'm not letting myself fall into the guilt pit. Yea, I'm being mean, but I can't stop myself.

"I wasn't high," Sandi insists. "You might say I was relaxed. My doctors added another med to keep my blood pressure from spiking." Sandi scowls. "And I haven't wet my undies. Don't mind Vivi, Art. Her Scorpio side is being paranoid as usual. She's mad that I asked you to follow us because I was sure she'd refuse your kind offer of driving us to my house. She turns to me. "See? I told you I could explain, but you're a typical Aries: so stubborn. Your transits are terrible, I told you. Excuse me for doing my best to protect you, if only from yourself. You should be damned grateful, not mad that Art cares about you so much that he's agreed to be your personal security. Do you think he's got nothing better to do? He's a busy man."

My temper flares. "Undies? What are you, a five-year-old? And I don't need a fucking bodyguard!"

"I think you do!" Sandi yells back.

"Ah, that's why she's giving me the cold shoulder?" Art asks Sandi. "Is that right, Viviana?" Art smiles and reaches for my hand, but I refuse the comforting gesture. "It's all right, Sandi," he says. "Let's wait until the tow truck arrives, then we'll get you home and deal with Viviana's car. What did you call it, Scorpio paranoia?" He addresses me this time. "Check that out: I'm learning. Aren't you proud of me?"

The tow truck arrives driven by a nice-looking Caucasian kid who promptly ticks me off when he asks Art and not me where to take MY damn car. When Sandi suggests the same place in Costa Mesa, Art gives her what I consider a peculiar look.

"Not this time," he tells the tow truck driver. "We'll have it towed to my buddy Robert's shop in Norco. I'm going to call him right now to expect it. Is that alright with you, Viviana?"

"Yes," I agree," I say. "Anywhere's better than Sandi's guys."

"Cool, sounds like a plan."

When the tow truck leaves, Art escorts us to his vehicle and off we go to Riverside and our "come to Jesus" chat.

Chapter 17

The Riverside property where Sandi has lived for the last decade or so with Jay isn't what your snooty coastal OC resident would expect. It's more rural than suburban, that's for sure. A rambling, gated, five-bedroom monstrosity with a smog-obscured hill view and at least a dozen no-longer-producing-fruit avocado trees. Yes, kids, avocado is a fruit.

The house comes with its own pond, although nowadays the pond is both sludge green and devoid of life. According to Jay, when his first wife was alive, she filled the pond with water lilies and koi. Naturally, he never forgets to remind Sandi that she's responsible for "killing" both the cranky flowers and the dumb fish.

There's also a substantial, mostly wasted area right in the front that's large enough to fit two zero-lot line houses you see in any of the new, disgracefully expensive subdevelopments just a few miles away. Since I've stayed at the house before, I noticed that some neighbors with similar properties use the space to build horse paddocks. Weird, right?

After those miserable years spent away from the beach in Texas, I'll never move inland. But hey, for some unexplainable reason, it works for Sandi. She's always going on and on about Riverside history, the orange groves, the horse ranches, and Spanish/Mexican California. For whatever reason, most likely because, here, everyone is from somewhere else, most people don't care about what took place before the gringos took over.

The gray gravel driveway is at least 150 feet long. I like the crunching sound my shoes make when I first get out of the car. To the left of the house, Jay put in artificial turf (paid for by the taxpayers), so he can park his Polaris Sportsman 450 H.Q. ATV next to a dusty, never-washed Toyota Land Cruiser, the car he actually owned before Sandi. Let's not forget the 25-foot Coachmen Galleria she bought him when they first got together. That man has more toys than he knows what to do with, and that's without the new fishing boat. Personally, I can do without the ATVs, but I'd love to take the RV to Sedona or Oregon, along with Sandi, of course. The Coachmen is small and handles easily, even for me.

Dream on, Viviana. Jay will never agree.

To the left of the main door, Jay had installed a dog run: One of his brilliant ideas was to use the property for a private dog boarding business. Just another one of his business "pipe dreams" gone up in smoke. That must have cost Sandi plenty.

Normally, I'd be jumping for joy to spend quality time with my friend without her jerk of a husband hovering, butting in and listening to my every word, but something tells me I'll regret my off-the-cuff decision. I should've just stayed at my little cottage and prepared for my date. Oh, crap, are we still going out Saturday night? What if Art forgot about it? I hope he did. I don't think I'm ready for normal.

Art dropped us off at the house hours ago, but not before stopping at the market, where he picked up a roasted chicken and a few mayo-laden salads for Sandi and me. He said he needed to get going, and I didn't ask him to stay. After eating in the front room (the only room free of boxes and bags of stuff Sandi needs to dump) and napping through an old episode of *Monk*, I help Sandi with bathing, brush her hair, and put her to bed. So far, the only bright spot of the entire debacle of being here is the scent of citrus, rosemary, and blue sage overwhelming my senses once I get settled in the second-floor guest room. The room is still filled with Jay's former wife's crafts boxes, something I find both creepy and sad. I wonder if something of my vibe will be left over after I'm out of here. Most likely not.

I don't take any chances getting any sleep by making sure I take my meds right on time. With the stress of everything I've been through since Thanksgiving weekend finally catching up with my raw nerves, I promptly drift into dreamless nothingness.

When I open my eyes, based on the bright light streaming through the grimy, cracked plantation shutters, it's mid-morning. My head throbs, I'm nauseous, and I don't exactly feel like playing caregiver. I could use a stiff double bloody Mary just about now. Then I try to take a deep breath and almost pass out from the stabbing pain in my ribs. Hoping I didn't crack them when I hit the steering wheel, I crawl out of bed and decide to take a long shower, seriously annoyed to have to cope with yet more injuries. As soon as I get myself together, I'm going to ask Sandi a few questions to clear the air once and for all.

It's another Southern California pre-holiday weekend: both hot and windy. Before I have time to check on Sandi, whom I'm sure is still in bed, I turn on my phone and see a slew of what I consider threatening text messages from a number I don't recognize. The last one is what my daddy would call openly hostile. "Pack up Ur shit and leave Cali before they find Ur body with no head."

If I had any sense, I'd be terrified, but my gut is telling me it's nothing but an attempt to bully me. Let's put it this way: If they were serious, I'd already be enjoying a few cocktails in the next dimension. When I reread the messages, I can tell whoever it is can't be an American, I mean, a native English speaker.

Aha. It's someone from Carlos's side.

I save the texts and decide to show them to someone, definitely not Art, whom I no longer trust. What I really want to do today is to hang out at the metaphysical book and supply shop, browsing as long as Sandi lets me. I need to learn more about herbs and tinctures, and if I'm lucky, get a psychic reading. I can't go on like this, not knowing if I can trust Art or my best friend. I need to call ahead, though. Fridays can be busy, being the second-best day to get a reading, Tuesday is the first. Tuesday is ruled by Mars and Friday, by Venus. Those are two good days to get married as well: not the weekends. Saturday is ruled by the old grouch, Saturn, while Sunday is a day more suited for spiritual work. No matter what Sandi says, I'm going to get an independent reading since I've admitted to myself that I need help in deciphering the appearance of the black-bearded man in my dreams. So far, he's been right on the money about not trusting anyone.

With the crappy, water-saving showerhead, I take what barely counts as a hot shower. It doesn't help at all. After making the bed, I go down to the kitchen to put some food into my rumbling gut, make some tea, and try to get Sandi up without too much hassle. When I get there, I'm surprised to see Sandi, still dressed in a nightgown, standing at the sink.

Whatever she's staring at outside has got her so focused that she doesn't hear me coming in.

"Good morning, Milady," I say, greeting her gently, not wanting to startle her. When there's no response, I try again.

"Hey there." I repeat, this time in my normal voice.

Sandi jumps as if she were napping standing up. "Crap, you scared me!"

"I said good morning, but you didn't hear me."

"Sorry, I was watching the dragon flies eat the bees that hang out on the pond. Did you know their eyes come with almost 30,000 lenses, so they can see all around?"

"Thirty thousand? I didn't, but now I do," I chuckle, thinking only Sandi would fill her head with such useless nonsense.

"I'm a hundred percent sure it's a Cosmic Message from Danny," she whispers, placing her index finger over her lips.

"Ah, Danny. I guess the dragonfly is a messenger of change and transformation. Bees mean visitors. Maybe not Danny, but someone new? Say, you want some chai tea and eggs or some granola and coconut yogurt? I saw a Zip-loc with granola in the pantry."

"No, I'm not hungry," she says, frowning. "Killing bees brings bad luck. Danny had bad luck."

"You must eat to take your meds," I insist, ignoring her comment about Danny's bad luck. Shit, no one has worse luck than me. "Well, I'm fixing something for myself. I'm starving," I say, "and then we're going to have a chat about 'our' renter, a chat you may not like. I mean it Sandi, after what I've been through, I'm not in the mood for playing mind games."

"Fine, I'll have granola, but no coconut yogurt. I want milk."

"Fine, I'll get you milk, even though you're not supposed to have dairy."

What in the world has happened in the last few weeks to make her act like she's going through the terrible twos? I think, but keep my big mouth shut and pour her a small glass of milk. (Jay drinks real milk by the gallon. That's why he's always on the can with the runs.)

By early afternoon, I've had enough of the "new" Sandi and I tell her just that. She bursts into tears and limps upstairs to bed before I get a chance to ask her about Art. Clearly, she's not going with me anywhere, at least not today. I have no choice but to order an Uber hoping the cost will be minimal, since the metaphysical bookstore I'm still determined to visit is nearby. Once the car arrives, I feel relieved. Not only do I need to understand my haunting dreams, but I need to see a fresh face.

When I arrive at the store, it's crowded, more so than usual, probably because of the upcoming holidays, especially Yule, the Winter Solstice, one of the Wiccan eight holy Sabbats. I can happily count at least ten women of all ages and races in the store. I consider this place my home away from home. The storefront, painted deep sage green and complimented by a cheerful marigold-yellow awning, isn't at all scary or weird. It's on the first floor of a vintage-looking brick building. The red bricks remind me of a small town in Texas, not Southern California. Everyone knows that earthquakes and bricks don't mix. A faux-rock wishing well, decorated with silk ivy and flowers, has a sign that invites visitors to toss in a coin and make a wish. I never do. It sounds hokey: "Stick to your goals and see it through, then your fondest wish is bound to come true." Right! I used to believe I was a Disney princess... once upon a time. Good thing I called ahead.

Before I begin browsing, I ask for Jackie, a clairaudient extra sense, a psychometrist, and my favorite tarot reader.

Jackie used to work in Costa Mesa, but couldn't afford the rent, so I followed her to Riverside even before I met Sandi. Our paranormal universe sure is small. Jackie's always been able to see through the fog of my mind, offering both guidance and comfort. When my gran died, I brought in a bracelet and a couple of rings Gran hadn't worn in years because her hands were swollen from arthritis. Within minutes, Jackie read the energy and told me things only Gran and I would know. Because of her paranormal hearing skills, she could hear my gran giggling, relaying a message only I would understand. She also told me where to find some hidden cash, and sure enough, I did! I wish I'd thought of bringing Carlos's boots along for my reading.

Jackie and Sandi used to be close, but Jackie couldn't deal with the changes that happened after Sandi's stroke. I also suspect Sandi's attitude about astrology being a superior method of divination didn't helped either. Wait until Jackie finds out how quickly Sandi's mind has gone down the toilet. She'll forgive Sandi and forget their quarrels.

A recent addition to the staff, a purple-haired, fully inked middle-aged gal arranging greeting cards, asks me to wait until she can inform Jackie of my arrival. Jackie is always running behind, but I don't mind. It gives me a chance to hang out and absorb the energy. I also like to people-watch. I pour myself a small cup of "today's witch's brew," finally releasing all the tension in my poor beat-up body. Even my sore ribs feel better.

As usual, I can see it's an interesting group of visitors in the shop. A stunningly exotic, African American girl with waist-length braids, dressed in a Gucci jumpsuit, is quickly gathering crystal gems in various shades of love spell pink. Something tells me she's done this before. When I focus on her, sparkling auric colors give off a Scorpio vibe. She gives me an intense look, signaling she's aware of me. I acknowledge her wishes and back off.

I notice two dramatically painted Hispanic women, a mother and daughter, standing by the register. The daughter is asking Lilly about an aromatherapy course. Lilly is as white as I am but speaks fluent Spanish. She's a student at UC Riverside. I'm acquainted with Lilly: She and I are always exchanging tricks about how to learn astrology faster. She's a computer major, smart, and hardworking. I bet she won't waste most of her life looking for love. It's a new world for women, thankfully. Still, girls will be girls. I smile toward the back, where a group of bewildered looking, nervously giggling teenage girls are playing with a small velvet bag of Ruin stones. Little fools. No one told them it's a bad idea to play with the spirit world. Two women in their seventies are waiting for their own psychic readers. They both look worried and sad.

No one told me how long the store's been around. I know nothing about the owners, but I bless them each and every time for offering the Wicca community a safe place. The staff divided the primary room into different areas, all carefully marked with hand-painted signs designating the different products for sale, including culinary herbs, healing herbs, crystals, incense, books on astrology, tarot, aromatherapy, and metaphysics, plus purpose jewelry and dragons. Yes, I mean, the entire store is a dragon lover's fantasy. There's a corner with stuffed dragons and a glass display with collectible dragon figurines and charms. The prices range from a few dollars to thousands. Dragons are hanging from the popcorn ceiling and dragons are displayed in the front window. So much whimsy and fun. It's the only place that makes me wish I had a baby girl of my own, but that thought passes quick enough.

A Victorian-era solid-oak table is piled high with handmade soaps and fabric scraps. The fabric rolls today are mostly related to Christmas, but I notice a few rolls of sparkling chiffon and silver lamé that remind me of my clubbing days. Another African American woman, nicely dressed in business attire, is picking up quilting supplies: a rotary cutter and a tin box holding multicolor clips. I've seen quilting groups meeting in the back room and often thought of joining one. Quilting is something I picked up during one of stays in rehab years back, but being an Aries, I didn't have the patience to stick with it.

Along the walls covered with flowered and striped wallpaper, the owners built several shelf units and lined their surfaces with scented paper. Sandi's favorite is the tea shelf, where she can find tea in tins, decorative strainers, and English porcelain teapots, some with matching cups and saucers. I prefer the candle shelf, organized by color, size, and Magik purpose. I like to pick up and examine all sizes of pillars and jars, votive and tapers, round and square, pyramid and flower shaped, giving preference to candles made of beeswax or ones scented with essential oils. The more expensive ones contain herbs or gems. Candles are essential for all ritual work, including making charms. (I burn a blue votive when I study astrology; blue is good when I need help geting my notes organized or adding some structure to my day. Deep blue is the color of water I need to cool off my overheated Mars.)

I'm in love with each section and can spend hours browsing and/or choosing what I need or don't need but want. Even without getting a personal reading, I'm happy, but I remind myself that I better focus on what I came here to learn. I'm determined to face the truth, no matter how painful.

As I'm about to ask the front desk about the timing of my appointment, Jackie pushes aside the multicolored beaded curtain separating the private reading space from the rest of the store and storms out. She's muttering something I can't hear under her breath, but I can tell she's pissed. She probably hasn't had time to eat. (Jackie's drug of choice is sugar.) She bumps into me without a glance and heads straight to the register.

Uh-oh. Poor Lilly. I don't envy her.

"I need a fucking break," Jackie screams at Lilly. "I told you not to overbook me on Fridays. Where's Chloe and Mike? Why am I the only one reading?"

"Chloe's sick and Mike's bike broke down, but he'll be here by six," Lilly says, trying to explain without raising her own voice. "I thought you wanted more readings. That's what you said last week, so I thought you'd be happy."

"Give me a break! More doesn't mean all. And I have my regulars who book me for an entire hour. Your stupid 20-minutes looky-loos only drain my energy. I haven't had my lunch or a bathroom break."

"Message received. Sorry," Lilly says, then waves me over.

"My apologies, boss," she winks at me. "Unfortunately, your reader needs a break, but if you can't wait, we can reschedule your session."

Jackie still does not realize that it's me. Her head's in the schedule book, so I play along with Lilly.

"Are you kidding me? How unprofessional are you people? No wonder you have such a terrible reputation. What happened to service? What happened to the customer is always right? I made an appointment and already paid. You better refund my payment and I mean right now. And don't you think I won't give you hell on Yelp, you dumb witches."

"My apologies again, but there's nothing I can do when your reader is psychically blocked. I promise that if you come back at six, you'll get a much better reading from Michael. He's not only a medium, but an authentic Hopi shaman," Lilly says, taking advantage of our little joke to put the screws in. Jackie must've really been a pain. "You'll love him. His aura is indigo, and he's a sex god." she adds with confidence. The girl's on fire. It's all I can do to keep a straight face.

Jackie finally looks up. "What did you just say, eh? And in front of my client? Mike is better than me, eh? Smoking peyote from morning to night doesn't make him a shaman. That's it, I quit, you evil brat. I'll show you."

Lilly and I break into hysterical laughter while poor Jackie turns as red as her Christmas sweater. She looks at Lilly, then me, then Lilly, back at me, and finally gets it, joining in.

"Merry Yule," I say, giving her a big hug during which I'm instantly enveloped in a cloud of her aura-grounding herbal essences of cinnamon and ginger.

"Hi Jackie. I'm your next."

"Shit," Jackie says, turning to Lilly. "Why didn't you tell me it was Vivi?"

"Sorry, I was busy at the register and Heather hasn't met her yet."

"I say you witches had me going. You too think you're funny, hey?"

(Jackie's "eh" is the only way I can tell she hails from Canada.

"You okay to read or should we get you something to eat first?" I ask, genuinely concerned for Jackie's well-being. "I don't have my car, long story, but we can walk over to the Mission Inn to grab some coffee and a muffin."

"I'm fine and I brought lunch. I was busting Lilly because the last readings were a waste of the gift." Jackie purses her lipstick-free lips surrounded by cobwebs of smoker lines. "Come here for another hug. I missed your face. How long has it been?"

"I've missed you too. Too long."

Jackie smiles. "Let me wash my hands and I'll take you back."

"All right, but only if you're sure. I booked an hour." She knows this won't be a waste of her "gift."

"That's great. It'll give us plenty of time to catch up. You're my last before Mike gets here, right, Lilly?" she asks her younger associate.

"That's right. Don't worry. I won't book any more clients until Mike arrives. And sorry about what I said. You realize, I think he's a smug douche. You're the best, Jackie."

"That I am. Love you, *duwies fach*."

"Love you too, *mom fach*, and thanks for teaching me Welsh."

Chapter 18

Jackie's readings always start with Wicca protection spells. She's one of our ritual leaders, a sort of high priestess, although in our world, any practitioner, female or male with knowledge, leadership skills, and a sincere desire to serve can be a high priestess or priest. I hope one day I can lead too, but not until I get my shit together. Sandi says I was drawn into the circle because I feel more comfortable among others who think for themselves and question all authority. We don't follow fashion or waste precious energy trying to be popular. We live by our own code.

Jackie's been an active Wicca for over twenty years. She came down to Southern California to start fresh after the failure of yet another miserable marriage. Unlike myself, she's also a mom to three grown kids from two different husbands. The last guy Jackie divorced was too old to donate sperm, she jokes. Last year, her oldest son made her a grandmother. While I don't envy her kids, one day, I'd like to get together with a man who has grandkids, so I can be a step. (Well, that rules out Nate.)

Jackie's still pretty, tall, and rail thin. My girl is also a natural blond with enormous hazel eyes and military-straight posture. Her low, scratchy voice reminds me of that crazy-hot '80s actress, Kathleen Turner. (Man, I used try and imitate her strong, sexy vibe, failing miserably.)

Jackie's worked in the hospitality industry, tried retail, and personal assisting, but couldn't make a living wage. Nowadays, she makes petty cash driving seniors to their doctor's appointments and the rest with psychic readings. Unlike Sandi, she's always struggled financially, but isn't a complainer. All parts of her family are Welsh. She's a true Celt. It was Jackie who helped me find a home with the Wicca family. Before her, I was dabbling here and there, but she's become my what I think of as a "spirit sponsor."

Our Jackie is a downhearted romantic, in love with love, an Aquarius with Venus in Pisces. She lets me read her chart so I can practice my astrology lessons on actual people, not just celebrities. Unfortunately, or perhaps fortunately, Jackie won't find her "twin flame" anytime soon, at least not here. Sandi's relocated her chart and has told her that while Southern California is a positive place for friendships and spiritual growth, money and sex aren't in the stars. Relocation is another technique I'd love to master. This is when the astrologer physically changes a client's natal chart coordinates to another location. Apparently, it's a big deal. Kind of makes sense if you think about it. Some people have rotten luck in their hometown or state or even country and then find happiness somewhere else. Others die while on a trip.

Jackie and I hold hands across a rickety card table, oddly free of candles, crystals, or other small knick-knacks. Jackie's not fond of other readers "magical" objects, which she says pollute her energy field. After several cleansing breaths, we say the sacred words in unison with our eyes closed: We call upon the White and Purple Light to surround us. We call upon our guides with harm to none. Then we open our eyes and continue with my favorite: "Living Goddess of Day and Night. Protect us with all your might." Finally, Jackie adds another incantation, the one about protecting her space with a pure golden haze and calls upon the Goddess. When she's ready, Jackie picks up a tiny, worn-out Tarot of the New Vision deck and lays out the cards while softly humming. I can sense the pull of the cards. It's a magnetism that's strong enough to make my stomach drop. I can't ignore the heat on my forehead and the tingling in my hands.

Yep, ready or not, here it comes, the truth and nothing but the truth.

"I'm going to spread out a Celtic Cross to check out the surrounding energy and then you can ask your questions," Jackie explains. The Celtic Cross is one of the most common tarot layouts, well-known for its accuracy. It's also easily misinterpreted by novices who read one card at the time without understanding the connections between the cards. As in all relationships, it's all about connections.

I rub my tired eyes and look closely at the spread of cards to see if anything jumps out. Although my metaphysical interests lay with the Stars, I've played with enough decks to have learned the basics. Jackie is too quiet. I'm getting nervous. I finally grow impatient with her theatrics. "What do you see?"

"Fog. I see fog. Nothing is what or where it should be. No one is who they say they are."

"No shit."

"No, I mean it. I've never seen this much occlusion or deception. What the hell's been going on with you?"

"Long story."

"I have time."

"Nope, you tell me. That's why I'm here."

"I need my personal deck to confirm. Can you go up front and ask Lilly to hand you my purse?"

"I'm on it." I get up too quickly and the dizziness and nausea make a troubling comeback.

"You don't look so hot, girl. Here, you sit. I'll go get it myself."

"I'm fine. I just got up too fast." I give her what sounds like a plausible excuse, not wanting to give her any more clues. This is how I recognize the reading will be right on the money. Most people give away too many clues to lousy readers or don't really want to know the truth. They twaddle on about this or that, obscuring the Spirit.

Jackie returns with her purse and lays out another Celtic Cross, this time using a deck I've never seen. "What deck is that?" I ask, curious about the gorgeous illustrations that remind me of Japanese graphic novels I got into reading thanks to Sandi's son Danny's obsession with everything Japanese.

"Mystical Manga. My home deck," she answers. "Beautiful, eh?"

"I'm grateful you're sharing them with me," I say sincerely. (Most readers have their own private decks they don't use for client divination.)

Thank the Goddess, I never told my gran about being friends with readers. She thought tarot cards were "the tool of Satan" and those who use them are nothing less than "Satan's own." I've known a few scammers and grifters, but never attributed any special powers to these pathetic creatures.

One of my favorite readers explained it in a cool way that made sense: Most people openly hostile to the Wicca community mix apples and oranges because they look at tarot as Divination in a biblical sense. We Wicca don't. And we don't work for Satan either. We don't believe he exists in the first place.

I see the cards as messages from my subconscious, which I choose to either block or misinterpret. That's all.

"Goddess, let's see what the cards say." Jackie chooses the Mystical Manga cards, examines them carefully, rolls her eyes, and whistles.

"What? Stop torturing me." I say, raising my voice.

"All right, here we go. They're telling me you're all messed up. Just look at the Nine of Wands in the Reverse. You want me to read reverse?"

"Goddess, yes! Do whatever you think will help."

"Sheesh, testy today."

"Jackie..."

"Fine. The first position is you and what surrounds you," Jackie says, starting slowly and then speeding up as she gets excited. "I see a problem with your attitude and perceptions. You feel surrounded by disloyalty and betrayal, eh? This time you are right. Trouble's ahead. Be vigilant. Get ready for a battle, a battle you thought you already fought and won. You are surrounded by people and relationships that make you wary and unsure. What's with all these people? I see two Kings. Look, this one is of the Rods suite and the other is a Pentacle. Do you get who I mean?"

"Affirmative," I say quietly, thinking of Nate, the Fire sign (Rods) and Art, the Earth element (Pentacles). I nod again but keep the names to myself so as not to influence Jackie.

"Ooh, I don't like this Page of Swords, either. Do you have a stalker? Incidentally, Pages can be females too."

I think she means Irma. "Actually," Jackie warns, I wouldn't take my eyes off the Queen of Rods either. This woman is a fire sign for sure: Aries, Leo, or Sagittarius. Aries? Wait, she could represent you!"

"Makes sense; it's my reading."

"Yes, but it seems no one can be trusted, including you. I mean your own judgement of the situation. Hmm, I'm getting confused, Viv. My readings aren't normally this convoluted. Let me use some clarifiers." She pulls out yet another deck, this time a beloved deck I recognize well, the original Rider-Waite. Jackie pulls out the Ten of Swords, followed by the Seven of Swords and the Devil.

"Crap. Tell me something I don't already know," I spit out bitterly. "I'm exhausted from constantly looking over my shoulder."

"Well, it's not the time to rest. Unless you do something different, you'll always be fighting the same battle over and over. Either fight on or stop the cycle of struggling. Change your mind—change your life."

"Easy for you to say."

"Not easy at all. Your choice, though."

"What else?"

"Oh, my dear, we've just begun. See the Tower Reversed?"

I nod. I was afraid of the dreaded Tower.

"Are you gripped by Universal Chaos?"

"You could say that," I say, trying to keep control of my emotions and play it cool.

"One thing is clear: The chaos isn't in your head. The Tower signifies something in your life is falling to pieces. See the Lightning Bolt?"

"Oh, double crap."

"Now don't freak. Everyone always freaks when the Tower appears, but I'm telling you straight up what's essential will be preserved. In fact, it'll hurt a lot worse if you try to hang on. You may feel like everything is crumbling, but trust me, because your Tower is reversed, I'm sure after the crisis, when your life calms down, everything should get much better.

Look at the Queen of Pentacles: You'll be happy by next May. Also, the Tower advises you to tread carefully or risk getting hit on the head."

"That's all I need. Another concussion."

"You had another concussion? What the heck, Viv? I thought your doctors warned one more head injury and your brain will not recover. What did Carlos say?"

"We broke up."

"Again?"

"Just before my fiftieth."

"But that was all the way back in April? Why didn't you come to see me?"

"I was crushed."

"I can understand that. Weren't you in love with that hottie?"

"If you can call what we had love."

"You're being ungrateful. Some of us don't have any luck with men, let alone good lookers. Admit it: Don't you miss that energy?"

"Like a giant wart on my ass."

"Ha-ha. I can't believe we haven't seen each other for that long. Let me ask the cards if you and Carlos will reconcile."

"Reconcile? Not this time, but go right ahead and check," I gurgle bitterly, but Jackie doesn't seem to notice. She draws several more cards and smiles with satisfaction.

"Look for yourself. Here's that same Queen of Rods—that's you—crossed by the King of Swords—Señor tall, dark, and handsome. Do you see Two of Cups between you? Two of Cups tell me that Carlos is not only your lover, but that this man also has deep feelings for you and only wants to bring you pleasure. No matter the obstacles or circumstances, he believes you two are destined to end up together."

"Bull crap," I whisper, not sure she heard me.

"Although," Jackie says, shaking her head and looking at me with disappointment, that judgy look I recognize only too well, "if you want him back, you'll have to be clear about your feelings. Sometimes this card shows you are torn between two men, the old and the new, and you can't move on unless you choose. Damn, witch, you've got it going on! I can't even hook up with one. Do you think I should grow out my hair? Men still like long hair, or do they? I think I'll go younger next time. Say, you want to hang out with me?"

When I don't respond, Jackie babbles on, "How blessed can you get? Now I pull the Nine of Cups, the card of wishes coming true. Finally, top the spread with the Six of Cups signaling reunion. I predict that by your next birthday, you two lovebirds will be tighter than ever."

This is where I lose it, bursting into tears. "Only if I'm dead. Do you see me dying?" I say, demanding an answer.

"No, of course you're not dying. What do you mean?"

I vomit all my unspoken guilt and fears all over her. "Carlos is dead. He was murdered. First, he dumped me, then, I saw him cheating, got pissed, and sicked the cops on him. He got busted for DUI and RA, but, of course, he got away with it again. The cops let him out, but he disappeared on the way home to his mama. Then they found his body without a head in Newport Coast at some construction site. His truck was there, too. So no matter what your cards say, Carlos and I aren't reuniting, not on this plane. I can tell with a hundred percent certitude that this time, it's over for good. And I've been seeing this young guy, but I dumped him and I'm in lust with my renter, a former cop, who thinks I'm nuts. Sandi says he's a good guy, but I don't trust her anymore. And I think Carlos's family is trying to kill me. And Sandi's losing her mind."

Now it's my turn to suck the oxygen out of Jackie's lungs. For the longest time, she says nothing. I can see she's trying to make sense of what I just told her. She looks at me, then back at the tarot layout, still not believing her own ears.

"No way. It can't be," she says. "It's right here, clear as the ceremonial glass orb. I see you and Carlos together. I don't understand. If he's crossed over, why are the cards saying you'll be reunited?"

"I understand only that I'm screwed!" I shout. "We'll be together again when I join him in hell because of this, I am sure. He is dead. I even studied his Fixed Stars, the stars that show the probable cause of death, and what did I see? Everything lined up," I say, now sobbing. "I'm sorry, Jackie, but this is not going anywhere. Your reading sucks. You made me more upset than before we started. I was trying to clear up my confusion, but now I'm more confused than ever. Hell, I'm terrified." I go to get up. "Look, nothing personal, but I will not stay for the entire reading. I'll pay for the full hour sure. I'm sure you can take another client. We're done. Obviously, you can't read today. You are too tired or blocked or something."

"I'm not blocked! Lilly's wrong. I was just hungry and needed a break. Sometimes, you can be such a narcissistic bitch, Viv."

"Are you kidding me? *I'm* a narcissist? If that's so, you're a jealous, old witch. No wonder Sandi can't stand you. Good luck with getting laid."

"Jealous of you? Who do you think you are? A druggie whore who can't make a commitment to anything or anyone. If Carlos is really dead, he's the lucky one, and if it wasn't for Sandi, you'd be living in a half-way house! Sandi and I fought over you. I warned her you're nothing but a user. Get the hell away from me!"

I can't believe what just happened. Yes, I can: Mercury Retrograde on my birthday.

"Fuck you, Jackie!" I say, jumping up and rushing past the register without saying a word to anyone.

Chapter 19

As I exit the store, more shocked than upset, a powerful gust of Santa Ana wind almost knocks me off my feet. I step off the curb clumsily, twist my foot and land on my ass.

"Whoa there. Watch your step," I hear a too-familiar voice say and I look up. It's Art.

You've got to be kidding me. What is he doing here?

"Let me help you up," he says with what I've come to loath as his "I'm your knight in shining armor" smugly annoying grin.

"I'm not a cripple or an old woman," I snap. "What makes you think I need your help. I can damn well get up on my own." Jumping up, I hold my purse close to my chest, ignoring his extended hand. "Are you spying on me, again?"

"If you see it that way," Art says, not taking the bait and continuing with the friendly bit. "Say, you've got dirt all over your backside. Here, let me."

"Don't you dare grab my ass!" I screech.

"I was just going to give you a handkerchief," Art counters, shaking his head in dismay. "You seem upset. Has something gone wrong with your appointment?"

"Yes. Wait. How did you find out about my reading? Did you 'bug' me?" My Scorpio paranoia awakens. All I want to do now is run or search my purse for a bug.

"Please calm down. I think you're overreacting. It's nothing that sinister. I have a logical explanation, but can we get inside somewhere? These wind gusts must be over sixty."

"I never overreact!" I proclaim, despite the fact he's kind of right. "Oh, you're going to have to explain a lot," I hiss, looking up at him with narrowed eyes.

"Let me buy you a cup of coffee," he says, showing sensitivity to my sobriety. "I parked across the street, right by that nice coffee place. Emery got me hooked on salted caramel mochas in the afternoon. Ever since high school I've been a regular-black-with-two-sugars guy, but I guess, it's a new world."

"I hate sugar in my coffee: too many carbs," I say and wrinkle my nose, still suspicious of his startling appearance. He is right, though, about the crazy wind that practically blows us across the street from the Wicca shop and the Mission Inn. How I'd love to share my passion for the historic inn with Art.

We'd check in late on a Friday, take a lingering walk in the garden, where I'd impress him with all my knowledge about the famous bell, the oldest bell in the Christian world, going back over seven hundred years. If only I was normal, we'd have just one drink in the President's Lounge, have a nice dinner, and end up upstairs in one of the romantic mini suites.

Cut it out, Viv, I tell my wayward mind. *That life is not for you.*

Another hurricane-force gust makes it hard for Art to open the door. We get inside and rub the dust from our eyes, the remnants of my mascara stinging so badly I ask the guy behind the register where the restroom is. When my eyes finally stop burning, I see that the wind has made a knotted mess of my hair and I try to comb it out with my fingers. By the time I leave the restroom, Art has paid for two mugs of steaming coffee and is waiting for me at a little table toward the back, away from the front door. Nate and Carlos would both be nose-deep in their phones by now, but not this guy. Damn, he looks great as usual in that unruffled, self-assured "I'm not aware I'm sex on a stick" manner that drives me nuts. Although he's not as dressed up as he was the other day, he looks comfortable in his pressed slacks and crisp denim shirt. His hair's more out of place than usual, but that's it. It's so unfair. While I look like a hag, his less-than-perfect hair only adds to his attractiveness. It's only been a day since my car crash, but if I'm being honest, I must admit I've missed his face. I wonder if he's going to blow off our Saturday-night date, and if we're still on, what in the world should I wear? I haven't thought about this stupid crap in years.

As I approach the marble-topped table for two, Art gets up, only sitting down again after I get comfortable. This time I skip my usual snarky remark about his old-school manners, realizing he's not play-acting at being a gentleman; he was simply raised to behave that way.

"Here you go," he says, handing me a large mug with an Italian flag. "Careful, it's hot. Hope you don't mind that I didn't get it to go. Black, no sugar, right? Hope you like French roast. I don't know much about the different beans, but the fellow behind the counter said it's easier on the gut. How's the nausea?" he rattles on, making me nervous.

"Thank you," I reach for the mug, jumping a bit when his fingers meet mine. I'm suddenly tongue-tied, painfully aware of my sad appearance. "It's all good," I say, lying about both the nausea and not mentioning the sore ribs. What man wants to hear a woman whine?

"Glad you weren't hurt badly, but you're probably wondering why I came to get you at that store, right?"

"You could say that," I say. I try to take a sip of the coffee and promptly burn my tongue.

"It's pretty straightforward, Viviana. I called Sandi to see how you were both doing and to tell you about what my buddy thinks happened to your Mercedes. Remember, my buddy the mechanic in Corona, where I had your car towed? Sandi told me you took an Uber to an appointment and gave me the address. She said you'd been gone longer than she expected and she was getting worried that you couldn't get a ride back with the winds and the fires. I called your cell and left a message. When you didn't respond, I came to get you since I was already halfway to Riverside. All the parking spots were occupied, so I parked across the street and waited. I didn't think you'd appreciate me coming in."

"That's right. I don't take kindly to people following me around. I didn't want to be bothered, so I turned my phone off, so I guess I'll buy your explanation, for now," I say, trying to show I know how to compromise. "Did you say there's another fire? Where now?" I ask. I'm not really interested, but figure if I keep him talking I can avoid thinking.

"Rancho Cucamonga. Where is that?" Art asks.

"It's just south of the foothills of the San Gabriel Mountains."

"Never been there, but Sandi said the fire could affect traffic."

"Well that area burns a lot. They had a pretty bad fire a few years back. It's the winds and the idiots who keep building, encroaching on wild brush areas. It's just like all those rich Hollywood types who live in Malibu: the fires, the mudslides, beach erosion, nothing stops them," I say, getting on my soapbox.

"I gather you're right. Anyway, since you didn't pick up, I waited and then tried to call you again. Do you want me to call Sandi to tell her we're together?"

"I can do it later since I don't really feel like going back to the house right now," I say with a shrug.

He doesn't let up. "I get it, but I believe she's worried and we probably don't want her to be alone. I understand. It's getting dark and my own folks have come down with 'sundowner syndrome.' Mom gets panicky and Dad doesn't understand how to deal with her."

I get irritated with his assumptions, wondering if he thinks I'm one cold-hearted bitch. "Sandi's fine. She spends her life alone in that monstrosity of a house. She's used to Jay running around with his friends."

"I don't like it, Viviana. She sounded distressed."

This man sure doesn't give up easily. I've at least got to give him that. I try again to explain my point of view, something I normally don't do. "Oh, please, she's just being dramatic. She's perfectly safe at home. I helped her bathe and there are plenty of snacks in the cupboard. I'm not her caregiver. If she wanted one, she's got plenty of money to hire help."

"If you're sure," Art says hopefully, finally coming around to my way of thinking.

"I am. Can I just enjoy the coffee in peace and have an adult conversation? Tell me about my car."

"All right," Art says, but I can smell his disapproval. He thinks I'm being a selfish bitch, but he wasn't there when I dropped everything to take care of Sandi.

Art clears his throat. "Sorry to say, but my buddy didn't see any obvious malfunction, but he doesn't think what happened is normal either. His experience tells him it's more like shoddy workmanship and negligence. You could've been killed."

"Tell him to check the accelerator cable," I blurt out, a hundred percent convinced someone tried to fuck with my car, to do damage or even harm me—again.

"Accelerator, hmm? Why, if you don't mind?"

"I can't explain. You'll just have to trust me."

"Did you friend at the psychic store tell you that someone messed with your car?"

"I don't need anyone to tell me anything, and Jackie isn't my friend. Is this what Sandi told you?" I ask, bristling, then wonder why she'd say something to Art who has nothing to do with our ways. A jolt of electricity hits me right in the pit of my stomach. There's something between Art and Sandi that doesn't add up.

"All right. I'll call him first thing tomorrow, before I pick you up."

"Pick me up? What for?" I ask, playing dumb.

"Pick you up for our date? Don't tell me you forgot."

He actually sounds disappointed, I think, but say nothing.

"Well, with all this crap going on and me staying with Sandi, I didn't think you wanted to take me out."

"I do. And we are going. I made plans, although I have to admit, I'm a little nervous. I haven't been out on a date in a long time, let alone with someone I really like."

"You, nervous? *I'm* the one who's terrified." I blurt out without meaning to, even though he just admitted the extent of his feelings for me.

"Well, I guess we both need a drink first," he chuckles, then sees my face and turns red. "Oh shit. I'm sorry. I didn't mean it. You must think me an idiot. No drinks, of course."

He looks clearly guilty. Now it's my turn to laugh. "It's fine, Art. Don't sweat the small stuff. I know you didn't mean it. That's the thing, though, I'm not exactly dating material."

"Stop," he says, then gets halfway up, leans over my coffee, and gives me the sweetest of kisses on my forehead. "I've been planning to ask you out for weeks. Please don't reject me."

I don't know what to say. My heart is beating so hard, I can't catch my breath.

"Reject you? I'm not about to walk away from someone I never thought I could..." I say before stopping myself, a completely new experience for someone who wears her heart on her sleeve.

Art widens his eyes, but wisely says nothing except, "I'm looking forward to tomorrow too."

We sit without talking. I fidget with my mug, feeling beyond awkward. I finally ask Art to get me a refill, but it looks like the coffee place is about to close.

"Let's get to Sandi's," I tell Art, suspecting he's ready to move on. Because the sun has set, the winds have calmed down. When we get to Sandi's, the house is unusually dark.

"Good thing we're back," Art says without looking at me.

"She's all right, probably on her laptop in the bedroom," I assure him, thinking something is odd.

"Why don't you just drop me off and I'll text you if I need help," I say, sounding more confident than I really am. "Remind me again how you two met?"

"I'll go in with you," he says firmly, shelving my question.

I jump out of Art's truck. He follows closely. I use the remote-control Sandi gave me to avoid fussing with the front door, which is always in need of work. Navigating through Jay and Sandi's garage is a tremendous challenge, almost as bad as cutting through the clutter in the house—piles and piles of junk, some boxed, others in black trash bags piled all the way to the ceiling. I stub my toe on the broken-down tread- mill, then trip over a box marked "Christmas." The smell in the garage practically makes me vomit. Thank the Goddess, I passed on Art's offers of pastries. I wonder what he's thinking right about now.

"Hey," I say over my shoulder to him, "watch where you step. I just saw rat droppings."

"Yeah, I'm getting the picture," Art says. "Wow. Do you think Sandi would mind if you and I clean this up?"

"Jay won't like it," I answer.

Okay, this is getting ridiculous. What's the deal?

"You probably think I'm being overly concerned about Sandi," Art says, as if reading my mind and puts his hand on my shoulder. When I turn around, I see the serious expression on his face and decide not to get into it, at least not just yet.

"Well, you must admit, it is weird how you're acting like you've known her for a long time or, better yet, like a relation."

"I care about Sandi, that's true. You notice, I'm a Boy Scout at heart," he jokes.

"I guess so but still, I have questions for both of you."

"I get it, and I will answer in due time. Here, give me your hand." Art reaches for me and shocks the bejesus out of me by placing an electric kiss on my wrist. I don't know how to deal with this, so I take my hand back and walk ahead.

In a second or two, we reach the back door and enter the dim hallway, decorated with Jay's lame fishing memorabilia. The house is eerily silent. I'm getting spooked. Maybe Art was right to worry.

"Do you think she's upstairs?" I whisper.

"Most likely, but my Spidey cop sense is telling me someone's in the house." Art whispers back, giving me goosebumps.

"Mine too. What do we do?"

"Stay back."

"No."

"Viviana, for once, don't be stubborn. I can't tell what's
ahead and I need to be sure you're safe just in case I have to...
you get what I'm saying."

As I'm about to throw a fit, telling him I've been through
rougher situations than this, a crashing sound comes from
the kitchen and makes both of us jump. I take off running
toward the sound, my heart pounding out of my chest. Art
follows, his gun drawn.

"Fuck, Sandra, you dumb, fat bitch. How many times
have I told you not to go barefoot." It's Jay. He's standing over
Sandi, who's fallen down on her side, her left foot bent in an
unnatural direction. Her eyes are closed and she's as white
as her underpants and bra. She must've come down from the
bedroom. Never the one to be embarrassed by a little skin, I
cringe at the injustice of it, knowing only too well that Sandi's
been body-shamed her entire life.

"Get away from her, you monster! I'm going to kill you!"
I push Jay so hard he tumbles over Sandi and lands on his
back.

"Help me get her up!" I yell to Art.

"Stop! Don't move her," Art says. "I'm calling an ambulance right now."

I see his point and back off from trying to lift Sandi but
continue to stay by her side. After placing the call, Art gets
down on the floor and checks her pulse. "Sandi, you're going
to be okay. Just rest." Sandi doesn't open her eyes, but I hear
a little moan.

"Did she hit her head?"

"I didn't see it, but you need to calm down. You're not doing her any good. Her pulse is steady and there's no obvious sign of a brain injury."

"What are you, a doctor too?"

"I was a medic in Iraq," Art says without looking directly at me.

"Why didn't you tell me?"

"I didn't have a chance."

"Get up, you useless piece of shit," I seethe with rage, turning to Jay, who's still hasn't gotten up.

"Fuck you, skanky bitch," he says, his eyes glassy, his speech slurred. I take a deep breath, recognizing the dick wad is high on something and it's not his favorite single-malt scotch.

How does the saying go? It's deja vu all over again, I think just as the paramedics come walking through the garage that Art and I left open. After asking the same old questions and slapping a 12 lead on the patient, the main dude informs us that Sandi should be taken to the hospital. All in all, they take no more than ten minutes to call for the ambulance. For once Jay is quiet. He most likely doesn't want to bring attention to his inebriated state. The ambulance arrives to take Sandi to the hospital. Again.

"I'm riding along," I inform Jay. "You, go to bed. I'll call you in the morning." He shakes his head, scowling at me, but says nothing.

Art takes me in his arms and gives me a squeeze. "Not a chance. I'll meet you there. No arguing." I'm not about to argue, so I give him a kiss on the cheek, my foolish heart oddly content.

Chapter 20

I t's barely 24 hours later, but here we are, Art and I, sitting across from each other at a beautifully set table in a fine dining establishment, all puffed up with a sense of accomplishment, experiencing what some folks call a date. After several stale coffee-fueled exhausting hours spent biting our nails in the ER, we got back to Sandi's, picked up my overnight bag, and drove back to Costa Mesa. There was no way in hell I'd stay with Jay one minute longer than necessary. Once the hospital staff assured us that Sandi would be admitted and was in stable condition, there was no reason for us to stick around. Her blood work showed low potassium and dehydration, just as I suspected. Jay's been starving her. She also had a hell of a UTI, which, according to the admitting physician, was the reason for her nutty behavior. With a couple of bags of IV fluids and antibiotics, Sandi would be fine. Another crisis averted. Phew.

When we arrived at the house, Jay was still up, playing with his computer, probably jerking off to online porn or gambling. Before we left, he tried to say something, but Art gave him a look that could stop a raging mama bear right in her tracks. It seemed oddly comforting to be around a powerful man, at least for tonight. Even though it was close to ten; the traffic was still heavy, so we stopped in Corona for a quick bite at a barbeque joint. The conversation centered on my car trouble and Sandi's health, nothing personal. Although I told Art that I barely had the energy to put myself together for our date. I was too beat to argue when he insisted he still wanted to take me out. After soaking in my not-so-clean bath tub, I took my meds and passed out, waking up late the next morning.

In the late afternoon, while Art was dealing with family stuff, I got the nerve to ask to borrow his truck, pretending I needed to run some errands, but what I really did was run over to a high-end resale boutique on 17th (no, I didn't get a doughnut) to find an outfit I hoped would knock his socks off. Normally, I'm perfectly content with picking out a few vintage items at a thrift store, but this was different. Often I can't admit how much money I pissed away at the mall when I was dancing. I mean, even the rich shop at resale boutiques. This is Newport Beach resale: nothing but designer stuff. And so, here I sit in my Saturday-night finery: a dark green velvet dress with lace inserts, topped with a white faux-fur jacket I removed as soon as we were seated to show off some cleavage, a move that was much appreciated by my date based on his body language.

The gals at the boutique helped me find suitable shoes: a pair of three-inch-high silver heels that must have cost someone a fortune. (The shoes reminded me of my dancing life.) After scrubbing my skin with a homemade sugar and rose oil scrub, I got sufficiently at ease with my forehead lines to pull my ironed frizz back into a low pony. I went all out decorating my hair with a sparkling silver headband, (hey, it's the holidays). I also used my old makeup tricks, the tricks that make me appear years younger, adding a pair of fluttery fake lashes and lip liner, something I haven't done in a decade. I learned how to project an illusion of youth from older dancers, the gals in their early forties who had no other way of making a living—if they still had a nice pair of tits. Once you're in the know, it's not a big deal to use a bit of highlighting and contouring to camouflage or emphasize what a man notices or doesn't. Beauty is an illusion after all. I wonder who said that? I probably heard it somewhere. Still, I could use one of Jackie's beauty spells.

For extra oomph, I mix my scent, a few drops of jasmine and ylang-ylang, topped with vanilla and cinnamon, blended into a scentless oil. Jasmin to stimulate, cinnamon and vanilla to seduce. Ylang-ylang helps me to relax during sex. That is when I'm sober. All this trouble just to make up not doing one double shot of vodka. Based on Art's reaction, I did a damn good job. He doesn't let go of my hand until he must. Pretending not to enjoy sitting next to him, I insist on being seated across, but not before brushing against his body, my flirty Chrissy side having way too much fun.

The place is gorgeous: warm, inviting, even elegant, but without being fussy. Who'd imagine he'd choose the city of Anaheim for our first official date? Anaheim, the blue-collar, fat tourist, Mickey Mouse, baseball, and hockey capital of the OC. I was expecting an old-school Italian joint in Costa Mesa or a fish place near the water. Am I ever glad I jazzed myself up.

We're sipping delicious mock cocktails and nibbling on freshly baked bread, neither of us entirely comfortable, both of us beyond thrilled we actually pulled it off, considering yet another act in the Sandi saga.

"That's the best thing I've drank in ages," I say to my handsome date, lifting the icy-cold copper mug to my lips, worrying about the intense burgundy lip color smearing, making me look like the mess I normally am. To be honest, I'd love a Moscow mule with a double Stoli, but I know better.

Art is wearing the same blazer he wore to his holiday party, neatly pressed Levi's, and a white button-down, his black laced shoes shining in the candlelight. None of Glenn's douche bag $400 shirts or Carlos's fake-ass Tony Lamas for him. Since the restaurant is part of an upscale country dancing club, Art's also wearing a low-key, western-style hat made of wool felt. I'm not exactly thrilled with the hat. It brings back way too many memories of my Texas years.

"Mmm," Art says, pointing to my mug, "your drink looks good. What's in it?"

"Mmm," I echo back, "I assume some honey and mango, probably with a few drops of fresh lime juice. Here, try it. I mean if you're not grossed out."

"Grossed out? Are you kidding? I can't wait to French kiss you. Oops, sorry. Do they still say that?"

When I giggle, offering him my mug, he samples the cocktail, making an approving sound. "And ginger beer. Emery loves ginger beer. Non-alcoholic, of course. I like how they used cucumber slices for garnish."

"I didn't think you're a drink-with-my-kids kind of dad," I say, smiling and dying to tell him he's delusional about the kid not sneaking booze behind his broad back, but I don't. I'm learning. I'm growing.

"Listen, before we order and enjoy our meal," Art says in his cop voice, "I wanted to give you an opportunity to ask me those questions you've been saving for a while now, right?"

I'm taken aback by his directness, but he's correct: Before I get in over my head, before that French kiss and whatever comes after, we need to clear the air. Or do we? Right on schedule, my anxiety coils up like a rattlesnake, demanding attention.

Damn, I need something to squash it. How do I sneak a shot?

"Okay, I'll go first," Art begins, as if sensing how nervous I am. "Before you ask your questions, I want to tell you about my past, that's if you still interested."

"I am," I mumble, adding direct eye contact, bracing for the bad news.

"Relax, Vivi, it's not that bad." He smiles, reaches across the table for my hand, and gives it a pat.

"If you say so. Is Arthur Russo even your actual name?".

"Yep. I am him."

"All right, that's a promising start," I say, trying to sound even-keeled.

"Where do you want me to start?"

"Wherever makes sense."

"I guess I wasn't that great in school, though I was fairly good at sports and screwing around. Definitely not book smart, not like Em's mom."

"What was her name?"

"Ann, without an *e*," he says. "Ann Charlotte. Her family came from the Carolinas. She was something: smart, brave, and gorgeous. Emery got her looks from her mom."

"I'm sure she was perfect. You married her," I say.

"It was my privilege," he responds, looking down, not acknowledging my compliment. I'm sorry I'm a cold-hearted bitch, but I'm glad she's a dead and not a live ex. I could never compete.

"I joined the military right after high school," Art says after taking a sip. "Served a couple of tours, then came back to Utah to work with my dad. He's a roofer. My folks moved to Utah from Wisconsin, where I was born and grew up."

"Milwaukee?"

"Nope. The northern part, about an hour from Green Bay. When I got back, I wasn't myself for a few years and working for the family seemed like an excellent choice."

"Wounded or PTSD?"

"Both. I mean nothing too dramatic, just enough to remember."

"So you've been out of the service since your twenties?" I ask.

"No, I went back after the Twin Towers were hit. I mean, a military career was always in the plan, that or law enforcement. I was never smart enough for the Bureau. My dad's a vet and a volunteer firefighter."

"Why did you leave the Marines in the first place?"

"Is it that obvious?" he asks, raising one eyebrow. "Let's say, I had a personality disorder; I hate assholes."

Something in the way Art sounds makes my skin tingle. He's got to have some Aries in him, or Scorpio or Aquarius. Active service, a need for justice along with a strong sense of duty. I wonder which one or perhaps all three? Shit, where's Sandi when I need her.

"I met Ann in Iraq. She was an MP. Long story. That's why I went in to law enforcement, to be near her," he adds, and just the way he says her name makes me crazy jealous. Yep, I'm in love.

"Good evening, folks. My name is Russ and it'll be my pleasure to be looking after y'all tonight. Any special occasions?" the server asks.

Taken by surprise, Art doesn't respond right away. The server winks and drawls, "Don't want to interrupt, but would you like another cocktail, or are you ready to place your order? We have specials." Since Russ arrived just before Art shared the possibly disturbing details about his "perfect" relationship with the wife, I take it as a sign from the Goddess, excuse myself and go to use the ladies, but before I leave, I ask Art to order me a BLT wedge salad and a coffee. It's going to be a long night. When I get back, my salad is waiting. Art is waiting. The server is waiting. Guess I better study the menu.

It takes a while to get through our supper. It's the best food I've had in ages. Short ribs for him and lobster mac for me. (The hell with not eating carbs. I've lost plenty of weight.) I'm too nervous and let loose, gobbling up the entire meal, ylang-ylang or not. Art stopped talking about his past, and I'm good with that. (Sure, I'm looking for answers, but for now I'm content because my inner psychic detective tells me everything he's divulged so far is the truth.)

We chat about Sandi's health, my car being fixed, and his upcoming trip to see his family. I tell him a few silly stories about my Christmas holidays in Texas, hunting wild pigs and shooting sandhill cranes with my brother and dad for supper. Nothing too intense, not yet. To be fair, if we have any chance to move our relationship forward, for once I'll keep my mouth shut, unless I have no choice.

"Get a load of that?" Art says, smiling and patting his flat stomach. "Me thinks we better go to the next room to work off some of this wonderful meal. You dance?"

"Salsa."

"Salsa? I'm impressed. How about a two-step or West Coast Swing?"

"Not on your life. I hate country dribble."

"Yeah, I remember, but I hoped you'd expand your play list. Plus, the new country artists are not that dribbly," he adds, laughing quietly, teeth gleaming in the soft light.

Oh, my.

"I've been kind of considering how good it'd be to dance with you. The way you move, I just know, you'd be a fun partner."

How does he do it? How does he turn vinegar into wine? It wouldn't hurt too badly to be held in those massive arms, my body molded to his, swaying to the music, country or not.

Stop! I almost scream out loud. I should've checked Neptune's transits. Neptune is the planet to watch for romance. It's different from Venus, though, higher vibration, more powerful to bring in a soul mate or your nightmare. Of course, I just had to be born with Neptune in Scorpio, the most intense sign, not to underestimate that it's sitting on top of my Ascendant. Lucky me. What a perfect placement for psychos, psychics, and addicts. Neptune or not, this man is way too good to be real.

"The thing is, Art, I have to come clean. To be honest," I start off, awkward as a teenager, "dinner's been amazing, you've been amazing, but you realize, I'm in recovery, and, well, country bars are full of boozers and I've got the jitters. I mean, it's just too hard. I mean..."

"Damn. I am so sorry," Art says, interrupting my lame speech. "I'm being what Emery calls a toxic male. Please forgive me. Of course, bars are off-limits. I'll find us a place to dance, like a dance studio or something where they don't serve alcohol. Emery takes lessons and sometimes they have socials for parents."

"Right, socials for parents," I say, feeling the walls closing in. He doesn't notice, chattering on, making me long for the old, strong, silent Art.

"Why don't we take this party home? I'll make you some of that grass tea you like and we'll talk—or not?" He gives his signature wink.

Crap.

"Right," I stammer. "How about a raincheck? I've had a great date night, but..."

"What's the matter with me?" Art responds, hitting himself on his forehead." You must be exhausted after everything you've been through these past few days. The concussion, the car accident, Sandi, and here I am thinking only of myself. I'm sorry, beautiful. It's just that I've been looking forward to this evening for months," he confesses. "Probably since you first took my breath away."

Oh my.

Now it's me who's forgotten how to fill my pipes with oxygen. He gets up, pulls me close, and plants a kiss so electrifying it blows out the candle on the table. The energy between us is nothing like I've ever experienced outside of my dream world. I don't trust myself to say no.

"I need to freshen up again," I whisper, licking my lips.

"Take your time. I'll settle up and grab the car, so you don't have to mark those pretty new shoes," Art says, his intimate tone sending shivers down my spine.

Wait, how did he learn about the shoes being new?

"Okay," I respond, asking no more stupid questions, desperate to quell my growing panic about what to do next, my Chrissy demanding satisfaction.

The drive back to "our" place is crackling with silent tension, the good kind, the kind that gives you butterflies in your stomach. Although I'm still dying to ask Art more questions, I'm afraid of his answers. Maybe we can leave it for the next morning. I bargain with my all-knowing gut. Just before we get off the 55 freeway, out of the blue, Art exhales loudly in what I take is excitement and starts off with, "All right, then.

Here goes. Listen, before we take off our clothes and get crazy with each other, I have to tell you something."

"Take off our clothes?" I moan, my overactive imagination kicking in.

"Hope so. The thing is, Viviana, your gut was right to hold back from me. I'm not exactly the man I told you I was. For one, I'm not a retired police officer and my renting from you, wasn't a coincidence, either."

I can't trust my ears. Oh yes, I can. All I can do is shake my head. I prepared for this. What do you know: I sure have zero luck with men. What do I expect with such a crappy Neptune?" I'm almost relived I was right. Almost.

"No, no, it's not that bad," Art continues. "I mean, it's not good since I was not entirely honest. I am in law enforcement, just not a cop."

An entire box of fireworks, my dad's favorite, Zeus Shells, goes off in my head. *No confíes en el. No confíes in el.* Don't trust him. Now I understand exactly what the bearded man in my dreams meant. He was warning me about Art. The men torturing him weren't the cartel, they were the Feds.

"You're fucking DEA? Pure evil! You dick wads are no better than the drug lords. I've been around enough. I've seen your methods. It's all about your ego. You'd sell out your own family to make an arrest and move up the ladder," I conclude, still hoping against all logic that I'm wrong. When he says nothing in response, I realize I'm right on the money. "Don't you dare lie to me. You're a Fed and you're here on assignment. I'm your 'in' with Glenn's drug operation. You're here to use me to set them up."

Art finally speaks up, his voice as distant as my future with him. "Affirmative on the first three points, except I'm not here to get you in trouble. I'm here to protect you. Unfortunately, you've been on the cartel's radar, and they're getting closer to making their move."

"What cartel?" I demand, raising my voice.

"The Arellano Felix group. They've been pretty active in Tijuana."

"You're shitting me! Everyone and their grandma are aware TJ is Sinaloa territory. Arellano is a big, fat loser. Don't you dare play the good guy. We're done. Do you hear me? Stop the car. Now."

"That wouldn't be wise. As far as the Sinaloa outfit, you're wrong. They made, shall we say, a special arrangement with the CJNG branch. You've heard of them? The Cartel Jalisco Nueva Generacion? These hombres are beyond brutal. Just last summer, they were surprisingly close to taking the Tijuana territory away from Sinaloa," Art says, sharing more info than I ever needed.

I break into sweat, flashing back. "I don't want to hear a word about those animals and their little wars. I've been done with this shit since Glenn landed me in the hospital with a hole in my head. Before that, I almost lost my life in Costa Rica. You can't imagine what it took for me to make it. But thanks to my family and the Goddess, that fucker is gone and I'm still here." "Stop the car," I hiss, on the verge of a full-blown panic attack, "or I'm jumping out."

"Please listen. I appreciate you're not involved, but you're right. It has to do with your past with Glenn," Art says, trying to reason with me.

"Bullshit!" I spit back, a wave of nausea hitting me so fast that my mouth fills up with saliva. "Glenn's been dead for nearly three years. It's Carlos's family who's after me and probably you as well."

"You need to calm down, babe. It's not that bad. I'll tell you everything as soon as we get home. I swear on my kid. I'm here to keep you safe as a personal favor to my Mexican counterpart. He's been working on the case longer than us." Art tries again to engage me in discussion, but I will neither listen to nor fall for his lies ever again.

"Nope. Not listening," I say. "You can swear on the Bible. I'll never listen to another word coming out of your corrupt pig mouth," I start to cry more out of self-hatred than anything. "I'm such a jerk to fall in love with a stinking Fed who doesn't give a rat's ass about me."

Oh shit, did I just say that out loud?

"I'm sorry I had to keep some things under wraps, but I care a great deal about you and your safety. I tried not to get involved, but you remember how that went?"

"I see. So now it's my fault?" I respond bitterly, now icy-Scorpio calm. "You know what? Quit manipulating. I've been nothing but upfront about everything: my addiction, my recovery status, my feelings for you. Actually, not you, the man you told me you were."

"I'm sorry you see it as manipulation. I truly am. Can we please talk? Just talk."

"No!"

"Vivi, you're being pigheaded. Come on, you owe me that much. We need to come up with a plan."

"Ram, not pig, and I owe you nothing."

"You told me I saved your life, more than once come to think of it, and you see me as sexy," he says, attempting to pacify me with a joke.

"Fine," I say, pretending to agree just to get him off my back. "Spill, and I mean all of it, and no touching."

"Yes, ma'am. As soon as we get in. I give you my word as a Marine. Yes, that part is true."

As we exit the freeway, turning left on University Drive right by the fair, the fog is as thick as New England clam chowder and I'm freezing. That fancy faux fur is worthless and I should've worn my old boots, not these silver heels. This evening sure isn't ending the way I hoped, just like nothing in my crummy life.

"I'm hungry."

"Sorry?"

"You heard me. Drive me to Jack in the Box on 17th. They have a late-night menu."

"I assumed you liked our dinner?"

"I barely touched the salad and gawked at you instead of enjoying my lobster mac. Since I can't get high, I want a chili cheeseburger and a Diet Coke, and I don't have my wallet on me. This stupid clutch holds nothing but a lipstick."

"All right. I could use a cup of coffee. Something tells me it's going to be a long night."

Chapter 21

"We are born at a given moment in a given place and like vintage years of wine we have the qualities of the year and of the season in which we are born. Astrology does not lay claim to anything else."—Carl. G Yung

The bloodied, barefoot, blindfolded man's captivity was ending. He knew it. His jailors knew it. Tragically, no one else had a clue. Ever since he came to, he counted days, which turned into weeks, which turned into months. He could tell by the way his two jailors talked Christmas was coming. That would mean, give or take a week or two, he'd been locked in this torture room for close to eight months. He'd missed the Mother's Day fiesta, the Memorial Day picnic at the beach, the Labor Day fishing trip to La Paz along with spending time with his departed loved ones on Dia De Los Muertos. Most of all, he missed seeing his own reflection in her *ojos azules*, the eyes that reminded him of the aquamarine-tinted, unpolluted waters of Punta Mita.

Nuestra Senora de Guadalupe forgive my sins and have mercy on me, he whispers, crossing his body several times. Will he ever have the opportunity to cleanse his soul at the Puerto

Vallarta flower-filled cathedral—la iglesia—that his family has worshipped in for generations.

He wasn't always blindfolded, only when he was left alone at what he suspected was a drug lab. The stump that was his hand had healed relatively well, considering the level of trauma and blood loss. His toenails were also growing back, if slowly. Although his ribs were perpetually sore and he lost tons of weight, it wouldn't be his physical condition that'd cause his imminent demise. If his luck held, it'd be a quick bullet to the back of his head. If not, well, he couldn't go there, not yet.

The prisoner suspected his kidnappers were well prepared for the long haul since they fed him strong antibiotics to treat a life-threatening infection, an infection that raised his temperature so high that he suffered a seizure and had hallucinations. Because in another life he was a medic, he recognized the stink of the meds. He was fortunate it wasn't Keflex, the one antibiotic he was allergic to and that would cause him to go into anaphylactic shock. After he recovered, the hallucinations became visions. He was still strong in both body and spirit, possessing something his *Norte Americano* partner called *bolas de acero*. *Bueno*, he'll soon get the *oportunidad* to see if his balls are really made of steel or egg powder.

As his eyesight dimmed, his other senses sharpened, including the emergence of something his family referred to as *la clarividencia*, the second sight. He couldn't wait to share this recent development, positive that his new gift would bring them much closer. And so he reached out through the walls of his confinement, using prayers as well as walking through her dreams. If anyone could find him, she could. That one, all-consuming, obsessive longing to hold her in his arms, begging her to forgive him, kept him sane. If only she weren't so damn jealous and vengeful, they'd be celebrating their first *Navidad* as a married couple. He'd already bought the ring, a delicate circle of blue diamonds, to match her eyes. He planned on asking her to marry him as soon as the case was finished. *"Muy bien, mijita,* let's try again." This time he spoke in his full voice, repeating over and over: "Find me. *Encuentrame. Salvame. Te necesito. No confíes en el.*

It's two weeks before sacred Yule, the Winter Solstice, and no one's around. I'm facing yet another holiday alone. I'm not in any condition to see my folks—I'm still having bad migraines and Sandi is stuck in rehab with a stubborn kidney infection I'm convinced made worse by the neglectful care she received at the hospital. Lady Katherine's boozing it up in South Florida. Poor Annie and Efren are spending Christmas at the "cult" church retreat. Nate is still MIA, and my hot renter, well, he's been having more drama with his kid than I care to deal with.

I'm better off on my own, prepping for a most interesting Yule, astrologically speaking, that is. Mars will be in Scorpio, sitting right on my Ascendant: whether it'll bring me a jolt of passion or anger, I'm not sure. What I know with a hundred percent certainty is that my fuse may blow at any moment.

The great alignment of the old grouch, Saturn, and Pluto, the dark overlord, promises to shake up everyone's world. For once, I won't be the only one fucked by the stars. It's get real time, folks. The year 2020 should be interesting.

The sole silver lining is that I had proved my special gifts to Art, whether he's made peace with the real me or not. I'm over trying to fit into his neat, little 1950's world. There's so much for me to do. I have to prepare my Yule alter.

After our fateful first date, when my worst suspicions about his motives were confirmed, I asked him to give me some space to process it all and he agreed a little too quickly for my taste. To be fair, I'm still not feeling well enough to throw myself into yet another ill-fated, lust-based affair. My mind keeps drifting back to Carlos: our first few months together, the fun we had dancing, all the hot sex. The guilt of what I've done to him is so overwhelming. Some nights I have no choice but to take a few extra meds just to drift off, something my psychiatrist doesn't like, not at all. Oh well, fuck her. At least I'm sober.

Art's Emery drama is another story. I'm proud of myself. My skills came in handy when I offered to help, although I can't get over how unreasonably upset he got with something my dad would've laughed off, chalking it up to normal teenage hormones. The entire situation just showed me what a right-wing dinosaur Art is. Maybe it's for the best that we never hooked up.

A few days after we have our fight, I go to the front house to ask him about the progress with my car and while he's calling the mechanic, he gets a hysterical call from Emery. The spoiled brat is crying and carrying on, asking him to get her because the kids at a party are popping pills and smoking weed. So I tell him to call her a cab or Uber but he calls his parents who don't drive after the sun sets. I can see he's pissed, but follows my advice, calling her a ride, even though he's huffing and puffing. About an hour later, he bursts into my place, all color drained from his face, looking like he's aged ten years. His usually "chilled to the bitter end cop demeanor" cracking like the asphalt in my driveway.

"My folks just called. Emery never made it home from the party. When the driver got there, she'd already left and now she's missing. Her phone is going straight to voice mail and she's not answering my texts. I called the sheriff and all of my local law enforcement connections. I've been trying to get a flight out, but it's Christmas. I'm getting on the road now, but I won't be able to get there for hours. I won't lose another baby, I can't. Not again. I promised Ann."

"Hey, hey, calm the fuck down," I say. "You're overreacting. Emery will be fine. She probably caught a ride with some boy she's afraid you won't approve of and ran down the phone battery. At her age, I used to do some crazy shit and I survived." I try to reassure him, sounding remarkably like my dad. "No news is good news."

Art says nothing. He just stands there, staring at me as if I'm the one losing my wits. Then he plumps his painfully gorgeous ass on my chair, holds his head with his hands, and says, "That's what I'm afraid of. You haven't turned out exactly normal, have you?"

"Wow, you sure know how to hit below the belt," I say, completely unprepared for his words.

"You see what I mean. We're both aware you haven't had an exactly peaceful normal, life."

"Right."

"You don't need to get defensive, but if your father did his job protecting you from outside influences, you wouldn't have people trying to... I mean, sorry, I'm losing it. Listen, Viv."

"What? Trying to kill me? Why don't you go to hell with your advice? My dad did the best he could.

Wait, I'm actually defending my dad?

"If you can't talk to me with respect, just leave. I'm sorry you're worried about your kid, but that doesn't give you the right to shit all over me."

"You're right. I apologize. I appreciate you were just trying to help. Forgive me?" Art reaches out for my hand, turns it over, placing a sweet kiss right in the middle of my palm, the gesture sending a jolt of energy straight into my heart. Now he's using his charm to get to me, and it's working.

"Fine. Let's agree to disagree on parenting," I bristle, pretending to still be angry. "I was thinking, until we hear from Emery or your folks, do you want me to check her birth chart? I assume you remember the time she was born?"

"Early morning if I recall correctly. Why?"

"If you let me use your laptop, I can find a free astrology software site."

I can check if there's anything obvious that would show danger. I can check the current transits too, I mean, where the planets are today and then cross check with her birth chart. I can also examine the position of the Fixed Stars at Birth for clues. Normally, when I lose something or sense danger, I have Sandi check. Lately, though, she's been pretty out of it. I have studied a little about forensic astrology, but Sandi has used it for decades. She has this book she wants me to read, but as always, shit happens. Wait—I remember now, something about forensics and the Stars. I'll search for the information online. I guess if you're positive about the time Emery left the party, I can cast a chart for the event. Actually, before I get myself frustrated, let's start with the event chart. It'll give us some clues."

If I can't figure it out, I'll try to connect with the spirit, I tell myself but don't say it to Art in case he sees psychic readers as the devil's own.)

"I don't get it."

"You don't need to understand. To be honest, I don't always understand either, but I have good intuition when it comes to astrology. I don't know if you noticed, but I've got this, whatever you want to call it, psychic thing going on, and it's getting stronger. You are aware of something called intuition? You've been in some crazy situations you can't explain, right?"

"Hmm, I see," Art says, shaking his head, taking a few seconds to process before shooting off his mouth, a character trait I find both rare and refreshing. "Come to think of it," he says thoughtfully, "I probably have. I've seen some, what you might call 'situations' that defied logic. Definitely in Iraq. I mean, the day Ann had her accident, I had the worst headache."

"Exactly," I say, trying to keep it light, avoiding asking more questions about his dead wife. "All you have to do is stay open and reserve judgement until you see if and how it actually works. It's pretty complicated. Remember when Sandi asked you to check on me at the beach because she saw danger from drowning? You didn't understand, but you came anyway. And lucky for me, you did."

Then a horrifying image hits me in the gut. What if it wasn't Sandi? What if Art was following me? How will I act if it was him who attacked me in the first place and then for some reason pretended to save me? What if the man in my dreams is my guardian angel trying to warn me about Art?

"Okay." Art seems to agree, if without enthusiasm, not that I expected anything different from a "normie" like him. "Guess, it can't hurt. I'll probably avoid getting stuck in Vegas traffic if I leave right away. Can we do it quickly?"

"I can't promise you a definitive answer, but if you go get your laptop, I'll start right away," I say, my self-confident—some say blowhard—Aries side taking control.

Within a few minutes, Art turns on his laptop and I'm able to find a free site for casting event charts.

"So what time do you figure she left the party?" I ask Art with cool confidence, as if I really knew what I was doing.

"Well, she called me around seven. Let's say around eight. Would you agree?"

"Makes sense. Where was the party?"

"My mom told me dad dropped Emery off before dark. Probably nearby. Try Kamas."

"Right on. Here we go. Let's plug in the data for December 7, 2019, 8 p.m., Kamas, Utah. Come to Mama."

"Viviana, stop making jokes. What do you see?" Art snaps, then gets uncomfortably close to me, placing his hand on my shoulder, looking at the screen as if he's able to understand the Astro-wheel.

"Give me a minute, will you?" I snap back, shrugging off his hand. How does he expect me to concentrate, given the effect his nearness has on my libido?

I try to remember what Sandi taught me. First, examine the Ascendant, the Rising sign. That would represent the person in trouble. Okay. It's Cancer, the Crab. Not too bad. She's not about to drown in Utah. Then let's see where the Moon sign is located and what planet, if any, is causing it harm. The Moon is in feisty Aries placed with Uranus, the rebel, Mr. Volatility himself. No wonder she wouldn't wait for a safe ride and took off, acting out of character. From what I recall, Moon with Uranus means the need to shock, to do things outside the norm, like acting young and stupid. That could be dangerous for an overprotected brat like Emery.

As if Art senses my mood change, he moves away from me and plunks his butt down on the chair.

"It's going to be okay," I say, trying to comfort him. "She's alive. I see nothing that shows otherwise."

"I'm sure. I would know it if she were gone. My heart would stop. You probably won't believe it, or maybe you will, but I physically felt her mom take her last breath even when

I wasn't with her." Art inhales, his even, quiet tone belying the utter heartbreak he must have felt.

Damn, is that what my dad suffered through all the times I was in trouble?

"Let's see if there's any car trouble," I say more to myself, not Art. "Yep. Look at you, sneaky Mars in the 4th house. Some folks say Mars only rules land, property, and shit to do with mothers, right?"

"Are you expecting me to understand what you're asking?"

"Nope. I'm talking to myself. Basically, something went wrong with her ride, probably something mechanical. Wait, Saturn is active too. Hmm. Sometimes Saturn shows dental problems or injury to the knees or even broken bones. Well, the good thing is there's nothing terrible on the cusp of the 7th house, the Descendant. I mean, there's Mars and Pluto, which means a possible attack by a perpetrator."

"What? She was attacked?" Art yells, jumping up.

"Hey, chill, I'm just speculating out loud. No, there's no square."

"Square?"

"The dreaded Mars square Pluto, not exact from what I can see. Wait, do you know if she has a boyfriend or a girl-friend? Nowadays you can't assume she's not a lesbian or a transgender kid."

Art's face shows he's shocked by my question. "Emery is not a lesbian. I'd be the first one she'd tell if she were. What the hell, Viv?"

"You sure about that? The poor thing is probably terrified to tell you when she sneaks a beer, let alone what you'd prob-ably judge as sinful sexual tendencies." My perverted Scorpio side keeps on pushing his buttons.

"Okay, we're done," he says in a huff. "I'm out of here. Clearly, you have wrong ideas about both me and my daughter. I don't know what I was thinking, asking you to behave if not normal at least decently."

Oops, I just crossed that invisible line.

"Shit, I'm sorry. I can be such a pushy bitch. I am truly only trying to help. Sometimes my mouth gets ahead of my intentions."

Art is about to walk out, so I make one last attempt. "Please give me another chance," I plead, following him out of my place, grabbing hold of his arm.

"I've got to go now. I can't deal with your character flaws," he says gravely, refusing to face me. "Have a good Christmas, or whatever nutty holiday you celebrate."

"I understand. I'm going to pray to the Goddess your daughter is found soon and safe." Then a flash of electricity moves up my body, sending chills up my spine as it settles around my neck. "Stop!" I scream. "I see her."

Art stops, turns on his heels, and looks at me with murder in his eyes. "Please. You've got to trust me. I can see her. She's all right, but I need to sit down because I'm about to pass out."

Something in the way I sound makes Art pay attention. He helps me back into the house and gets me a glass of water.

"What do you see?"

"Call your folks and ask them if it snowed."

"All right," he says and makes the call. "Yes, the snow started right after Dad got back," he tells me.

"Good. Then my vision is right. I see the car in a ditch. Does she have a license?"

"Just a permit."

"She was driving. There are two more. Yep, Mercury and the Sun in the 5th house. I feel some pain. They are injured., but not badly. I don't see blood. Wait, the two in the back seat are passed out. "

"Emery?"

"She awake. Freezing. It's her leg."

"Broken?"

"I can't tell, but she can't get out of the car. I see lots of snow. If I'm right about Saturn, then yes."

"Can you see where?"

"No."

"Okay. That's enough information to go on. I'm calling my dad and my buddy at UHP. I pray they'll find the car, but I'm driving there right now."

"You'll find her," I insist, sounding more confident. "She's frightened, but not hysterical."

Now I'm so tuned in that I'm overwhelmed by an energetic pull and hit by an all-too-familiar wave of nausea and pain. Sandi says because I'm not balanced, I'm vulnerable to absorb negative vibes that cause a real physical reaction. That's so lame.

"Of course, she's scared. Not for herself. She fears hurting you. It isn't a kid's job to worry about her parents."

The impressions of Emery I'm getting are so strong that tears pour down my face. "Please don't be angry with her. You're way too tough on her." I say for some dumb reason as if I genuinely care for the girl.

"What the hell, Viv? You are crazy!" Art finally snaps. "Thanks for trying to help, but never tell me how to parent."

Wow, I never expected him to get this angry with me.

"I guess we'll see if your stars are right," he adds, then frowns and walks out. "I'll call you once I get there," he says without turning around.

"Please do. I'll stay awake until I hear from you," I say, trying to reassure him that despite my rough edges, I'm still a good person who cares about him and his kid.

"Up to you," he mumbles, still angry.

Just as well. What was I expecting? Was I too hasty breaking it off with Nate, after all?

Chapter 22

The Winter Solstice, Wicca's sacred Yule, has come and gone without me doing anything I planned. I'm not sure if I'm depressed over Art or, as my dad always warned me, "lazy as a South Florida gator."

Instead of harvesting the traditional log, dusting it with flour, and decorating it with the three candles, cloves, and rosebuds, I've spent the last two weeks in a stupor: eating crap, binge-watching *Law and Order* and *The Walking Dead*, waiting for Art to call, which he hasn't, except for that one call to tell me Emery was safe. I was right: She was driving her two drunk friends home when the car ran into a ditch in a heavy snowfall. Her ankle was broken and she came down with a nasty cold, but otherwise, the kid was all right. I didn't ask when he was coming back, and he didn't offer.

I finally heard from his mechanic pal who'd been working on my car. He told me there's been a delay getting a needed part because my funky diesel is "too old and should be retired."

Since I've got nowhere to go, I've been making food runs to 17th or sitting around on Art's porch studying astrology while drinking loads of dark roast coffee with Leroux French chicory, my family's Christmas gift. (I guess they've been kicking their heels up in New Orleans without me.) It seems like the entire world has left me behind. Funny how I consider the porch as Art's and not mine.

Sandi was moved to a different rehab place in Corona, but we've been talking up a storm. Turns out she's not suffering from dementia. Once her UTI cleared up and her kidneys started working again, all the mental stuff resolved and she went back to being herself, as clever and funny as she was before all the troubles. Was I relieved. She'll be back at her place by New Year's and hopefully my car will be ready, so I can visit. She asked me to spend New Year's Day with her, watching the Rose Parade and the ball games and I said yes. I'm hoping she's finally seen through Jay's bull crap and is ready to make some permanent changes.

I am better. Even my bad dreams about the tortured man haven't been bothering me as much. I guess my concussion is finally healing.

Okay. Enough moping around, I tell myself. *He will not surprise you and come home in time for New Year's Eve. This is dumb. Come on, Viv, let's work on those resolutions early. You know you're better off on your own.*

I decide to start right away by making a to-do list: Take down my fake Christmas tree, store away the silver and white plastic garland, throw away my grandparents' moldy Santa knick-knacks, wash Sandi's Christmas blanket, and take the decorative pillowcases to the cleaners. So far, so good.

Then I scribble a few affirmations in red pen: I promise myself that next year, I'll take Lady Katherine up on her promise to take me somewhere fabulous. I will go back to the gym and lose all this holiday weight. I will forbid myself to dream about Art, Nate, or any other man until Sandi says my chart shows a positive Venus transit. I will see my neurologist and my psychiatrist and ask them to help me with my nightmares. I will save money and take a trip to see my dad.

I'm feeling so good about myself that I continue to scribble down my thoughts: I've got to clear my cupboards and fridge from every crumb of cake, cookies, and chips still lying around. That should take a day or so, then I'll clean out my closets, and give myself a pedicure and a rose facial. I'll get some exercise by walking to the fresh market and buy only non starchy veggies and vegan cheese. Time to clean up my act.

By late afternoon, after a lunch of a Cup o' Noodles and the last bag of salt and vinegar kettle chips, I'm too exhausted to do anything else, so I lay down for a bit, just to rest. I can't tell how long I'm out, but when I open my eyes, I almost have a heart attack from fright. Someone is standing by the door and I can't see who it is because it's dark. All I can smell is fear and malevolence.

"Help! Rape!" I scream at the top of my lungs, the adrenaline sending my pulse sky high, giving me a jolt far stronger than a gram of coke, then realize I'm aware of who this is. It's the nightmare man. I'm still asleep or in a dream state.

"Who are you and what do you want from me?" I demand of the apparition, sick and tired of his games. "I'm a medium for the dead." No response. "Tell me who you are or go to hell, where you probably came from."

"You know me. Find me. Help me. We're running out of time."

Did I really just hear a voice or did he get into my crazy head and I'm hallucinating? Maybe the damn Chinese put some weird shrooms into my soup.

"Okay. I can play this game too," I say. "Tell me where you are, and I'll find you."

"Hurry, *mi amor, mi tesoro*. I'm close. *No mas tiempo*."

"Stop it! Just stop," I sob, my heart pouncing out of my chest. "I'm no one's treasure."

"Hurry..."

With that last word, the man or whatever he was dissolves into nothingness and I will myself to wake up. It's dark, but I had left the lights on in the kitchen. I'm cold and hot at the same time, my left hand is numb from lying on it. All I want is to drink my nerves numb. I get up, turn the rest of the lights on, and take a quick shower. I want out of here. It's drizzling, but I don't care. I put on my boots and my old leather jacket and leave the house. Any place on 17th will do, even a bar.

It takes me only 15 minutes to reach the Harp, the last authentic Irish pub around. I walk straight into the bar, wet like an old chicken, my bones rattling, terror drying my mouth, positive I'll be spending the next few hours poisoning my liver and hating my guts.

Paranoid as usual, I peer around, noticing a familiar rush I get anytime I step into a drinking establishment. It's still early, and the place is mercifully quiet: Perhaps I can still get something to eat, like fried zucchini or chicken tenders or a juicy barbecue burger with onion rings. Or I can order that big Irish breakfast with baked beans and blood sausage. They serve it all day. If I can get my blood sugar up, I can skip the hassle and the guilt of falling off the wagon.

Something in my peripheral vision snaps me out of my reverie. Oh crap. It's Nate, and he sees me. That's all I need. Another fucking loser. He looks like shit and that makes me feel better. Why should I be the only one suffering? What did I see in him in the first place? He's so not Art. I watch in slow motion as he approaches, dressed in the usual stupid Tommy Bahama shirt and cargo shorts, his head covered by a Raider's team beanie. He's unshaven, his expression almost menacing. Nate, menacing? I must be really losing it and WTF with the beanie? He thinks he's a teenager. Shorts in December? What I thought was him being casually comfy is really him being an immature idiot.

"You're back," I say, sounding as composed as I can. "I haven't seen you since before Thanksgiving."

He makes a lukewarm attempt to pacify me. "I am, I mean, I've been back. Happy Holidays, Viv. I was going to call you, but..."

I interrupt, sounding suspiciously bitter. "But what? Broken fingers? Lost your phone? Sick kid? Crazy ex? Got busted for DUI again?"

"Well, based on our last communication, I didn't guess you fucking cared," he responds, not exactly sounding like his usual, easygoing Sagittarius self.

"I don't."

I'm sure I don't care, so how come I'm biting his head off? Go figure.

"Yeah, that's what I thought. Still hooking up with the cop?" Nate asks, lowering his voice and giving me a dirty look as if I'm not wearing clothes.

"Who I'm seeing is none of your fucking business," I say, ignoring the comment about Art *(Wait, how did he know about Art and his being a retired cop?)*. "But no, for your information, I'm not seeing anyone. I'm totally free and for once ready to focus on my personal growth, my sobriety, and my joy."

So there!

"I don't give a shit about your personal growth, but I can see you're working really hard on your sobriety. You sure found a perfect place, a bar." he says with a sarcastic cackle.

Something in his laughter causes shivers to run up and down my spine. Who is this guy? I've heard this laughter before. My psychic sleuth awakens. I decide to follow my hunch, change my tone and investigate further.

"That wasn't nice, Nathan. I thought we were friends. What happened to you in Lancaster? Did something go wrong with your son?" I say, taking another approach. I can tell it's working because Nate's expression has changed. Now he looks more like old Nate.

He offers an apology, softening his tone. "Sorry, Viv. You're right. I guess my ego got a little bruised when you dropped me."

"I didn't drop you. I like you very much. It was just, you understand, our timing was off. The planets didn't align, and you have your hands full with being a dad. I mean, I get it. I guess I got jealous," I lie. "You get me: I don't have the easiest of personalities."

"I wouldn't say that," he says and finally smiles, showing off his dimple. "You know what? You're right. We are friends, so how about we wish each other happiness and hug it out?"

"You bet." I sat, smiling back. "Let's start the year right, friend." I give him a hug, smelling whiskey and weed on his clothes. "How about you buy me a nonalcoholic ginger beer and something to eat."

***

Several hours later, after I eat myself into a fried food coma, we end up at his apartment. The place is dark and smells like rat shit, but I'm too lonely to care. Nate gorges on edibles and I get sex. Afterward, instead of cuddling, Nate goes on and on about this major business opportunity to buy some cryptocurrency that will make him a bundle. When I don't seem to care, he gets irritated and says it's the only way he can gain custody of his kid. Then he tells me I shouldn't trust Sandi's gift of the house. When I disagree, he switches his strategy and plays with my boobs, twisting my nipples and telling me I'm not getting younger and not exactly employable. Why don't I plan for my future and get in on the deal? He swears on his kid if I come up with something he calls a seed investment of, let's say half a million dollars, we both are guaranteed to become rich and can take off for some island. When I laugh, assuming he's kidding, he gets furious.

"I figured you were, you know, smart, psychic, always talking about planets and shit. No wonder you're always counting every penny!" he yells. "Five hundred thou is nothing. I'm around guys selling their Newport houses and buying as many coins as they can. We can make ten times our investment. One Bitcoin was thirty bucks just a few years ago, and now it's selling for tens of thousands. Ask your fucking charts or cards."

"Are you crazy? I don't use spirit for getting rich schemes." I say, finally putting an end to his pipe-dreaming Neptunian dribble. "I don't even get what you're talking about, and even if I did, where would I get that kind of money?" I feel the heat rising off my back and I'm becoming angry. This fucker is pushing my buttons.

"You must have saved some money when you were dancing," he insists.

"I did, but that that money is long gone. I haven't danced in ten years." What do you think I've been living off?

"What about your ex, the older guy, the one who was a major player with the Mexicans? He must've been in the middle of a big deal when he died."

"Glenn? Wait. How do you know about Glenn's business?" My stomach goes into a spasm. I push his hands off of me and jump up. "I've never said a word to you about my ex."

"Sure, you did. How else would I remember details about him? You're the one who told me you met him when you were dancing. He wanted you to stop, so you did, and then he brought you into his world. You said you lived with him in Laguna Beach and that he was loaded and then you almost died in the car accident that killed him."

"I did not."

"Damn, Viv. Now I'm worried. That concussion you had has really messed up your head." Then he adds, faking concern, "You need to speak with your doctor about the memory loss. Want me to go with you? Concussions can affect the memory."

"I didn't tell you about my concussion either." And then it hits me. I truly don't know shit about this guy, and I suspect if I keep pushing it tonight, I may find out something I'm not yet ready to deal with.

"Yeah, you're right," I say, pretending to seem confused, putting my hand to my forehead.

Goddess, just let me live though tonight, and I'll ask Art to check this worm out when he gets back from his holiday cruise.

"My mind hasn't been right since Thanksgiving," I say, agreeing with Nate, praying my acting gene kicks in. "Sorry, babe. Of course, I must have told you about him. I tell everyone everything about my past. It's those damn 12-step meetings, blah-blah-blah. You're right about my memory, though: brain fog. You know me, such a ditz." Making a cute face, I return to bed, hoping he believes I believe him. Just to be sure, I ask if he wants a nice, long BJ.

"Ah, you're so sweet and I like how you do oral, but I'd feel guilty. You sound tired," he says, smiling, back to his usual easygoing self. "I have an idea: Why don't I make you a cup of that tea you gave me and then we'll get some shut-eye. I've got a lot going on with the crypto deal. Let's talk about it more in the morning. You'll see, this is an amazing opportunity for us to move to the next level in our relationship. I've missed you."

"I'd love some tea," I say and smile. I pretend to yawn but I'm fully awake thanks to the fight-or-flight adrenaline jolt. More lousy sex I don't need. Come to think of it, nor do I want to continue this relationship, let alone move it to the next level. Missed me? Bull!

I don't recall drifting off, but when I come to, it's the middle of the day. The dirty plastic blinds are broken, so the bright light hits the bed just in the right spot to get me up. Nate is nowhere around. There is no note or messages left on my phone. I'm more groggy than usual and have a dull headache. I'm sure I didn't take a drink, not even a beer, and I forgot my sleep meds at home. This was odd.

Dragging myself up, I go into the bathroom and use the filthy toilet. Thank goodness for working on my quads. The place also stinks of black mold. Since I'm allergic to black mold, I promptly get dizzy. Even I am not crazy enough to take a shower here, so I put on last night's clothes and go snooping. The place is a mess. It doesn't look like he's been living here at all and the other two bedrooms are empty too. There's no coffee or tea or even a beer. He must have used the last tea bags last night. The fridge is empty too. I pour myself a glass of water straight from the faucet and throw up. Did he slip me something after we did it so I would pass out? The tingling in my hands must mean something shady took place.

My mind drifts back to last night's creepiness. For once, sex wasn't good. To be honest, it stunk. With Nate, it's never been great, but this time something felt even more off. I don't even think we kissed.

"Now, slow down, Viviana. There must be a logical explanation," I say out loud. Could be he's still pissed off about you dumping him or he's serious about the money he thinks you can get him. Nah, he's just a pothead Archer."

Then I realize we've never really made love when he wasn't using. I remember in the beginning, when I was a little smitten, asking him to do it sober, but he just laughed it off. He wasn't mad or anything, just completely insolent. Why didn't I see all the little warning signs? Because I never do. I'm too damn desperate for male attention.

I mean, I wasn't exactly honest with him either. I used the few minutes of lousy banging to fantasize about Art. Before I leave, I check inside the hall closet and that's when I'm convinced Nate is not right in the head and it has nothing to do with him being stressed out over his kid. I see duct tape, ropes, boxes with needles, serious drugs paraphernalia, bondage crap, a few unrecognizable instruments that look like surgical instruments that gave off a strong topo scent. Was it blood? Fuck. I've got to get out. Now. I grab my purse and take off but run straight into one of Nate's roommates, the small Indian-looking kid whose name I can never remember.

"Whoa! my man said you may be up by now. Where do you think you're going?"

"I have a doctor's appointment and I'm late. Tell Nate I'll bring dinner around eight." I try to respond coolly, hoping he notices my resolve.

"Right. Not going to happen."

"Get out of my way." I say, raising my voice, narrowing my eyes, giving him my warning stare.

"What's the rush, you crazy bitch?" he says, grinning menacingly. His expression shocks the hell out of me. "Turn around and get back into bed. Nate asked me to keep you here until he gets back. And if you get bored, let me know. I hear you're pretty handy with your mouth for an old slut."

"What did you just call me, you limp dick, towel head? Get the fuck out of my way, or I'll cut you!" I yell, hoping to shock him right back with my racist rant, my adrenaline kicking in as it usually does when I realize I'm screwed, and that's when he slugs me in the jaw, sending me to the ground.

"Is that all you've got, you, stinking man-gina!" I yell, grabbing his lower legs and shoving him backward. I'm strong and I've done this maneuver before. He goes down hard, hitting his head on the door jamb. It makes an awful snapping sound.

Shit, I think I just broke his neck.

I get up, tasting blood inside my cheek. I approach carefully and check to see if he's still kicking. Now that he knocked some sense into my stubborn, trusting head, I'm prepared to hit back harder if needed. Unnecessary. He's out.

Grabbing my stuff, I ignore the pain in my face and practically run all the way home. I'm praying the cop friend Art asked to watch me is around. I search for an unmarked car. No such luck. I have to do something before Nate catches on or someone discovers the Indian kid. I know I can't stay at the house and I still don't have my car. I panic. I need to call the cops, but something stops me. I can't admit I was at Nate's without getting into a shitload of trouble if that dick wad is dead. And then it hits me: Why was Nate so desperate to keep me at his place, enough to bring in a reinforcement?

I don't have money to lend him, but he doesn't seem to get it. And what was he saying about Glenn? I feel like our conversation came straight out of that new show I stumbled on, *The Ozarks*. I need to grab a change of clothes and get the heck out of Dodge, as my dad would say.

That makes me think of my dad and decide to call him, but then I think why? What can he do other than bitch me out and say I told you so? I dial Art's phone instead, knowing he won't pick up. I leave a dumb message, rattling on about needing help, suspecting Nate, and missing him. Naturally, I keep the incident with the roommate to myself. He doesn't call back. It figures. He's probably sunning his gorgeous bod on a beach, drinking margaritas.

About an hour later, when I'm fully awake, I get some food into my gut, swallowing several cups of chicory coffee and an entire Heath Bar. Then a brilliant thought hits me. I need a psychic reading. There's a small place not too faraway that Nate would know nothing about. I can take a bus and then walk the rest of the way. Then, I stop myself, recalling vividly the last time I had a psychic reading, the one that ended in a nasty fight, topped by the loss of a friend, if Jackie was ever a friend. Fuck psychic readers and their lies. What I need is to shadow Nate, a Glock 26, and a pair of cajones. Now I'm cooking, but have to be smart and check with today's planets for directions. I grab my planetary calendar and write out the transits for the next 24-hour period.

First, I make sure there's nothing life-threatening falling over my Sun or Moon, something like Mars-Uranus or Mars-Pluto fighting each other and me, kind of like the *Clash of the Titans*. I used to have a major crush on Harry Hamlin in that Greek tunic.

Here we go again. Focus, Viv, focus! Damn brain fog.

Okay. I'm back: basically, negative meetings between Mars and the other two planetary villains touching my chart can signal being attacked. Sandi uses it to predict a probability of any type of violent confrontation. That goes double for me because the God of War is the most important planet in my life, what you can call my Cosmic Boss, me being Sun sign Aries and a Rising sign of Scorpio, both ruled by Mars, Mars being involved with head injuries, like my propensity for concussions. One more knock on the head and I'll be toast. I snicker. Actually, more like a veggie.

Chapter 23

No matter how hastily I glance at the daily planetary chart and decide on a plan of action, the late-afternoon light fades into a deep gray fog that resembles the furry coat of a field mouse. It makes me miss Lady Katherine. I haven't been called *mausi* for ages. I wonder if she's back home at the beach. Damn, I miss the beach, despite almost drowning. I even miss Annie's scowl.

"Focus, Viv, focus," I command myself again, this time in full voice. If I'm to solve the mystery of why Nate was so weird, going as far as sending his roommate to keep me at his place, I need to go back there and sniff around, naturally in disguise. Hopefully, the jerk-off came to and left to get some medical attention. Suddenly, I get that feeling, that special Scorpio tingling all over my skin anytime I put my nose where it doesn't belong.

Let's see: Whom shall I be tonight? Clearly not Chrissy. I think I need to retire Chrissy. I'm getting too old for her she-nanigans. How about someone no one wants to see, let alone remember? Then it comes to me: I'll dress like a street bum. No one wants to see the homeless, let alone smell them. Sandi, who knows random crap, told me she read somewhere that the brain of a regular person looks through someone homeless as if they aren't even human, just a lifeless object. I believe it. I was only on the streets once and only for a few days before Daddy found me, but I learned well what it means to be invisible. Luckily, I was so high that my mind blocked the memory of most of what happened. I recall it being scorching hot and wanting to pee so bad that I did it right in the parking lot of a 7-Eleven, in front of others. There is no place for modesty or human dignity on the streets. Looking back, I think that was when I hit rock bottom. I don't understand how folks survive, some for years on end. I mean, I've had plenty of friends go through a spell of bad luck and end up a throwaway, but the majority don't make it out alive. That's why no matter what, I'll be forever grateful to Sandi for making sure I'll always have a roof over my head. Note to self: MUST STAY CLEAN!

Now glad that I haven't showered since yesterday, and just to be authentic, I pull out some not-so-fresh underpants and stinky socks from the wicker basket I use for dirty clothes. There is a silver lining to being lazy and not doing laundry. I'll just have to get used to my own B.O.

The bum getup is no problem: I'm a pack rat with piles of old shit anyway so I have plenty of choices. I quickly decide on the pair of forest-green-and-red, Christmas-plaid, heavy wool pants for inspiration. When I peek inside, I notice a large, mostly faded Marshall Field's label. I didn't even know I had these pants hanging under some moth-eaten sweaters. Marshall Field's: That brings back memories of my fastidious, ladylike grandma, who'd always make an annual birthday trek to her hometown, Chicago, to buy things she told me could only be found at Marshall Field's. I wonder what she'd think of Amazon and the ease of buying anything, anytime, and at low cost. Or it could be that the pants once belonged to a fancy-ass gal, probably from the Midwest. That's why I probably picked up the dumb pants, most likely in a Salvation Army store. I don't know why I'm trying to cling to illusions of a happy childhood. Goddess knows, I have plenty of unhappy memories.

The bad news is that now that I'm not loaded, the plaid pants are hideous, but the good news, the waist is huge, falling-off huge. Wow, I must've lost at least twenty pounds since I stopped drinking. If I'm about to die, at least I'll look good for the viewing if they find my body. That thought sends a surge of electric energy up and down my arms, meaning it's a real possibility. Before choosing what top to wear, I use a man's tie to cinch the waist of the pants.

"It must be Glenn's," I whisper. Just saying his name makes me nauseous.

Carlos was never one for dressing up. Out of the blue, I remember his gorgeous, sexy grin and my eyes get suspiciously blurry. I rub my eyes dry and locate several musty-smelling sweaters, damaged by time and bugs. I end up piling one on top of the other, the colors clashing with each other and the pants. Good thing it's getting cold. I find a perfectly tattered, full-length wool coat at least two sizes too large for my new sexy bod, and a horribly stained knitted cap. Most of my shoes aren't exactly glamorous or new, so that's a simple choice. I put on my favorite pair of tattered, grungy Toms flats, marveling about how long I've been able to wear them.

When I pull the coat out, I notice a carton that was covered by the long coattails. When I open it, I find a long-lost, gray-haired witch's wig. I wore the wig back in the days when having Halloween drug and booze parties was the highlight of my year. I suspect the wig is a gift from the Goddess herself because it is the perfect cherry on top of my character cake.

What shall I call this alternative version of me? Hmm. Whom do I hate right now? Jackie! Hello world, meet Jackie.

Normally, I'd try to clean and comb out the matted wig fibers the best I could, but that wouldn't serve my purpose. I slick back my unwashed purple mop, put on the wig, and decide to add more props. I need bags. I think Sandi left her entire collection of Trader Joe's reusable bags under my kitchen sink. I'm right. I sing out the line from *Poltergeist*: "They're here." (When I was a kid, I hated that movie. Howie Jr. used to make me watch it over and over, just to see me pee myself from fright. He only stopped after I threw up a box of Cheez-Its crackers all over the sofa and Daddy took a belt to his mean ass.)

Within a few minutes, my new persona emerges. Yes! I appear and smell disgusting. What else? For good measure, after I lock the front door, I smudge my entire face and hands with real dirt from Art's mostly empty herbal pots, smearing dog poop someone left on the lawn on the bottom of my Toms. Finally satisfied that this is the best I can do, I take a deep, calming breath in and exhale. Even Art the cop wouldn't recognize me now. I borrow Sandi's metal pull cart, stuff the bags with trash, papers, and leftover takeout food cartons and pile them in the cart, set on my quest for truth, and if my luck holds, revenge, or at least Cosmic justice. I try to push aside memories of what happened the last time I followed one of my crazy plans.

This time, it'll be different, I reassure myself.

Retracing my steps back to Nate's rental is easy. I'm glad it's foggy and dark. No one is around the neighborhood. I mean, no one is nuts enough to walk to restaurants and bars, although the holiday car traffic on 17th is insane. I wish I could grab a Sidecar doughnut and a cup of something sweet and hot, like an Irish coffee with plenty of scotch. I'm shivering underneath my rags, mostly from excitement and a little from the temperature drop. It's turned windy and wet. Good. I'll appear even more pathetic. Sure enough, a trendily dressed young Asian couple is walking toward me just as I turn left onto Nate's street. I know I should ignore them, but when have I ever done what I should? I decide to have some fun by yelling out obscenities and sexual slurs, moving aggressively toward the girl. The horrified couple takes off, crossing the street without looking at me. That made me feel better. At least I have possible witnesses if I get pummeled.

Enough fun and games, Viviana. You are on a discovery mission, I remind myself. Nate's apartment is a little unusual for our neighborhood; it's more like a private residence, but that's why I always liked it. He rents a three-bedroom cottage, set smack in the middle of a group of one-story bungalow-style houses. Most of the bungalows, covered by unruly vegetation, have seen better days, making the entire setup very private and not in keeping with the east side Costa Mesa hipster set.

I approach slowly, bending over as if I have a hump in case someone inside is watching. Interesting. Nate's place is completely dark. Even the front porch light is off. I turn my head right and left several times, waiting for an occasional car to pass by. As I move toward the back entrance, the light rain turns into a downpour, as bands of showers flow right off the ocean. I take out a plastic bag and put it over my knitted cap. Why in the hell not? I hide in the bushes near the kitchen window, patiently waiting for something, but nothing happens, not for a while.

Then, suddenly, the lights go on in almost every window. It must be close to dinnertime. Folks are home after a miserable commute. I'm about to give up when I hear the roar of a massive engine. Overcome by dread and a warning gurgle in my stomach, I give myself one more chance to back off, recognizing that what is about to happen is a game changer. Why does it always feels like a poorly acted *Law and Order* episode every time something bad happens to me?

Inside Nate's place, the light goes on. There must be an automatic setting. Slowly I creep toward the street to take a peek at the vehicle making all that noise, wondering if the second of Nate's roommates showed up, scared out of my wits, heart in my throat. Thank God, I mean Goddess, Nate doesn't drive. I rub the raindrops from my eyes and realize what I assumed was a large truck isn't that at all. It's a car, and what a car: a gorgeous black, no, dark maroon, Maybach sedan is parked in front, right by the entrance to Nate's apartment. I recognize the lines, pure class and elegance. Honestly, it looks more like a sculpture than a mode of transportation. Who said only men have hots for cars?

Way back when we first hooked up, before all the trouble with his cartel "partners," Glenn drove a black Maybach. He was thrilled with everything the car represented: a rare, standout, ultra-luxurious brand that regular folks didn't even know existed. Not getting the usual wowed response, he asked me what I thought, so I lied, rolling my eyes, pretending I didn't care. Just to rattle his chain, I told him it was a pretentious, insanely overpriced toy for guys with "small assets." Then I made it clear, I was pretty used to all those fancy bells and whistles because many of my "fans" drove luxury cars. Later on in our relationship, he confessed that my response made him determined to prove me wrong. Of course, he made a point to help me appreciate how much the car set him back.

"I could've bought a Bentley or a Maserati, but they're a dime a dozen in Orange County," he'd said.

Blah-blah-blah. Asshole. There are rules to this game, namely when you're doing business with a cartel, you keep a low profile.

Someone turns off the engine and opens the door. I crouch down behind the bush, keeping myself in the shadows, hardly breathing. I see a tall, broad-shouldered man dressed in what I think of as "Vegas douche style." He's wearing a heavily studded black, leather jacket with a flashy animal embroidery design, sleek black leather jeans, and high-heeled neon-blue lizard boots. Since I've been around players and such with serious money, I can appreciate the crazy cost of Philipp Plein leather, plus I'd been gifted a sleek, borderline skanky LBD or two from the same label back in my Vegas dancing days. Even though I've lost tons of weight, nowadays I couldn't pull one of those dresses over my thighs.

I can't make out the Maybach owner's face, but I would stake my life on it: He's as gorgeous as his car.

Shit, and here I look like a bag lady. Wait. What are you thinking?

Before the man turns around, he bends over and extends his hand to someone. I see a shiny high-heeled black boot with a red sole, then the face of the woman belonging to the boot. Man, she looks familiar. What the heck? It can't be. She looks like that Vietnamese gal who told her girlfriend that Carlos was too cheap to sleep with, the one from the tavern.

Knock it off, Viv. This is racist. Not all Asians look alike...

And then the woman laughs. Yep, it's her. I will never forget that flirtatious laugh and that chimney-black horse-tail extensions; they must be extensions. Unreal. Then the man in the Plein biker jacket turns toward me and I almost pass out looking at his familiar—terrifyingly so—features. He is bold, clean shaven, and harshly good looking, with a deadly expression and that undeniably life-threatening scowl. It's my ex, Glenn, returned from hell itself.

I rub my eyes again, biting down on my lower lip hard enough to draw blood. It can't be. A dizzy spell followed by nausea hits me right in the gut. I saw the pictures of his bashed-in brain and broken body. The cops forced me to identify him, even though I was banged up pretty badly and lying in the hospital.

Breathe. In, out, in, out...

No way. It can't be Glenn. This man is at least two decades younger. And then the truth hits me in the face, and I am certain what my delusional brain has been hiding for months. It isn't Glenn, it's Nate. How? Why? Who? The questions crowd my shocked mind. I've got to pull myself together. I'm so screwed.

Something in the way the guy I now believe is Nate is looking at the young woman tells me they are not a love match. He whispers something in her ear and she winces, then grabs onto his arm. He twists away and pushes her toward the house by the neck. Looking back, then to both sides of the street, Nate clicks the button on his keys, locking the Maybach.

Now that I'm positive I've been played, an icy calmness settles over me, as if I'm not the one operating my body. I wait. I can't hear or see what's happening inside. Time stands still. I close my eyes and ask the Goddess for guidance. I see light and then I hear a voice. The trunk is not actually closed. There's something not right with it. I'm taking a chance, but I also have an out in case Nate comes out. I'm just a looney, old, homeless woman looking to steal something. I approach quickly and press the trunk lock button. It opens. The idiot probably forgot to check the battery or the actuator is malfunctioning. Glenn used to have this problem all the time.

You'd think a car that costs more than a house would have a better trunk mechanism. My decision is made.

A while later, I hear the front door open and close. The pair emerges with Nate carrying a large dark travel duffle. Whatever is inside is heavy: probably weapons or a major shipment of something illegal and expensive. I've got to do something. My opportunity comes when Nate clicks the open button and shoves the duffle into the massive trunk, telling his gal friend something I can't make out. Now that whatever he removed from the apartment is safely in the trunk, Nate relaxes enough to raise his voice. Good. I need information about where they're going. I move closer, stabbing the front of my foot on something sharp, those old flats not offering any protection. Quickly, I put my hand to my mouth to stifle the sound.

"Where I go?" I hear the gal plead in poor English.

"Not my problem. Go to hell, for all I care."

"Why you mean to me?" she asks.

She doesn't give up easily, I'll give her that much.

"I help you when you ask me. I take a chance. What you ask, I do: I need money. My kid needs food. You and me, we go inside. I give you good sex," she says with a pout, tossing her hair side to side in a well-practiced move, trying to hold on to Nate.

Bad move, honey. Your charms are lost on this dude, that's if he's anything like Glenn.

"Listen carefully, you little whore. I don't have time for your BS. I told you, scram. Disappear. Go back to Vietnam or wherever else no one can find you or I'll make you disappear. But first, I'll make sure it'll hurt. One more word and I'll get to your kid. In fact, he's more valuable than you when it comes to sex."

"No. You leave my boy alone. I go. Just give a little money and I go."

Bad move, honey.

To shut her up, Nate hits her hard in the stomach and she goes down like a sack of rice.

Geez, I guess Nate is not a nice guy after all, I think. *It seems Nate is the one the man in the dreams was warning you about, not Art. I've got to figure this out. Here's your chance, Viv.*

Since Nate is still preoccupied with his companion, I wait until a large SUV slowly passes by, leaving Sandi's cart well hidden in the bushes. Quickly I crawl over to the back of the Maybach, open the trunk halfway, and get in. I roll to my side in a fetal position, pushing the duffle to the side, closing the trunk. One thing about these super-luxury cars, they sure don't make a lot of noise. The trunk smells like weed and shit. Or is it me? Once we get going, I'll try Art again. Just his name brings a rush of emotions. I can't believe how I misjudged him. I should've trusted Sandi when she told me he was the right man for me, and now I'll probably never see him again.

Sandi... what if... stop. No more ifs. As Daddy always says: no guts, no glory. In just a few minutes, Nate turns on the engine and off I go to meet my Alpha Centauri destiny once and for all.

Chapter 24

ate's been driving for a while. By now, I'm having doubts about my plan. I can't tell where we're going but based on the high-speed flow of traffic at this time of night, we're going south, toward San Diego. The freeways inland or to LA would be parking lots. I keep my eyes closed, trying to astral-project out of my cramped, nausea-filled body.

Without warning, Nate slams on the breaks and I roll over the duffle. I decide the stench isn't me. After all, it's coming from the bag. I take out my phone and use the flashlight feature to poke around. The zipper is stuck on something. I pull and tug, realizing I probably need a special incantation for moving stuck energy. Incantations are what I most love about being a part of the magical Wicca world, not the only thing, but definitely most useful when I need some other-worldly helping hand to get the job done safely and quickly. Unfortunately, I don't have time for proper prep like fasting and lighting candles, but magic is all about intention, right? Let's see, what do I use for stuck zippers? Not sure, but the duffle must have some money or drugs that make money and I've used money spells before, just not successfully. At least I ought to try? First, I imagine lighting a bright green candle, then I say three times, keeping my eyes closed: money surrounds me, money astounds me, money rushes toward me. I open my eyes, turn on my phone light again and pull. Nada. Clearly, it's not the right spell. How about I try something to find what's been lost. Could Nate have put something that belongs to me in the duffle? I think I wrote this one down on a piece of paper I carry in my wallet because I'm always losing stuff. I open my Coach cross-body bag that has seen better days, reach inside the middle pocket, and find a red paper scrap. Even with the phone light, I still can't make out what I wrote because I used a fucking pencil. Where are my damn readers? There, on the bottom, stuck to gum. Double damn: One of the lenses is missing. It isn't Mercury Retrograde again, or is it?

Finally, I give up and pull on the offensive zipper with all my strength and it gives. Who needs spells, anyway? I open the duffle, clenching my teeth to face what's inside. What the heck? It looks like a dark wig. So, I reach in and shine my light on it. FUCK! The wig belongs to a human head with glassy eyes open and the head belongs to Nate's roommate, the Indian guy whom I left passed out after he hit his head on the door jamb. Wait, but where is the rest of him? Oh my God. I killed him! I've got to get out of the trunk before Nate stops to dump the body and realizes I've been tailing him.

Pull yourself together, Viv. You've been through worse.

Hmmm, not really. This is homicide. Who'd believe me, an ex druggie over a clean-cut, innocent looking IT millennial? Daddy was right about me. He was convinced I would end up with a life sentence. A crazy idea stops my oncoming panic attack. The next time Nate stops, I'll throw out the head and get inside the duffle. Can I do that? Probably not. What I can do is hide way in the back and pray I'm invisible. Right. The car stops, but I don't have time to close the zipper. Maybe it's for the best. It'll keep Nate busy as I scream, hopefully scaring the bejesus out of him until I zap him with my trusted old Vexor MK-3 bear spray (What? You think I'm really nuts to go on a mission without self-protection?) and run for my life.

Several minutes go by and I realize Nate isn't opening the trunk. It's now or never. I try to ignore the head in the duffle and slowly open the trunk just to check my surroundings. My gut is telling me I'm in no immediate danger and I trust my gut more than anyone else. I open the trunk wide enough and get out. Nate has parked the car at the side of a small, one-story ranch house. I check around carefully, reminding myself that I'm still in full homeless gear just in case someone comes out. The residential neighborhood street is dark and quiet as I walk to my left, noticing with relief that an almost identical ranch one-story next door is all boarded up. Where am I? I should probably go over to the corner to check the street name. The fog is as thick as milk and that tells me I'm in an area within ten miles or so off the coast. An elderly man, wearing a windbreaker and a fisherman's cap, shuffles slowly toward me. He's accompanied by a dog dressed in a sweater. I try to cross the street, but the dog, some type of beagle mix, howls.

"Hi there." I say, trying to sound more normal than I appear.

"Good evening, miss," the man says, surprising me with a friendly smile. He must be blind or suffer from some form of dementia. "Hell of a night for a walk," he observes, "but my Gus here, he doesn't care. Are you new to our street?"

I engage him, hoping he can tell me where I am. "I wish. What a quaint street. I just love your jacarandas, especially when they bloom."

"Sorry to disagree, but we hate jacarandas. You should see the mess and the stains on our cars," the man complains while his pet is trying to hump my leg, clearly attracted by my scent. "Are you lost? You need directions?"

"Nope," I say, smiling. "Thank you kindly. My boyfriend left me at the corner. We had a minor disagreement if you get what I mean. I thought I'd drop in on some old friends."

"Oh, sure, me and Karen used to fight from morning to night. Now that she's passed, I miss our own little disagreements."

"Sorry about your loss."

"It's okay. I've been a widower for a while. I'm kind of used to it. Now I do what I want, go where I want."

"I understand. Like I said, I needed to cool off. I used to have friends living close by, but I can't remember the address. I remember the trees, though. I guess my memory, or my eyes, aren't what they used to be." I chuckle, finally being honest.

"Join the party," the man says, laughing along. "Two cataract surgeries and night blindness."

Well, that explains him calling me "miss."

"I think my friends lived in that yellow house," I say, waving behind me to the house next to the one Nate was at. I'm not sure he can see my gesture, "but it looks abandoned."

"Could be. There was a couple living there, but they were renters," he says. "The house has been empty for a while, at least a year."

"Shoot. That's too bad. Yeah, it's been a while since I've been over here," I say, trying to come up with a plausible explanation.

"Nowadays, it don't pay to rent. Rents are cheap. It's the investors who are coming in, grabbing whatever they get their dirty paws on so they can build, what do they call them? Oh yeah, mega-mansions. They sure offer crazy money to all of us. Well, screw them. I have a pension and my SSI. I'm going to die in my own bed."

"Why is that?" I ask, playing dumb. "I've been mostly living in Reno."

"Why? That's easy: location, location, location. Have you seen home prices in Encinitas and Carlsbad? Anywhere costal brings mega bucks."

"Ah, that makes sense." Now I realize where Nate took me and the head in the duffle. I was right. We're in North San Diego County.

"Me and Karen moved here to Vista from San Diego when I left the navy. That was in the '70s. We still had more avocado trees than jacarandas. Karen calls them purple menaces." He speaks of the past like it was yesterday, luckily giving me more information than I hoped for.

"Nice. I love avocados," I say nodding, my mind spinning, trying to remember if I know someone, anyone, in Vista. "Well, it's been nice chatting with you. Reminds me of times when folks were friendly. I'm going to call my boyfriend and apologize for my temper. I'm sure he's not far."

"You're smart. I can tell you from personal experience, you never can predict how much time you have left with your loved ones. I have so many regrets. It's sure been real nice talking with you. You take care, young lady, and thanks for listening to a lonely old man. Let's go home, Gus."

Out of the blue, I shock myself by giving the old man a quick hug, hoping he won't notice how I smell. (Mostly the old ones don't, because if they did, who could live in those God-awful retirement homes?)

He squeezes back, then shocks me by pointing to the road: "Here's another scum bag investor in a fancy car," adding bitterly, "I wonder who else he bullied out of their home." The car passing by is the Maybach with Nate in the driver's seat and most likely the severed head in the trunk.

"Have a nice evening," I say, trying to end our conversation, desperate to snoop around the house now that I know Nate's gone.

"You too, young lady. If you need anything, my house is the one with the Nativity scene, just ahead," he says, rattling on and getting on my raw-as-they-are nerves. "Can you believe it's past Christmas? Still, I hate to take it down since I don't get trees anymore."

"Thanks. I'll be fine." I start to walk away.

"Karen was sure strong in her faith. Did I tell you she was a good Catholic girl? Me? Nope. I'm not much with the priests and nuns and the rules. Say, how'd' you like a cup of coffee?"

"Sorry, it's too late for coffee," I say, shaking my head, "but thanks again. I'm sure my boyfriend will come and get me, but if not, I'll call an Uber."

Crap. I feel bad for cutting him short. He seems genuinely hospitable. Man, I hope one lonely night, he doesn't invite in the wrong kind of street person.

"Uber, you say. That's what my granddaughter says: Don't drive Papa, get an Uber. Beats me why she thinks some dope-smoking stranger is safer than me."

Damn, he won't shut up.

"Good night now," I say with a wave and take off in a different direction from the man's house, praying the poor, old dude gets the point so I don't have to get mean. What is it with me and old folks? It's not like I'm one to worry about being mean to anyone else, even little kids. Must be the same old Saturn in the 11th House. When this is all over, I vow to myself, I'll try to make younger friends. Heck, I'll even give Art's kid a chance.

***

Just to make sure I'm all alone, I walk around the block before going back to Nate's house. It looks dark and empty. I send yet another unanswered text to Art and enter the side yard through the freshly painted white iron gate. The side yard is neat, covered by some sort of gravel; not very practical if you're digging up dirt to bury a plastic bag with a head, or severed extremities.

The back door is locked, but I don't care because I have experience with breaking and entering. (Howie Jr. and I used to practice picking locks, sneaking into our grandparents' house for a few beers and a little cash way before we were teens.) Then a terrifying thought hits me. What was I thinking? Nate is the sneaky type. I'm sure he's installed some sort of security system. I don't want to take a chance with the cops, at least not just yet.

I close my eyes and try to "feel" my way in. Where the heck is my so-called gift when I need it? I rub my hands together, creating energetic heat, place my hands on the wet, cold metal doorknob, exhale tentatively and turn it to the right, squeezing my eyes shut, ready to run. The door is locked, but there's no alarm sound. Okay. I can deal with one silly knob.

Now, everybody knows these doorknobs have a twisting lock mechanism on the inside, but it could be one with push-button. Let's see. I need light, so I take out my phone, noticing the battery is about to go. I better hurry. The light helps. I'm able to make out a little round hole in the center for those special moments when you're stuck in the right place, but in the wrong time. It looks like I need something thin and pretty long. I mean a screwdriver or a hex wrench would be nice, but anything thing will do. I dig into my bag, locating several items I can try.

First, I try a paper clip, but it bends. No problem, I should have a hairpin somewhere in my makeup pouch. Nope, but I find several used cotton swabs. All I need to do is get rid of the used-up fluff. Yet, another case of me being a lazy slob or a as Carlos used to call me *la dejada*, paying off. Fuck you, Carlos! Oops, I guess it's kind of crappy of me to tell off the dead.

I make sure the swab is nice and clean, insert it into the hole, sweep it around, twisting several times before it catches on something. I apply some pressure, but not too much so as to not break the swab and hear a long-awaited click. Yes! Who said you need a locksmith when you have me around?

I open the two-panel door, still apprehensive about an alarm, but again, all is quiet. Creeping toward the front, I pass two empty bedrooms, then a typical '70s-style, all-oak kitchen with white tile. Although it's dark, everything looks completely normal, eerily so. What the hell did I expect: heads on a stake, bloody body parts, piles of drugs? Sometimes, my imagination gets me in trouble. Sometimes? Ha!

I should check out the living room, but my bladder needs easing so badly, I either have to pee or wet my pants, not that it would make much difference in how I stink. Still, it's cold enough to get a nasty UTI. I might as well check out the master bedroom. Maybe Nate left something behind that can help me understand what he's been up to. As I enter the largest of the bedrooms, my inner alarm bells go off. I close the metal blinds, turn on a night light by the bed, and look around.

Still, nothing suspicious, except for my nausea returning with a vengeance. Why does this room seem so familiar? I stare again. But first, I have to pee and then I'll snoop inside the two matching night tables.

The door leading to either a walk-in closet or to the en-suite bathroom is closed. I turn the knob, realizing its locked. Weird. I'm not about to repeat the swab thing again, so I exit the bedroom and use the half bath, grateful there's toilet paper.

Well, strike three, I think. *Come on, Viv, better take off before Nate finishes the job with the dead Indian guy. Wait, before I leave, I better poke around the deserted place next door.*

Actually, why didn't I go over there first? It kind of makes sense to hide illegal things over there. And what a good excuse: I'm going to develop the property. (Nothing suspicious: everyone knows it takes forever to get permits and environmental surveys in California.) I'll bet my favorite Alan Leo astrology book that Nate owns the house next door as well.

As I'm about to leave, something inside forces me to go back into the bedroom. It's not my imagination. I'm hearing something coming from behind the locked bathroom door. (I know it's a bathroom because I looked inside the empty closet.) I'm thinking it could be a dog. No, it would bark. Is there a cat? Why would anyone lock up a cat? It could be rats or a six-foot python. I knew that several of Glenn's hombres kept deadly snakes, just to frighten their *putanas*.

Man, this is nuts. I've got to blow this joint. Turning around, I notice an unframed vintage poster that piques my interest. The poster, hanging above the bed, is an advertisement for Placentia Girl Brand Orange Company. Way back when Orange County had acres and acres of citrus orchards, art posters of orange crates were all the rage. I remember the design. Yes, here's the rendering of a young woman with dark hair waving in the wind. She's riding a horse. The horse's mane matches that of the rider. The rider is dressed in old-school Western gear.

Now, I get why I recall the poster. It reminds me of the orange crate poster Daddy had hanging in our little Laguna beach cottage. It's the same poster from my dreams! It's then that the energy hits me right in the gut. I almost vomit. I was in this room before, so many times. This is the room where I see the poor, tortured man, the man from my nightmares.

Chapter 25

I take another minute to jimmy the lock on the bathroom door. It unlocks. With my heart pounding out of my pericardium, I turn the knob and feel for the light switch, first to my left (I'm a lefty), and then to my right. Figures. When I flip the switch on, the harsh, bluish light is so bright, it takes my eyes a second to adapt. I notice the dull, metallic odor of dried blood. The bathroom isn't as modest as one would expect, with faded orange pavers laid out on the bias, cracked white tile, dual sinks, and a separate spot for the toilet. But I already recognized the details. Without hesitation, I head straight for the tub, drawing the opaque plastic curtain out of the way.

My breath catches somewhere between my lungs and my larynx. I stop myself from screaming, swiftly covering my mouth with a shaking hand. It's the man, the tortured man, who's been crying out for me from my darkest nightmares, the man sending me warnings, though it looks like the danger was coming from Nate and not Art Russo. One dumb mistake and it could cost me my life.

The guy looks oddly peaceful, his eyes closed. I drop to my knees, right on the hard Mexican pavers and reach inside the tub to probe for a pulse. He's alive. Barely. The pulse is way too slow for someone his age. The bastards drugged him, of course. That would make sense in their world. Praise the Lord, I'd already seen this horror in my dreams or I'd pass out. Completely nude, the miserable soul is marked with mauve and yellow bruises, his feet and hands knotted up with thin plastic cords. To be fair, he looks like a luau pig before being roasted. A ridiculous notion crosses my mind: Here's another grand reason not to eat meat.

His face, including the wild beard, is covered with semi-fresh blood. Whoever held him has been enjoying beating him to a pulp for the sheer pleasure of it. I search for the missing hand I saw in my dreams., Yep, it's there or actually, not there. It looks like the stub healed. Perhaps he's been kept a prisoner for as long as I've been having my visions, or were those nightmares my first authentic out-of-body experience? Have I been astral-projecting all alone?

Get yourself together, Viv. You need to get him out of here before Nate returns.

After pulling the bloodied gag out of his mouth as gently as possible, I tap my finger on his shoulder. "Hey, mister, wake up. Can you open your eyes?" He doesn't respond. What am I expecting? This is a bathroom, let's try to find scissors. Sure enough, I find an enormous pair in one of the under-the-sink drawers and try to cut the plastic, but with zero results. What I need is something sharper, more like a Swiss army knife, and that one I've got. Daddy's personal safety rule number 1: When doing something potentially perilous to your health, never leave your trusted Swiss knife or bear mace behind.

As I attempt to emancipate the victim, he opens one hazel green eye, framed with thick black lashes, so like Carlos's, except for the color. (I used to ridicule Mr. Peacock about those lashes, accusing him of getting lash extensions.)

The guy's left eye is swollen shut, badly in need of cutting. (My high school boyfriend, Mike, was a major star at our local boxing gym.) We'll just have to deal with it later. After I finish getting him loose, even though he's bone thin, I realize I may require his cooperation to drag him out of the tub.

"Hi there," I try to reassure him. "Don't worry. I've got you," I add with relief as I tear up from sheer exhaustion. "What's your name, dear?" I ask, trying not to sound freaked out. He still doesn't respond, except for a lone tear I see crawling down his face. It shatters my soul.

"Any busted bones? Can you try to get up?" Then it dawns on me. The guy probably doesn't speak English. "*Ola, amigo. Estas securo. Como te llamas?*"

Hmm. Does he speak something other than Spanish? He certainly looks Hispanic. Poor guy probably forgot his name. Must be all the beatings he took. And then the man licks his cracked lips and gives me the shock of my life.

"I felt in my blood you'd find me, *mi amor*. I never stopped crying for you. Never stopped trusting your gift and our love."

When I am frozen, flabbergasted and speechless, he lifts his mutilated arm trying to touch me to check that I'm real. "*Gracias a Dios*, it is you. I'd recognize these eyes even in this getup."

Wait. I recognize this voice, but it can't be. I'm in a trance. That's it. I must've blacked out again.

"I love you so much, baby," he professes. "Please, tell me you still love me. It's the only thing that's kept me alive, Vivi. Is it that bad? What did they do to my face? You don't recognize me? It's me." He makes some effort to smile, wincing from pain.

I gather my wits and demand an explanation. I'm not out of my body now. "Who the fuck are you, mister, and how do you know my name?"

"I must be hideous, but it is me, Carlos. Baby, I'm a hundred percent alive. I've been calling out to you from the gates of hell," the man says, pleading with me. "Believe me. I'm so sorry I broke up with you before your birthday. Remember? It was April. I had no choice. We were about to wrap up the case."

"Stop it!" I scream, unable to control my rage. "How do you know about Carlos dumping me? He must have told you. Yes, that's it. You were held together. He was murdered, but you lived." This is the only logical explanation I can think of. "Stop messing with my head and help me get you out of the damn tub. I'm not about to call the cops if that's what you're worried about. I've got my own problems. (Like the IT geek I accidentally whacked). I'll even get you to the border, but then you're on your own."

The man struggles to sit up, his atrophied muscles cramping. I climb into the tub behind his back. Hooking my thighs around his hips, I use my upper body to get his back up. I've used this maneuver before helping Sandi after the stroke, never understanding why Jay wouldn't install a walk-in tub.

"Get as close as you can to the side and stay there," I bark unceremoniously once he is sitting straight up, holding onto the tub lip. Clearly in terrible pain, but cooperating, the man turns to one side, gets on his knees, swinging one long, hairy leg over. I step over the lip of the tub and use all my strength to pull him onto the matless floor. Mission accomplished.

"If I didn't love you so much, I'd strangle you," the broken man says and gives a weak laugh that turns into a dry cough as he rubs his bruised ribs. "Listen to me, for the love of your crazy Goddess or your Stars," the insane man says, continuing to play with my emotions. "I'm not with the cartels. Call 911 now. We don't have time before they return. I am law enforcement a Mexican Tactical. I can't explain everything now, but you'll have to trust me."

"Oh no, you don't. What the heck is a Tactical?"

"*Puta*. Fine. I'm a member of an elite anti-cartel force."

"Aha! That makes sense. Now I believe you. You Feds have no shame. You had something on Carlos. Probably blackmailed him into cooperating with you, threatened his family. You learned how much he loved his family. You forced him to get you on the inside. Something went horribly wrong. And they got you both. I told Carlos cartels have no mercy."

"Viviana, look at me. "

"I'm looking, and I don't know who you are. Even your eyes are not his eyes." I'm shaking with anger.

"Come here, baby. Let me hold you. Look inside your heart. You'll see me."

"No." I refuse to face him. "I studied Carlos's chart. I saw the Fixed Stars. They showed how Carlos would die and it matched with what the cops found."

"Oh, is that it?" the fake Carlos says with relief. "Let me explain, but once we get going."

"I'm not going anywhere with you. You have one minute to give me your pitch and I mean one minute. I'm sure Carlos told you how stubborn I am."

"*Bueno*. My actual name isn't Carlos, well, it's one of my middle names. I'm sure you know that in our culture, kids are given several *familia* names. I'm Ivan, named after my *abuelo*, who was a police officer too. See how much we have in common? And I wasn't born in July. I'm an Aries, just like you, born on March 29 in Guanajuato state. So see? Your astrology mumbo-jumbo couldn't possibly predict my death."

"Mumbo-jumbo?" Now, I'm really ticked off.

"Sorry, *mi amor.*"

"You think you're like me? Like *me*? No way! And what about your eyes? Carlos had beautiful espresso eyes." I try to make sense of what I'm hearing.

"Tinted lenses,." he explains, adding, "I've been also wearing prosthetics. I pray you like my real nose. My *abuelo*, you know, great-grandad, was one of the white Russians who fled to Mexico after their revolution. And my hair is kind of light brown. I look more gringo than Latino. Sorry. I remember how much you love my sexy Latin lover vibe."

"Fine. Let me see your cock," I say, feeling a mortifying hormonal flush creep up my chest.

"With pleasure. Hopefully, my *pene* is still, as you used to call it, 'pretty.' I haven't been giving it much attention, but maybe after you forgive me, we can pick up where we left off?" he asks jokingly.

"Shit, Carlos, you're such a stupid *cerdo*." I smack him on the arm in a too-familiar gesture, and then I'm sure. It is my Carlos, come back to life. My Scorpio jealousies and a pathological need for revenge didn't cause his death. It is as if a load of bricks has been lifted off my chest. All this time, all the guilt, all the anger, all of it melted like Crayola crayons under the Palm Springs sun. He isn't a moody mama's boy Cancer, he's a brave Warrior Aries. Just like me.

"That's my Vivi."

"Carlos..." We embrace. He pulls off my gray wig, running his remaining hand over my flat frizz, whispering, over and over: *te amo, te amo*, as our tears mingle. As much as I wish I had more time to process, that's one thing we no longer have.

"We have to go." I break away from our reunion hug. "Here, Carlos, let's get some clothes on you." (Little did I plan when piling on my homeless get-up that the layers would come in this handy.)

Quickly removing my outer coat along with a long knit skirt, a moth-eaten sweater, and one pair of socks, I put the rags on Carlos's boney, battered body. Almost sobbing, I flash back to how gorgeous he was. I'd like to apologize for my body stench, but something tells me he's too far gone to notice. I guess his nose has been broken several times. When he shivers, I place my hand over his forehead. Oh, no. He's on fire. Must be the drugs, made worse by the emotional shock. I need to get him to the ER stat.

"I came in through the back," I inform my long-lost, not so dead, ex-boyfriend.

"Does anyone suspect where you are?" he asks, looking as if he's about to pass out.

"Yeah. I texted a friend. Long story."

You have no idea how long. What am I going to tell him about Art? It's raining men. Hallelujah!.

"Let me help you up. I'm strong as an ox and hungry as a bear," I say, trying to lighten the mood. It takes a little more of an effort on both of our parts to get Carlos to his feet, but as soon as I let go, his muscles give out and he crumples, luckily, on the bed.

"I'm sorry. I can't seem to stay on my feet," Carlos says, apologizing, even his bruises look pale.

"No apologies. Ever. It's just your muscles are weak from being tied up. Doctors say it takes just days to lose one's mobility, but with therapy, I'll get you back on your feet. You should've seen Sandi after the stroke."

I sound as if I actually know what I'm talking about and I'm liking this new, confident me. "Just stay put. Plan A: I'm going to check for a landline in the front room. Plan B: I may have some battery left to dial 911, but I'll have to take off when I hear the sirens." I don't want to have to explain.

Carlos nods and says, "*Si, mi amore, gracias.*"

Wow. No more arguing? I pull Carlos up on the bed, propping him up with a pillow. "Don't close your eyes. Stay awake," I command. Leaving the bedroom door closed, in case he falls off the bed, I move into the kitchen, praying I find a phone. The kitchen is free of signs of any use, except for two enormous bottles of acid, the kind the cartels used to dispose of dismembered bodies. That's why they threw Carlos in the tub. This is worse than I could've ever imagined, even in my nightmares. Nate is evil incarnate on par with my ex, Glenn.

Chapter 26

As I leave the kitchen and enter the front room, I bump into a shadowy figure. "Who the fuck are you?" the figure yells, pushing me backward with the barrel of what I assume is a gun. Shit.

"What are you doing in my house?" he demands. I recognize the voice: It's Nate returning to finish Carlos. When I don't respond, he turns on the light, takes one look at me and cackles with enough malice to make my skin crawl. "Finally, showing your correct age, hey, Viv? I always knew you were a skank. And you stink like shit. Thanks for getting rid of that weak towel head for me."

Towel head? That's classy. Here I assumed they were friends.

"Fuck you too Nate. And I did nothing wrong. Your roomie is the one who attacked me. All I did is defend myself," I respond, puffing my chest out in defiance.

"That's what you'll have to tell the cops, but something tells me your word stinks as much as your old ass," he says, adding with blood-curling malice, "Guess you saw what I do to my enemies?"

"What do you mean?" I ask, playing dumb, trying to prolong the inevitable.

"Even you're not that dumb. What do you think about my 'Mexican' friend?"

"I don't get what you're talking about: that dude is Indian. Dot, not feather, Indian." I say, trying to come up with plausible angle and deflect his attention from Carlos. "Sure, I followed you here to see what you did with your roommate's body because I was afraid that I was the one who killed him, but when I saw his head in the trunk, I finally understood it was you. I waited until you left and broke in, but I didn't see it. How did you learn I was here? I checked for an alarm system." I keep my voice nice and even and my cool, collected Scorpio side fully in control, reminding myself it's just Nate. This is not the time to lose one's head, in more ways than one. I guess my strategy worked because I can tell from his body language, he's softening.

"Listen, I need no more trouble with the cops. And about my past, it's a lot more complicated than I told you. There are folks on the inside who'd love a chance to even the score with my family. I'm not going inside, ever. Nate, you can trust me. You've got nothing to worry about. Why would I say anything to the pigs? What do I care about some geek douchebag?" Then I add, "can I sit down?"

Nate shakes his head and looks at me like I'm crazy, but finally waves his hand in the direction of the futon sofa. "Sit. Be my guest." I plop my ass down, looking as if nothing bad is about to happen—just two exes talking things over. Without a word, Nate comes to the sofa and slaps me hard in the face.

"Damn, that felt good! I've been wanting to do that ever since we met."

My head snaps back and I bite my lip hard, drawing blood, to stop myself from crying. Then he touches his P7, (if you can call that overpriced toy an actual gun), to my forehead.

"You are a tough, old broad. I give you that," Nate says. "You might as well know you're not getting out of here with your head connected to your body unless you tell me where you hid the product. If you already sold it, I want all the money, and I mean to the last penny. I wasted enough time, hating every sec I had to spend in your company." The he adds sarcastically, "No more fun and games, not that being your 'boyfriend' was ever fun."

"You're being mean, hon. I hoped we had some laughs," I try again, using my Chrissy voice.

"Laughs? Oh yeah, that's what it was." He grabs a chair and sits down, keeping the gun pointed at me.

I try again, at the very least, to buy some time: "You're not a murderer. I'm psychic. You realize I'd sense something dangerous. You just got in over your head. And what about your little boy and the custody fight? You'll lose him if you get busted and eventually you will. Whatever you've got yourself into, is it worth it to lose your kid? It's bad karma. I know you believe in karma; we've talked about it."

"What kid? Did you ever meet him or ever ask to see photos? I don't have any kids; at least, not that I'm aware of. I had you drive me to Lancaster in your junker because it was safer to transport. You really are a brain-damaged wacko. All the booze and drugs didn't make you psychic, just stupid. My karma is to spend my life in Monaco or the Maldives, driving Lamborghinis and fucking eighteen-year-old exotic models, not used-up old whores."

My temper flares. "I've had just about enough of your insults! Shut your mouth! I figured you were a nice guy, pathetic, but nice. But you're a creep and a liar!"

I jump off the futon and rush toward him, desperate to claw his eyes out, but I'm stopped by the cocking sound of his gun.

Nate pushes me hard, using the gun. "Stand back, bitch. Now, it's your turn to listen. You shut the fuck up and hear me good. No more stalling. I want the stuff my father left you. I don't give a rat's ass if it's fentanyl or cash. No way I'll end up like him. I'm going to be a crypto millionaire. This is why I let you live, even though you don't deserve it," he shouts. "I want everything you have. Now if you're dumb enough to die for it, I'll ask my south-of-the-border partners to take care of your cop lover or better yet, the old woman. You have one minute to respond." He looks down at his watch.

"What are you talking about? You must be using the same shit you're pushing. You're nuts. If I had money, would I live in a moldy back house in Costa Mesa? And why would your father leave me anything? Incidentally, who is your father?"

"Who was he, you mean? Who do you expect?" He raises his voice, dripping malice.

"I don't fucking know. You tell me." My eyes leak from sheer frustration.

"Look at me." Nate gets up to his full height, pulling back his shoulders. The change in posture instantly makes him appear taller. He gets right in my face and scowls and then I admit to myself what my mind was trying to tell me all along. It all makes sense, the familiarity, the instant connection, the lousy sex.

"You're Glenn's son."

"Finally! I was worried I was losing my good looks, the looks I got from my dad, although, I clearly have better taste in women," he snickers, insulting me one more time.

"I didn't know. Sorry for your loss," I mumble, offering a semi-sincere apology, my mind spinning with questions. "If you hate him so much, why would you want to follow in his footsteps?"

"What loss? I'm glad he's dead. He deserved worse after what he put me and my mother through. Let him rot in hell but give me what he owes me. The last call from him was a waste of time, except for him putting the screws in by telling me you were the only woman he ever loved and if anything happened to him, you would be well taken care of. Yeah, I used some of his connections to make money, but it's the seed money for investing in crypto I need, you ignorant slut. I told you, I got some info, a guaranteed opportunity to make twenty times what I put in. I only need a million to turn it into twenty. Why would I want to spend my life being the mule for the cartels and then end up like him?"

I don't understand his gibberish. What's a crypto, and where would I get a million dollars? "Nate, listen. You don't understand what you're talking about. Glenn was a monster. He was a liar. He promised the world and gave zilch. I'm sorry you had a shit for a dad, but you've been had. Glenn didn't love me. He hated my guts. I have plenty of broken bones and per-manent brain damage to prove it. He raped me and used me as a sex slave for his cartel partners. He left me nothing. Nothing. I lived on the streets, doing things my mind refuses to admit."

Sickening memories, moving pictures come crushing over my head like high surf at the Newport Wedge, each wave forc-ing my lungs to seize with unimaginable pain. "I wish I was dead," I sob, the dry heaving turning into hysterical laughter.

For a few minutes, Nate sits without saying a word, trying to process. Then, without a warning, he jumps to his feet, grabs the chair and tries to hit me with it, screaming, "You're dead! I'm going to smash your brains in or even better, gut you while you watch."

I duck. He misses my head, hitting me on my right shoulder. He grabs my neck and tries to choke me awkwardly. Well familiar with the move, I fight back, shaking my body from left to right. I use my feet to slam his shins. Neither of us is strong enough to end this comedy.

"Stand back or I'll shoot."

Nate let's go of my neck just long enough for me to reach into my pocket for the bear mace.

It's Carlos, bluffing his way in, holding a kitchen knife, barely hanging onto the door jamb. When Nate realizes there's no gun, he advances toward Carlos, who falls to his knees. As Nate's about to shoot him, I scream, rushing toward both men. "You're going to meet your daddy in hell, motherfucker," I say, shoving Nate away from Carlos and spraying him with the mace.

As Nate yells out in pain, Carlos uses the knife, slashing Nate's calves and thighs. Nate's gun goes off and my heart stops as Carlos gets hit in the chest. This is where I lose it. All my emotions expand: all the pain, all the anger, all the love, merging with Goddess Magik, filling me with a force I've never imagined.

Strength of Day, Strength of Night, Give me strength, Beyond my sight.

Jumping on Nate's back, I grab his hair and yank it hard. He jabs me with his elbow, just missing my ribs. On instinct, I wrap my arm around the back of Nate's neck, pushing his head to the side. (I've practiced the guillotine choke hold just for these occasions.) I use my wrist to cut-jab into his throat, just below his Adam's apple. Nate continues to make a half-assed attempt to get me off his back, but the wounds on his legs are bleeding heavily and I sense his life force slipping away. He goes down, but I don't stop. I use my feet to kick his sides, his head, anywhere I can reach, the power surging through my veins, taking away any pain or fear. I don't pay attention to the noises coming from behind me or the sound of sirens.

"Vivi, stop. You're killing him." A familiar voice enters my blood trance, but I can't stop.

Strength of Day, Strength of Night, Give me strength, Beyond my sight.

"Stop!" Strong hands take hold of me, pulling me back from the brink of hell.

"I get it, I truly do, hon. He deserves it, but you don't. Please, try to breathe. Come on, one, two, three in, one to three out." I turn around and stare up into Art's eyes, those amber eyes looking at me with nothing but compassion and worry. I black out.

Chapter 27

open my eyes refreshed, filled with an odd sense of peace. My ever-present headache has vanished. Yeah. I'm dead. Sunlight is streaming through a large window overlooking the ocean. I smile and fill my lungs with air: This is my heaven. Then my dumb bladder makes its presence known and I realize I'm still on the earth plane, once again lying in a hospital bed. Weird. I haven't felt this good in ages. Locating the long, plastic bed control panel on my right, I press the button to move myself up into a sitting position, then call for the nurse. Because it's taking a few minutes, I swing my feet to the side, grab on to the IV cart, and go into the bathroom. When I come out, a nurse is standing by the bed, resetting the screen.

"Good morning, Ms. Glover. How are you doing? How's the head?"

"I'm great, actually. Where am I?" I ask with a friendly smile. This is new. Why am I being so nice?

"Excellent," the nurse, a pleasant looking Caucasian woman, says. "There's no need to worry," she adds with competence. "Your police friend checked you in for observation, but the doctor will explain when he does his morning rounds. Are you hungry?"

"No, thank you, but I could use a shower."

"I'll have to check with your charge nurse, but I don't see any issues with that." She introduces herself. "I'm Caroline, the night nurse. We're in the middle of a shift change. Thanks for your patience. Let me help you back into bed."

"No problem, I understand. Thanks." No problem? Did those words just come out of my mouth? What the heck have they done to me?

"You've been sleeping for a while. I hope some rest and the meds helped your head. When you came in, you were in pretty rough shape."

"What happened?"

"The doctor will explain, but you have a visitor. He's been here all night. I'm sure he'll fill you in."

"Hi there. How's your head?" Art asks, walking into my room with a small flower arrangement of pink carnations and spray roses. Neither the rare stubble nor the heavy shadows under his eyes detract from his beauty. Damn. My foolish heart skips a beat.

"Hello," I whisper, once again self-conscious of my pitiful appearance, hoping he remembers I can look nice. "I'm great, better than I've been in ages. The headache is gone. What was wrong with me?"

The nurse interrupts us. "Well, I'll give you folks some privacy. Glad you're feeling better, dear. Heather should check in on you in a while. I'll leave her a note about your requesting a shower."

"Thank you for taking such great care of Viviana, Caroline," Art says to the nurse and hands her his card. "I appreciate it was a long night. Anything I can ever do for you, don't you hesitate to call me." Art extends his hand, but the nurse gives him a quick hug. Of course. Who wouldn't want to get closer to this rare specimen? My green-eyed nature awakens. Thank God, I mean Goddess. I was worrying I'd had a lobotomy.

"You remember anything?" my savior asks after grabbing a chair.

"Not really. Did they sedate me?"

"I don't know the exact medications, but yes, the doctors in the ER kept you after they saw your brain scan."

"Fuck! I mean, I have a brain tumor? I knew it. All the hits I took on the head finally took their toll."

"You don't have a brain tumor." Art chuckles and says reassuringly, then reaches out for my IV-free hand, kissing it gently. "The doctor will explain. I checked. He's on the floor."

"Don't you laugh at me," I say, realizing I sound like a spoiled brat, but a brain tumor is nothing to sneeze about since I have a double whammy in my chart from Mars, the most important planet for my Sun and my Rising sign, although I don't mind having my hand kissed. I can't be that sick if even his slightest touch makes me this horny.

He lets go of my hand and says with force: "Never. I'll never laugh at you again. Not after what you've done. You're my hero. Not only did you save my best friend's life, but you also got the bad guy, and I mean all by yourself. We came in to mop up. I'm so sorry."

"Hang on for a sec. Your best friend? You mean my Carlos? Where is that liar?" I don't remember why I'm asking and then my memory lockbox clicks open, flooding my mind with moving pictures. My heart skips several beats. The pictures move with speed, one replacing another: Nate calling me horrible names, Carlos tied up like an animal in the tub, the old man with a dog, the head in the duffle, Nate slapping my face, Carlos being shot.

"Carlos is not even Carlos, and Nate is Glenn's son," I admit, more to myself than Art.

"I'm sorry. He is, but there's no need for your to give that bastard a thought."

"I'm not scared of that limp-dick loser," I say, squaring my jaw in defiance.

"Guess not." Art looks at me with a curious expression. "We've got him, although barely. I thought you'd almost killed him with your bare hands. Carlos, I mean Ivan, is alive. They removed the bullet. He made it through surgery. But it's still touch and go because of, well, you know. He's here, just a few floors up, in the ICU. I assume you want to see him, but first, you best talk with the neurologist who saw your brain scan."

"Right," I acknowledge feeling doubly betrayed, not believing Art can sound so damn matter of fact about what I've just gone through. I want to throw something at his head or at the very least throw up.

"Say, how did you know where I was? Wait, I know. You had a tracker on me somehow all this time. Didn't you and don't lie to me now!" I hiss.

Art's head is saved when my doctor enters. A tall, ridiculously cute Asian physician followed by a group of two young women (yay!) and an African American guy (double yay!) extends his hand to Art and smiles at me with that look I recognize, that certain expression that means nothing good.

"Bad news?" I blurt out, unable to stop my heart from taking off.

"Why do people always assume I bring bad news? Do I look like the Grim Reaper?" the doctor asks, making an inappropriate joke.

"Something like that," I mumble, bracing for the worst-case scenario.

"All kidding aside, we found some abnormalities, Viviana. You're pretty lucky I was doing late rounds when the ambulance brought you in."

"It's Miss Glover, if you don't mind," I snap. What's with all these teenagers being in charge of my life? "Well? Are you going to tell me what's wrong with my head or do I have to call my lawyers?" I threaten, finally acting more like myself.

The doctor now looks a bit annoyed. "No need for that, Ms. Glover."

Good.

"When you were brought in, you were dehydrated with tachycardia, which means your heart rate was well above normal range."

"I know what tachycardia means."

"Viv, knock it off," Art butts in. "I'm sorry, Dr. Park, she's still in shock," he says, making an unasked-for excuse. He addresses the doctor. "Viviana was led to believe that a very close friend was murdered, but he's alive."

"It's perfectly all right. I'm a brain surgeon. We have no feelings to hurt."

He's kidding again, or is he?

"Here's the deal," Park pronounces, now as serious as my ensuing panic. "You've clearly suffered from more brain trauma than I've seen in a while, let's say, since Iraq."

Shit. He's not a kid, after all. Well, he's Asian, they never show age. Me and my big mouth.

"Can the damage be reversed?" Art inquires, looking concerned.

"I'm afraid not. Ms. Glover has had several concussions that can cause brain degeneration. We also found a small blood clot that most likely will have to be removed, at least at some point. She will have to follow up regularly with her own specialist. Right now, she's in no immediate danger, but I am concerned about CTE, chronic traumatic encephalopathy, something we usually see among football players. Unfortunately, we can only confirm CTE after the patient has succumbed. The good news about CTE is that it is very rare. Ah, yes. The scan also showed increased activity in the right area of her brain. Have you heard of parahippocampal gyrus?"

WTF? I scream inside, devastated by the unfairness of it all.

"What does that do Dr. Park?" I ask quietly.

"Mostly, significant mood swings, depression, behavioral problems related to aggression, and some dementia like degeneration of the thinking processes. In rare cases, we have also seen suicidal ideation."

Hmm. Makes sense since I have all the symptoms, including playing Russian roulette with substances. I sure have banged my head more than I can remember.

I keep my train of thought to myself. I'll be damned if I'm going to give it more energy by putting into words my deepest fears.

"So what do we do?" Art asks, continuing to advocate for me as I go silent, trying to go within and ask the Sprit for guidance.

"Well, as I already explained, Ms. Glover will have to be seen regularly. She'll need to avoid additional injuries, and, of course, manage her stress."

"Fat chance," I sneer. "Everything will be fine, doc. I'm an Aries with a Scorpio Rising. Alpha Centauri will protect me. The Goddess led me to Carlos and she'll save us both. My psychic visions are getting stronger and stronger."

I turn to Art. "Why don't you tell him how I found and saved Carlos?"

The doctor and Art exchange looks, those "lovely" familiar looks I've been facing all of my life.

"Enough about some phantom brain disorders. Can I see my boyfriend? He's here, in the ICU," I demand, ignoring a cringe from Art.

"We don't see any reason to keep you here," Park responds. "I'll write the order to discharge, but you'll have to check with your boyfriend's AP, the attending physician, to see if he can have visitors."

"I'm also aware of the meaning of an AP," I snap again, sick and tired of being treated like a mindless bimbo.

"I'm sorry, Doctor," Art says, apologizing for me again. Who asked him to?

"Incidentally, Doctor Gonzales here," Park says, motioning to the male resident, "has done some research while in med school regarding patients with acute so-called psychic experiences that can be viewed as paranoid delusions or even schizophrenia. Can you explain what you read to Ms. Glover? She may find it interesting."

"Hi, Ms. Glover," the resident says, smiling, showing off his dimples and dazzling smile. "Not to tire you with the details, but basically, we've seen several studies linking some rather unconventional brain activities such as ESP and intuition, or remote viewing, with the right cerebral hemisphere, in particular the right posterior cortical and hippocampal regions."

"Can you repeat the same thing in English?" I ask, smiling, charmed by his accent.

"Sorry, I'm a science geek," González says, returning my smile. "We think by using brain imagery we can actually pinpoint the area of the brain that shows a connection between brain activity and paranormal experiences. Maybe if I leave my card with you, you would consent to work with me at some later date?"

"Hell, no. You're not going to pick my brain and make me lose my gift."

"Sorry," Art tells the junior resident. He's becoming a broken record of apologies and it's really pissing me off.

"No problem," Gonzales says. "Her behavior clearly corresponds with her condition." The men talk about me as if I wasn't there. To keep myself from really losing it and giving them an excuse to keep me in bed, I cross my arms, ignoring the IV pinch.

"Good luck, Ms. Glover. Follow your instructions." Park ends his visit and leaves my room with the three stooges following.

"Fine!" I yell after him. Art shakes his head and leaves me alone. I close my eyes, trying to ignore what I just heard, my poor brain shutting down. When I open my blurry eyes, I'm shocked again, this time by another visitor. It's Carlos's sister, Irma, looking really odd—older and somehow taller. She's wearing an all-black pantsuit, a white button-down shirt, and shiny black, high-heeled boots. Her long, curly hair is pulled back into a slick bun and she's wearing dark glasses and red lipstick. She even smells like the law.

"Hey, Captain Russo. Long time," she says, extending her hand to Art for a shake.

"Hello, yourself, Major Saucedo. It's been too long."

"Hi, Vivi. So happy you're doing better."

Irma, or whoever the fuck she turns out to be, smiles and approaches my bed. I shake my head and turn toward the window.

"Is she going to be okay?" the traitor asks Art.

"Eventually. She's in shock. "

"Understandable. She's been through an ordeal. What can I do to help? Does she need me to talk to her? Did you tell her?"

"I'm not in shock. Ordeal, you say? You set me up to get Nate! I almost died! Wait. I know what you can do for me," I say sweetly, then scream at the top of my lungs: "You two pigs can just go and fuck each other."

"Uh-oh. She's still angry," Irma says.

"Guess so."

"Let me talk to her alone, Russo."

"Sure. Give it a shot."

Even though my eyes are closed, I feel Art leaving my space.

Irma tries to manipulate me. "*Ola, mija.* I'm truly sorry for everything you've suffered. We never intended to put you in danger. I mean, not after we realized you weren't involved with your ex's business." "Yeah, that and a peso will get you nada."

She loses her cool. "Okay. Enough. You want me to tell you the truth or you'll just hold your Scorpio grudge?"

"Your so-called cop truth? No, *gracias.* Are you even Carlos's sister?"

"I am not."

"I knew it. And here I was so good to you. I was your friend."

"I know, and I appreciated every minute."

"Even when you thought I was with the cartels?"

"Listen to me, Viviana. For once in your life, be quiet and listen."

"Fine. Talk fast."

"For obvious reasons, I can't tell you everything, but you're right. We played you, but you have to understand, Ivan and I come from the same place. We fight on the same side. I knew his family before they were kidnapped, tortured, and dumped on a highway. The woman you thought was his mother is a close family friend and she took a big chance working with this Tactical team. The Jalisco group is out of control. They've gone after the local Feds, tortured them, got the names and addresses of police officers and butchered them at home in front of their children. We've got outstanding officers deserting, grabbing their families and fleeing into hiding. Ivan is unique, *un hombre muy especial*. He is a dual citizen and loves your country so much that he fought side-by-side with Captain Russo in Iraq. We thought you were still involved with your ex-boyfriend's business with the Sinaloa and since Sinaloa and Jalisco are at war, well, we were hoping you'd lead us somewhere ."

"Seriously? You think I believe your bull crap? I'm a nobody. I know nothing. First Nate, and then you."

"I know... it was a coincidence. Clearly he had his reasons to go after you."

"There's no such thing as a coincidence. It's my rotten Aries luck. Everyone's been playing me, even those who claim to care about me," I say bitterly." And...

"Okay. That's enough." Irma putts her face near mine, stopping me with a look that chills my blood. "Ivan realized you weren't involved. He cared enough about you to move the investigation in a different direction. But no, you with your loco jealousies, you're the one who almost got him killed. Even Art dropped everything, including leaving his daughter behind, to help keep your cranky ass safe."

"You're telling me, Carlos, I mean, Ivan, suspected I was in danger and he said nothing to me?" I try to make sense of what she is telling me.

"I don't know. He's not exactly in shape to tell me. You better pray he makes it or I swear on his soul, I'll feed you to the cartels myself. On top of it, because of you, both Ivan and I have blown our covers. He even thinks he loves you, you insane woman."

Before I have time to respond or apologize, she storms off.

Chapter 28

It's yet another blissfully sunny, beach-scented Southern California April, and that means I'm another year closer to the end of my journey. I woke up fifty but will go to bed closer to sixty. The only silver lining to this year's birthday is that Mercury isn't retrograding, although according to Sandi, Uranus, the nervy rebel, isn't happy with my natal chart, signaling major surprises, which in my understanding means the shit hitting the fan.

"Can I ever get a break from the Stars?" I asked Sandi just last week when she did my annual birthday forecast. (My fairy Goddess Mama is blessedly back to her normal self, that is, once several rounds of antibiotics cleared a series of urinary tract infections, resulting in her kidneys working as they should.) Her answer ticked me off.

"If I were as young as you, I'd go Solar Return chasing. I'm sure we can find a spot on this planet where everything is in perfect planetary alignment."

Yeah, if I were a rich man, but something tells me that would be way too monotonous.

As a birthday gift, Sandi and Katherine, my two BFFs pinkie-swore to skip last year's drama, promising a low-key "do-over" get-together. Ever since I found out what was really going on behind my back, I've adjusted expectations of my relationships.

I'm still without my car, but the car is fine. It's that little cherry inside my head that's preventing me from driving. Everyone, including my doc, agrees, I'm a moving violation. So I've been getting rides and using crappy OC public transportation just in case it pops. For once, I've been a good girl. I've had several follow-up brain scans, I've kept my stress to a minimum—I mean my minimum—and I've cooled it on my sleeping meds.

Also, I'm in a committed relationship. Carlos, aka Ivan, my on-again, off-again dude, and I have reconciled, which on the surface is not that unusual, except that this time, he claims we've got a real chance to make it work because "he's being real with me." I guess time or the next Mercury Retrograde will tell. I must admit, we are getting along, keeping our disagreements to a minimum. I mean, I'd taken on a real piece of work, caring for a guy who barely survived being shot in the chest. His recovery has been slow and painful, but me standing by him has made all the difference. I still care about him very much and we have a strong psychic bond. How else would you explain him being able to contact me through my dream state during the eight horrific months of his captivity?

Apparently, without astrology, I'm a horrible judge of character. Nate, whom I thought was a ne'er-do-well, limp-dick kid, turned out to be a major douche bag, just as evil, if not more, than his daddy, my ex, Glenn. How sick can you be to chop off folks' hands and heads? And for what? Something not even real like imaginary money.

All the months I thought I was in control but was cruelly played make me angry beyond measure. I sure am a master of self-delusion. Everything about Nate was fabricated. I still don't get how he found me, but he was stalking me for several months before my vengeful Scorpio self gave him an opening. He won't admit it, but I recognize as surely as I perceive the Goddess's watchful eye, that he was the one behind the Laguna beach attack—maybe not him exactly, but someone doing it for him.

Now Nate's being held without bail. But I know the Feds. They will try to turn him because of his connections with Glenn's cartel hombres. He will be offered one sort of deal or another. Heck, he'll probably end up suing me for trespassing and attempted murder. That's our justice system. Anything for a deal.

I've been so worried about just that, that Carlos asked Art to monitor Nate, and, of course, he agreed since Carlos and he go way back. Carlos promised to come clean and tell me everything once he officially retires. I can't wait.

Note to self: must work on gratitude.

After all, Art dropped everything, including his Emery, to keep me safe for Carlos just before Nate took Carlos. I'm still confused, but grateful. Growing up around law enforcement taught me to not ask too many questions. I mean, do I trust what these two characters tell me is the truth? Probably not. Hell, Carlos isn't even a Cancer. Go figure. His first name isn't even Carlos, but he agreed to still let me call him by the name I've been used to. Irma, who's not Irma either, has been visiting regularly, and it turns out we have remained good friends. We can joke about the past, make fun of men, and dream about the future.

Art and I are cordial. Now I get it why he kept his distance. He was always aware of Carlos's feelings for me. I get it. Still, it hurts. Even Sandi kept the truth from me. She knew all along who he was and what he was doing in my house. Of course, I forgive her. I just can't forgive myself for being such a village idiot.

The bus stops a block away from my favorite yogurt shop, but this time I'm the one who's late. Because I've lost more weight, I'm wearing white skinny jeans and a floral boho top I found at the vintage store. The girl who helped me said it was originally super expensive. I'm growing my hair long, but today, I fix it nicely into two braids, making me look younger. I wish Carlos was here, but he had a PT session. His mutilated arm is giving him trouble.

The ocean is sparkling, the birds are chirping, and Laguna is as fresh as the ocean breeze. My life is crap. Even a drink wouldn't help my mood.

As I cross the street, I notice Katherine's Rolls with Efren standing outside, but no one else.

"Happy birthday, Viviana," he says, giving me a hug and a double cheek kiss.

"Where's everyone?" I ask? I can't believe another birthday is ruined.

"At the beach house, miss. I'm here to pick you up in style," he clarifies, sounding conspiratorial.

"Fine. But that wasn't the plan," I mumble, getting in the front, despite Efren's opening the car's back door.

"Don't worry. You will like your birthday surprise."

"Fuck surprises," I mumble again, hoping he won't hear me and take it to heart. Uranus is already causing havoc.

It takes only five minutes to get to Katherine's, but I'm feeling even worse, if that's possible. Efren opens the garage but asks me to get out. I do. The house is dead quiet. For a moment, I flash back to the last time I was here, my heart jumping up my throat, nausea returning. And then I hear music. It's a mariachi band, playing my favorite, "Guadalajara." The musicians approach as I stand with my jaw on the ground. There are five of them, including one who looks familiar. I blink my eyes several times. It's Carlos. He's all dressed up and looking gorgeous. Behind him stands Sandi and Katherine, holding hands with a tall, gray-haired gentleman, Annie, and Efren. Even Irma, Carlos's fake sister, is there. I'm speechless, almost in tears.

"Feliz cumpleanos, mi amor," Carlos says, taking my hand and dropping to his knees. I gasp, tongue-tied and in shock.

"Viviana, *mi amor*. Will you marry me?"

WTF just happened?

"I love you more than I can tell. Without you, I wouldn't be standing here asking you to share your life with me. I know I don't deserve you: I lied, I made you cry, but I swear on the Virgin, if you marry me, you won't regret a single day. Will you? Please say *si*."

****

"Hi Daddy, it's me."

"Hey, baby girl. How's it going there in wacko land?"

"Fine, I mean, I have news."

"Again? What now? Money or the law?"

"No, nothing like that Daddy." I swallow hard. "It's like this. I'm getting married. Carlos proposed on my birthday. He got on his knees. He hired a band. Everyone was there."

"No shit."

"You're not happy for me?"

"Sure, I'm happy. Surprised you'd say yes to one of our own. I knew I liked that Carlos of yours, Mexican and all, but I also know how you feel about the force."

"He's about to retire on full pension. His injuries are pretty bad. I owe him big time and I'll make good on my promises to be the wife he deserves."

"That's great, hon. Hey, Judi Ann, get a load of this. Viv's getting married," my father yells to my stepmom, who picks up on the other line, while my dad drops off, I'm sure to get back to the game. Yep, my folks still have a land line.

Judi Ann gushes, "Oh goodness. Vivi. I'm so happy. I've always told you. Carlos is one of the good guys. Congrats. When is the lucky event? You'll let me plan it with you, right?"

"Yeah, if you wish," I say, not wanting to rock the boat. "Can you put Daddy back on?"

"We're happy for y'all, but I'm watching my Rangers kicking the crap out of your Angels," Daddy says impatiently, dying to get off the phone. "How about your stepmom and I call you later? Want me to tell Junior?"

"Sure, Daddy. I'm going to be a bride!"

"Guess so, honey."

Just not the bride of the man I truly love: Arthur Howard Russo—my Fixed Star soul mate.

9 781951 943912